AN HIST

DAVID

MW00893510

SHE SEES
GHOSTS

THE STORY OF A WOMAN WHO RESCUES LOST SOULS
PART OF THE ADIRONDACK SPIRIT SERIES

outskirts
press

She Sees Ghosts—The Story of a Woman Who Rescues Lost Souls
Part of the Adirondack Spirit Series
All Rights Reserved.
Copyright © 2021 David Fitz-Gerald
v3.0

This is a work of fiction. Names, characters, businesses, places, events, locales, and incidents are either the products of the author's imagination or used in a fictitious manner. Any resemblance to actual persons, living or dead, or actual events is purely coincidental.

The opinions expressed in this manuscript are solely the opinions of the author and do not represent the opinions or thoughts of the publisher. The author has represented and warranted full ownership and/or legal right to publish all the materials in this book.

This book may not be reproduced, transmitted, or stored in whole or in part by any means, including graphic, electronic, or mechanical without the express written consent of the publisher except in the case of brief quotations embodied in critical articles and reviews.

Outskirts Press, Inc.
http://www.outskirtspress.com

ISBN: 978-1-9772-3357-8

Library of Congress Control Number: 2020917173

Cover Image © 2021 www.shutterstock.com.. All rights reserved - used with permission.
Cover design by: @padrondesign

Outskirts Press and the "OP" logo are trademarks belonging to Outskirts Press, Inc.

PRINTED IN THE UNITED STATES OF AMERICA

Dedicated to the memory of Bosley, a black cat (2006–2019)

Chapter 1

December 1799

The sound of church bells hung heavy in the foggy morning air. Four bodies were stitched into threadbare blankets. Next to the bodies a man labored to breathe, and occasionally he had enough energy to moan, almost silently. His clothes were tattered from months of imprisonment and shredded from dozens of whip-strikes. The bodies lay in a row just beyond a tall dark building next to a red brick church.

An old man slowly rolled a clunky wooden cart up the road and parked it near the bodies. He groaned and struggled to lift the emaciated bodies onto his death cart. He mumbled complaints about his sore back and his tired old arms, not that anyone would hear them. He lifted the body of the man that clung to life and rolled him onto the dead bodies. He chuckled, and said, "Someone to talk to," as he took up the handles of his cart. After several loud grunts, he got the wooden wheels moving again. He said, "I'll be leaving you in a trench at the edge of the city. If you are able to get up, you are welcome to walk away. I don't reckon you have any fight left in you anyway." He finished his thoughts with a snort and a laugh. At the edge of the city, he dumped the cartload of bodies into a shallow ditch. With no further obligation to his passengers, he rolled his empty cart back up the street.

The battered, bloody man drew his last breath in the muddy trench. He was finally free of the horrible prison—free also from the confines of his beleaguered body.

Mehitable saw his spirit essence separate from his physical body. It floated above him for a minute. He looked directly at her. She thought he looked sad. His spirit-form hung above his body, looking this way and that, as if searching for something or someone, then the spirit slowly evaporated into the air, and she woke up from her nightmare. She rubbed her eyes, realized it wasn't time to wake up yet, then replayed the scene in her mind as she tried to fall back to sleep.

She slept undisturbed for several hours. Just before dawn, another dream came to her. It was a frequently recurring dream. In it, she and her grandmother sat in cozy chairs by a warm fireplace knitting thick wool blankets.

Granny paused, holding her work in her hands, and looked down into Mehitable's face. She loved to say her granddaughter's musical name and insisted that everyone say it correctly. She pronounced it Muh-hett-a-BELLE. Granny's head was slightly tilted. She smiled with her whole face, not just with her lips, but well into her rosy, wrinkled cheeks. Her hazel eyes sparkled as she said, "You have a precious gift, Mehitable. You are *chosen*. Sometimes, it might not seem like a gift. You will have to be brave. You will have to be strong. It will be hard, but people need you to do this. 'Tis God's will." Then she whispered, like it was a secret just for them, "I know you have this gift because I have it too. I will help you." Then Granny quoted her favorite Bible verse, "God is my savior; I am confident and unafraid. My strength and courage is the Lord, and He has been my savior."

At that point, Mehitable always woke up. Whenever she dreamed of Granny she liked to linger in bed, happy to remember the sweet woman who had spent her last years doting on her. She shut her eyes tightly and pictured Granny with her silver hair piled on top of her head. Tiny, curly, escaped strands hung symmetrically, just in front of her ears. Granny had passed away a year earlier, and still Mehitable had no idea what Granny was talking about. *What gift*, she wondered. How would Granny help her, dead as she was? Mehitable stretched her arms, yawned, and swung her feet to the floor.

The cow needed to be milked.

At the end of the day, Mehitable sat on a plank bench in front of a small table. She stretched her fingers, then she balled her hands into fists. She repeated the exercises several times. It had become a ritual for her. She shook her hands like she was trying to dry them in a breeze. She tilted back slightly and rolled her head from side to side, sending her long, chestnut-brown hair flying over her shoulders and cascading down her back. She was wearing a new, burgundy colored dress with a black satin bow above the small of her back. Her parents and her five brothers and sisters sat attentively, as they did each night after dinner. She placed her fingers on the keys, closed her eyes, and began to play.

The ancient virginal was the most colorful, resplendent furnishing in a house full of ordinary, homemade objects. It was so old that nobody knew its story. It had been passed down through generations on her mother's side of the family. Mehitable liked to imagine what stories the virginal could tell. She imagined the perilous journey across the ocean, perhaps 125 years earlier with one of her mother's ancestors. She thought about the artist that carefully painted the scene of eight men and twice as many dogs engaged in a lively foxhunt, surrounded by red, black, and gold swirls that looked like vines and onions. Sometimes she imagined Granny's ancestors were wealthy and lived in a castle on a tall hill overlooking the ocean. Mehitable thought it was a miracle that the sound of a piano could fit into a box only sixty-six inches long, 20 inches deep, and 10 inches tall. Though she played it every night, she never failed to appreciate its beauty and its lovely sound. When she said her evening prayers, she thanked God for her family's many blessings, and never failed to count the virginal among them. Granny had patiently taught her to play it before she died, and she often thought of Granny when she played.

Mehitable finished her first song and opened her eyes, her daydreaming interrupted. The few songs she knew, she had mastered so well that she played them by heart, with no need to concentrate. She played them flawlessly, memorized by rote, having repeated each song hundreds of times. It was not hard for her to daydream while she played.

Wilhelmina sat in her favorite chair by the hearth. Between the rocking of her chair, and the clicking of her knitting needles, Wilhelmina's activity served as Mehitable's rhythm section. Her chair was a short distance from the virginal. Wilhelmina couldn't take her eyes away from her beautiful daughter. Wilhelmina hummed quietly and knitted prolifically. Now and then, Mehitable would glance at her mother while she was playing and give her mother a quick smile or nod before closing her eyes once again.

Mehitable's father, Horace, sat in a chair next to her mother. After dinner Horace smoked his favorite pipe. As Mehitable played, he rocked from side to side, as if he were floating on the blue-gray, apple scented ribbons of smoke that swirled above his head. Sometimes when Mehitable looked at her father she saw transparent floating images over his shoulders, even when he wasn't smoking his pipe. On rare occasions, she saw similar images elsewhere. Looking away usually took care of the problem, though it seemed to Mehitable that those apparitions appeared more frequently the older she got.

When he finished his pipe that night, Horace joined Mehitable, adding his deep baritone voice alongside her crystalline soprano. Horace's rich tone warmed their home even on the coldest nights.

That summer, Mehitable began working at Tommy Todd's store, a two mile walk down Lewis Road. Her earnings had allowed the family to generate a little savings. She was permitted to spend ten percent of her earnings however she wished. Her purchases included an oak hairbrush with bristles made from porcupine quills. She purchased fabric to make her new dress, a project which had kept Mehitable and her mother busy for months. Thirdly, Mehitable purchased sheet music. The half dozen songs she bought doubled the family's collection. She purchased the more complicated compositions. The simpler ones she memorized, line by line, while she looked at the sheet music in Tommy Todd's store.

Mehitable and her father had just completed learning a new song called, "Adieu to the Village Delights." It had a lovely, yet haunting melody. It made her think of Romeo without Juliet. Sometimes she stopped by the little library before walking home from town after work. She felt guilty idling at the library when there were so many chores to do at home. Usually she would read just a couple of pages and savor them in her thoughts until the next time she was able to spend a half an hour in the small town's tiny public library. She was slowly working her way through all of

Shakespeare's plays. On a couple of occasions, she used the library to avoid walking home with a boy her age. Anson Smudge worked at Tommy Todd's distillery. He lived two miles to the north of Mehitable, and often seemed to be walking up the path at the same time as she was. Nothing about Anson appealed to her, but she tried to be polite. For some reason he had taken a keen interest in her since she began working at the store, though they hadn't been friendly as school children. Mehitable was smitten with the idea of a man, but so far, no specific man had caught her fancy. In any case, she didn't think of Anson Smudge as a *man*.

She began to play the new song, and her father joined in.

Adieu to the village delights
which lately my fancy enjoyed
No longer the country invites
To me all its pleasures are void
Adieu thou sweet health-breathing hill
thou can'st not my comfort restore
Forever adieu my dear vill!

My Lucy alas is no more
is no…
…no more
My Lucy alas is no more
She was the cure of my pain
my blessing, my honor, my pride
She never gave me cause to complain
'til that fatal day when she died

Her eyes, that so beautiful shone
are closed forever in sleep
And mine, since my Lucy is gone

have nothing to do but to weep
but to weep...
...to weep
have nothing to do but to weep

Could my tears the bright angel restore,
like a fountain they never should cease

But Lucy alas is no more
and I am a stranger to peace
Let me copy with fervor devout
the virtues that glowed in her heart
Then soon, when life's sand is run out
We shall meet again, never to part
Never to part...
...to part
We shall meet again never to part

It was the first time they had played the new song in its entirety, without mistakes or restarting. It was the last song of the evening. Wilhelmina's cheeks were covered with tears, thinking of Lucy's lover's loss. Mehitable imagined Lucy and her lover, reunited in heaven.

Except for Mehitable's brother Perry, the rest of her brothers and sisters had fallen asleep in a pile on the sheepskin rug at her mother's feet, the warmth of the hearth, the slow pace of the long, sad song, and the soothing deep voice of their father having slowly sent them to slumber. One by one, Horace scooped up his children and placed each one in their own beds. The boys, Perry, Noble, and Otto shared one small room. The girls, Mehitable, Lavinia, and Permelia shared a second room.

Mehitable's brother Perry asked her if she would hunt rabbits

with him the following morning. It would be cold, two days after Christmas, but it was easy to find rabbit tracks in fresh snow.
Mehitable and Perry had enjoyed hunting rabbits with slingshots
for many years, and they always knew just where to find them, with
or without tracks. Rabbits were plentiful. After Perry went to bed,
Horace kissed Wilhelmina on her cheek, and went to bed himself.

Mehitable and her mother spent half an hour checking every
inch of Mehitable's new dress for the last time. She had plenty of
homespun dresses, and one bright blue dress for church on Sundays.
The burgundy dress was planned especially for her sixteenth birthday party. Normally, her family would have celebrated in a more
intimate fashion, with close family and nearby neighbors. Because
Mehitable's birthday was on New Year's Eve, her sweet sixteen col-
lided with the dawn of a new century. She was looking forward to
a festive celebration. She was glad to be sharing her birthday with
the whole town. She hoped that the celebration would help improve
the dour mood everyone had been in since learning of the death of
the country's very first president. Though he had died on the 14th
of December, it took many days for the sad news to spread from the
nation's capital to their remote country town.

Chapter 2

December 1799

A light snow fell overnight. Horace had agreed to do the morning chores himself. Half an hour before dawn, Perry tiptoed into the girls' room, grabbed Mehitable's foot, and gave it a light shake. Her eyes opened wide. She popped from her bed, feet moving, and ready to face the opportunities a new day provided. Like her brother, Mehitable liked to spring from bed and start her day with gusto. They were properly dressed for a winter's morning outdoors, fifteen minutes before dawn. Right on schedule, the chanticleer that Perry had named Dinner crowed loudly in the barn across the street. They grabbed their slingshots and headed out.

It was early in the season. Early enough that they didn't need snowshoes yet. Early enough that the fresh blanket of snow was still a welcome sight. Perry scooped up a handful of snow, blew it into the wind, and confirmed the wind was blowing from north to south.

There was a small hillside across from Lewis Creek, a creek so small they could jump across it without a running start. The hill was three hundred yards from their saltbox styled house. They had always had good luck on the opposite side of that hill. They took a turn to the right so they could approach the hill from the south, facing into the wind. Slowly, they moved from tree to tree, hoping to surprise some rabbits enjoying their early morning breakfasts of dried grasses. They got as close as they dared. They had pockets full of perfectly picked round river rocks. Mehitable loaded a rock into the basket of her slingshot and waited. Perry's slingshot was also ready. They watched as a rabbit zigged and zagged through the snow to a clump of grass, looked in one direction, then looked in another before venturing to chomp on the grass. Perry made the slightest motion with his head, indicating to his sister that she should take the shot. Mehitable's rock hit the rabbit square in the head, just below its long ears. It dropped to the ground, motionless. She ran to the rabbit and popped it into the woven sack she had tied to her waist. Then she darted back behind her tree.

It would be a while before they were likely to see another rabbit. They darted from tree to tree, taking up a new position further along the hillside. They waited fifteen minutes, and were rewarded with the sight of three rabbits, nuzzling under the snow in search of something to nibble. Perry loaded a stone in his slingshot. He looked at his sister. Her eyes widened and she very slowly pointed away from the rabbits. Perry turned his head and saw what Mehitable had seen. A red fox with a black nose was slinking low through the snow, taking cover behind a bump along the hillside. The fox was intent on surprising the rabbits. It wasn't watching its own backside. It was very close to Perry. He quietly pulled the sling back as far as he could and let his rock go. An instant later, Mehitable also let a rock fly. Perry quickly reloaded and sent a third rock. All three rocks hit the fox in the head. The rabbits had bolted. There was no telling which rock killed the fox, not that it mattered. Perry sunk his knife into the fox, letting its blood spill onto the white snow. He quickly gutted Mehitable's rabbit as well. In all the excitement over the fox, they absentmindedly left their slingshots on the ground at the foot of the rabbit-rich hillside.

They had always been a highly successful hunting duo. Rabbits were small and wary, making them naturally hard to hit. For years they had spent the better part of their days as kids roaming the woods with their slingshots perfecting their skills with tens of thousands of rocks flung. They didn't hit every tiny-headed rabbit or addle-brained turkey they aimed for, but they hit enough to provide their family with a significant additional source of food.

Since Mehitable had taken the job at the store, Perry had been left alone to work the woods. He had perfected the art of setting snares. He was proud to show Mehitable his route as he checked from snare to snare. He had been hoping to catch his sister alone anyhow, and he had been looking for just such an opportunity for several weeks. He was nervous to ask, though they were almost as close as twins. Desire overcame his nerves, and the question spilled from his lips, "Pray, do you think Aurilla fancies me?"

Perry's question surprised her. She stopped in her tracks, and looked at him, almost as if he were a stranger. Aurilla had grown up with them. She was just one of a handful of children their age. They had all attended their tiny school together. She had never thought to imagine her friend and her brother as a couple. Mehitable couldn't visualize *herself* with a beau. How was she supposed to imagine her little brother, a gallant swain, romantically involved with one of her closest friends?

Perry interrupted her thoughts. "If I marry Aurilla, she would officially become your sister-in-law."

Mehitable shuddered, shaking off her surprise. She was days away from turning 16. Her little brother had just turned 15. They were still young, but they weren't kids anymore. She put her hand on Perry's shoulder and asked him if he would like her to ask Aurilla for him.

"Pray, please do," Perry begged.

Mehitable nodded. "The first chance I get."

"Before the party?" Perry pushed.

She laughed. "Aye, I shall ask her today if I can."

Perry seemed to leap from snare to snare as they wandered the woods from trap to trap. Mehitable noticed the spring in his step and she thought he had taken on the spirit of a rabbit. He practically bounced through the woods that morning.

They found a trap that had been sprung. There was fresh blood on the snow near the base of the trap, and fluffs of fur in the vicinity. Perhaps it was a fox that had raided Perry's snare. Further down the line, two of Perry's traps had rabbits hanging from the saplings that had snapped back to their fully upright positions. Perry showed Mehitable how to reset the snares.

At the end of Perry's snare-trail there were two large boulders, side by side in the woods. They decided to take a break before returning home. They sat facing each other on the rocks and talked about many things. When Perry had finally finished talking about Aurilla, at least for that moment, Mehitable decided she had something confidential that she would like to share as well. She said, "Perry, I want to tell you something I've never told anyone before. Do you promise to keep it a secret?"

Perry turned his head slightly and twisted his face in confusion. Then he nodded his head earnestly, agreeing to keep her confidence.

Mehitable put her hands on her kneecaps, leaned forward, and whispered loudly, "Sometimes I think I can see ghosts." Then she nodded, as if to confirm all the questions that might be asked. The questions came nevertheless.

"Ghosts? Like the Holy Spirit? Like dead people?" Perry asked excitedly.

Mehitable held her index finger up to her lips, reminding him that she would like him to keep such information to himself. Of course, there wasn't anyone within the sound of her voice. It was the first time she had ever mentioned it out loud.

Perry asked what the ghosts looked like, and whether they were scary.

"Most of the time 'tis like a flash. A quick flicker of movement I see from the corner of my eye. Like a mouse scampering along the base of a wall, gone from sight before you fully realize what you've seen." She shuddered at the thought of seeing a mouse, something she found more unpleasant than ghosts. "Sometimes 'tis like fog in the shape of a person. If I look at it, it starts to come into focus, so that I can see what the person looked like. Usually I just close my eyes or look away."

Perry asked, "Have you always seen the ghosts?"

Mehitable placed her right hand on her cheek, and looked off into the woods, as if she might find the answer to his question in the forest. "I guess I have always seen them. I have always had the good sense to look away. Maybe the spirits knew I was afraid. Since I started working at the store, I have been seeing them more and more. The ghosts no longer seem content to be ignored. They don't seem to care that I wish they'd stay away." She looked at her brother having admitted her fear. She nervously bit her lower lip, and a wrinkle of worry dashed across her forehead.

Perry tried to lighten the moment by joking, "If I ever die, I'll come back and haunt you. You best not be afraid of me!"

Mehitable laughed and flung a woolen mitten at her brother's face. She was glad to have shared her secret, and she was glad the conversation was over. She thought, perhaps, that having given voice to her concern, the ghosts would refrain from showing themselves to her in the future.

They returned home just before noon. Three rabbits and a fox made for a successful morning. Perry worked on tanning the hides. On the way home Perry told Mehitable that he thought the fox skin would make a nice gift for the pretty girlfriend he hoped to have. He confessed that he imagined kissing Aurilla in the moonlight on a cold winter's day, and he imagined the fox's fur, at her neck, tickling his chin. Mehitable rolled her eyes, laughed, put her hand on Perry's shoulder, and asked, "How could she possibly resist such a hopeless romantic?"

Immediately upon returning home, Mehitable turned to the kitchen. She combined oats, pumpkin, and maple syrup into cookies. When they had cooled enough, she put them in a basket, covered them with a cloth, and headed up the road to visit her friend. The first farm she passed was the Lewis farm, where her best friend Polly lived. Normally she would have stopped there, but she was in a hurry. A bit further up the road she came to her friend Aurilla's house. Mehitable was surprised to hear Aurilla say that she had been winking and smiling at Perry for two years before he had finally noticed. Mehitable shook her head back and forth, shrugged, and opened her palms, as if asking God why she had missed the signs of Aurilla and Perry's impending, inevitable romance.

Having asked Perry's question, Mehitable left the cookies on a plate at Aurilla's house, hugged her friend, and set out for home, swinging her empty basket as she walked. Perry would be happy with her news. Mehitable planned to suggest that Perry ask Aurilla to stroll around the village green on New Year's Eve.

A blast of excitement shot up her spine. There were only four more days until the party.

Mehitable worked at the store the following day. It was dark when she woke up, and very cold. She bundled up as tightly as she could before making her long walk to town. She was early, but the proprietor had already arrived. She made a fire in the fireplace, striking flint on steel and igniting a tiny nest of dried lichens.

Tommy Todd had some questions for her. Mehitable's family was well-known for their sheep, and Mehitable had mastered the art of carding the wool with paddles, spinning it into thread, and dyeing it different colors. It had been on his mind for some time.

Tommy's questions led to his decision to invest in a carding factory. Mehitable happily encouraged him. Carding was her least favorite part of the process. She thought people *would* pay to have the carding done in Tommy's factory.

Mehitable loved everything about working at the store. She enjoyed visiting with the customers, helping them find whatever they were looking for, and tidying up the merchandise so it always looked most presentable. She even enjoyed sweeping the floors and cleaning the windows. There were very few customers that day, and Mehitable kept herself busy, absent-mindedly cleaning things that were already clean, the fine silver, the delicate china, and the fancy fabrics. As she cleaned, her thoughts kept returning to the party.

At three o'clock in the afternoon, her friends Polly and Aurilla met her in front of the store. They were dressed in their Sunday best, though it was only Saturday afternoon. They both carried large baskets full of baked goods. They walked together from the store to the library. The library was just as deserted as the store. Since nobody else was there, the librarian permitted them to practice the reading they intended to share with guests on Tuesday evening. The selection was from Shakespeare's Macbeth, and the girls quickly assigned among themselves the roles of witch number one, witch number two, and witch number three. Of course, none of the girls intended to *dress* the part. The librarian let the girls take the book from the library, though there was only one copy. They planned to *make do* by passing the book back and forth during the reading.

Polly chided her friends, "What are we doing, reading about nasty witches' recipes on Holy Innocents Day? Is it wise to tempt the fates?" Then she cackled like she imagined a witch would cackle, making the other girls laugh. The librarian also chuckled and warned the girls that she would be closing the library in a couple of minutes.

Polly, Aurilla, and Mehitable bundled up, picked up their

baskets, and left the library. Their first stop was at widow Martin's house. Mrs. Martin had agreed to chaperone them from door to door, and had warm cider brewing at the edge of her hearth fire. The tradition of wassailing meant delivering warm cider and cheerful hymns to their neighbors' homes. In addition to carrying cider they also served their baked goods. They received many compliments on their harmonies, and even more praise for their cookies. Alexander Murdock, the proprietor of the Inn at Eagle Tavern reminded the girls that Holy Innocents Day was a solemn observance of King Herod's order to kill all the baby Jewish boys at the time of Christ. Mehitable shuddered at the reminder, and a vision of a swirling pile of the ghosts of countless dead babies appeared to her behind Mr. Murdock. They thanked Mr. Murdock, Polly handed him a cookie, and they were off to the next stop.

It was ten o'clock when they arrived at Mehitable's house. Polly's father, John Lewis, met them there, and escorted Polly and Aurilla home. It had been a long day and Mehitable was tired. Her little sisters had been asleep for hours. Mehitable lay there in the dark trying to shake the image of piles of dead ghost babies. She alternated between excited thoughts about her upcoming party and the ghoulish atrocities, neither of which permitted her much rest. It seemed like she had just closed her eyes when her 11-year-old sister Lavinia shook her, telling her it was time for breakfast. Their 8-year-old sister, Permelia, had crawled in with Mehitable in the early morning hours, as she often did. Waking Permelia often required significant effort.

Chapter 3

December 29, 1799

Polly and Aurilla met Mehitable in front of her house, shortly after breakfast. Mehitable had a sled loaded up with clumps of dried flowers, hunks of bark, and sacks full of dyed corn leaves collected in August and September. She also had a bag full of dried aromatics, including peppermint leaves, rosemary needles, yarrow, and lemon grass. The girls took turns pulling the rope, dragging the laden sled behind them. They chattered happily all the way to town and arrived at church late. Mehitable dropped the sled's rope in the snow, and the girls slinked into church, joining their families. After a very short night of sleep, Mehitable was challenged to stifle yawns throughout the service. Several times during the service, she recalled the gyre of ghost babies that kept her awake the night before.

Finally, the doors of the little church opened, and families spilled forth into a crisp, sunny, early winter's morning. Polly, Aurilla, and Mehitable met just outside the church on their way to retrieve Mehitable's sled. They pulled the sled across the green, buried beneath a couple of inches of snow, and passed a couple of men who were talking about their plans to build a proper, Congregational church, suitable for the needs of the growing town. They dropped the sled-rope in front of Union Academy and stepped inside.

Bright light spilled in from the windows of the small, two-story schoolhouse. Mehitable sparked a fire in the stone fireplace at the back of the room on the first floor. Polly used a flame on the tip of a twig to light several oil lamps to further brighten the room. Aurilla began sweeping the room with a straw broom. When the fire was made and the lanterns were lit, Polly and Mehitable wiped the surface of each desk and all the walls with damp cloths. Mehitable wondered where dust came from. After an hour of cleaning, the girls turned to decorating.

On a hot day in September, the girls had gathered to dye dried corn leaves. Mehitable had been working on the barrels of dye all summer. She had used raspberries and beets to turn one barrel of water red. Barberry and onion skins turned a second barrel of water orange. Blueberries, grapes, and indigo from Tommy Todd's Store turned a third barrel bluish-purple. The dried corn leaves soaked up the rich, deep colors. The leaves also soaked up the pungent vinegar which helped lock the color into the leaves. In addition to dyeing the corn leaves, they soaked the white fronds of Queen Anne's Lace in the barrels. In the months since, most of the vinegar smell had subsided. Mehitable was glad the colors hadn't faded much. Ironically, each of the girls' favorite colors was represented: purple for Polly, orange for Aurilla, and red for Mehitable.

While they fashioned bark into vases for their dried flower arrangements, they reminisced about their school years together. They told stories, laughed, and joked. They matched all the unmarried boys and girls in town, beginning with Perry and Aurilla. When they had finished, only Mehitable, Polly, Anson Smudge, and Reuben Sanford remained unmatched. Mehitable's mind had wandered. Polly offered to take Reuben Sanford, and suggested Mehitable could have Anson Smudge. Aurilla nudged Mehitable, to see if she cared to offer a thought. Polly watched Mehitable's face, expectantly. Mehitable apologized for letting her mind wander away. Polly repeated her offer. Mehitable was surprised. First Aurilla, then

Polly. She wondered why everyone was in such a hurry. The only thought she had to offer her friends that day was simply, "Nay! No, thank you, just the same!"

The vases were finished. The girls turned their attention to arranging the dried flowers. They placed the tall, brightly colored corn leaves in the middle of each vase and surrounded them with dried wildflowers. They finished each arrangement with the Queen Anne's Lace. Finally, they tied fabric ribbons around the base of each vase. Mehitable thanked her friends for their help and commented on the mass of color that the flowers created. They spread the three dozen arrangements throughout Union Academy, bringing a splash of festiveness to every dark corner of the building. Then they got the sacks of aromatics from the sled-wagon. They covered every square inch of both floors with the concoction.

It was late afternoon when the girls finished their decorating. Aurilla blew out the oil lamps. Polly extinguished the fire. Mehitable packed up the last of their supplies and loaded them into the sled. Then she hugged her friends and thanked them again. They stood in the doorway, surveying their creation. Mehitable breathed deeply through her nose and exclaimed, "It looks beautiful and it smells delicious. I can't wait for the party. Two days to go, friends."

The girls walked lazily together up Lewis Road as day gave way to night.

After a happy day of decorating, a hearty Sunday dinner, and a few songs with her family, Mehitable fell asleep easily, with no thoughts of dark spirits. She slept soundly and awoke the next morning feeling rejuvenated. Her feet were moving the moment they touched the plank floor. She felt like her ordinary self as she dressed quickly and hurried to the kitchen. Her mother had breakfast ready. Mehitable bundled up warmly, grabbed a strip of bacon and a biscuit, hugged her mother, picked up her basket and headed out of the front door, well before dawn.

She hummed her way down the road, enjoying the brisk frostiness of a dry, early winter morning. It was dark, but her feet easily followed the wagon wheel path down the road to town. When she finished nibbling her biscuit, she cleaned her teeth with a frayed sassafras twig. She arrived at twenty minutes to seven, clearly early for work. Nevertheless, Tommy plucked the watch from his vest pocket to verify Mehitable's punctual arrival. He smiled at her kindly, her reward for arriving early. She started the fire and put on a pot of peppermint leaves. Mehitable had suggested serving tea to shoppers. Tommy noticed that shoppers tended to stay in the store longer and buy more when they had a cup of tea.

It was a busy day at Tommy Todd's Store. Townsfolk were busy making final preparations for the party. There was great interest in things such as hats, scarfs, handkerchiefs, neckerchiefs, broaches, hatpins, ribbon, buttons, bows, and perfume. In addition to looking their finest, ladies competed to outdo themselves and each other by baking their finest recipes. Mehitable sold a lot of sugar, milled flower, and the exotic fruits, brought in from New York City, imported from the Caribbean islands along with the sugar. Her mouth watered as Tommy's customers cleaned out his supply of limes, oranges, and lemons.

Aurilla and her mother stopped in to see Tommy with a large collection of handcrafted hat pins. After an hour of negotiations, Tommy purchased half a year's worth of their handiwork, and they seemed to be pleased with the prices they received. It seemed to Mehitable that Tommy spent more time purchasing things than selling things. A couple of times a week, Tommy would venture to nearby towns, and trade goods like Aurilla's hatpins for something *they* had that *he* could add to his stock.

Mrs. Martin stopped in for some kerosene for her lamps. She enjoyed the taste of Mehitable's peppermint tea and asked how it was made. Mehitable told her it was made simply from sugar and dried peppermint leaves. Then Mehitable whispered behind her hand that it cured flatulence. It wasn't the first time Mehitable had seen an, "Oh really" look on a customer's face. Mrs. Martin was motivated to leave with a quarter pound bag of Mehitable's peppermint tea leaves. After Mrs. Martin left, Tommy looked at Mehitable, smiled, and knowingly shook his head from side to side. They were in between customers at that moment, and Tommy asked, "Doesn't Mrs. Martin know that she has a huge clump of peppermint that grows right in front of her house?"

Mehitable smiled back across the store, and asked Tommy, "Aye, but does Mrs. Martin's peppermint cure flatulence?"

Tall and angular, Tommy covered his ears with his knobby knuckles, as if shocked to be hearing such a suggestion. The look on Tommy's face struck Mehitable, causing her to laugh, and she thought, *Tommy Todd is odd.* She liked working with Tommy and listening to him dream of the other businesses he would establish someday. Mehitable also liked Tommy's wife, Betty, who was always most kind. They had a houseful of kids, and Mehitable wondered why none of them worked in the store instead of her. Sometimes, Betty would appear for a couple of minutes in the store with their 2-year-old baby named Relief on her hip. Sometimes when Mehitable saw Betty carrying the baby girl, she wondered what sort of "relief" Betty might have been experiencing to name her little girl, Relief Todd. Maybe it had something to do with the line of potions, pastes, powders, oils, and miracle cures Tommy carried in his store.

It was nearly quitting time when Anson entered through the back door of the store, surprising Mehitable and making her jump. He enjoyed surprising her in that manner, and he was able to surprise her almost every day. Mehitable knew she should expect his arrival at five minutes to three, every afternoon. As usual, Anson laughed at her expense on his way to talk to Tommy. He began reporting on the day's work at Tommy's still, next door.

Just then, Reuben Sanford came through the door. Anson looked up from his conversation with his boss and saw Mehitable smile at Reuben. Anson frowned, and returned to his update. Reuben wandered over to say hello to Tommy and Anson, joining in their conversation. Mehitable noticed that Reuben appeared to be fascinated by Tommy's interest in business and machinery.

Mehitable brought Reuben a cup of tea and smiled at him again, interrupting a conversation on the details of operating a still. Reuben thanked Mehitable and returned promptly to Tommy's lesson on fermentation. Mehitable's workday was over, and she was glad to slip out the back door of the store, unnoticed. She was happy that Anson was stuck in a conversation with Tommy and Reuben. She never knew what to say to the moody young man who always wanted to scare her. They had nothing in common, and in Mehitable's opinion, they had never had an interesting or engaging conversation, despite having attended school together for ten years.

When Mehitable arrived at home, her mother was busy baking pies. The house smelled like burning sugar. Wilhelmina smiled at Mehitable, confessing that the sugar had gotten away from her. Sometimes her brothers and sisters were a handful, but they had finally settled down. Mehitable took over tending the conversion of sugar to molasses. Wilhelmina asked Mehitable about her day at the store while she peeled potatoes. Then they talked about the party. "What's everyone baking?" Wilhelmina asked.

Mehitable answered, "It seems everyone is making their specialties." Polly's mother was making Apple Brown Betty. Aurilla's mother was making Blueberry Buckle. Betty Todd was making cider donuts. Mrs. Martin was making lemon cream puffs. Mehitable smiled naughtily at her mother. "I think I'll skip dinner and just have dessert."

Wilhelmina raised an eyebrow, looked up at her daughter, and asked, "Who's going to eat my Shoo-Fly Pie, with all those rare delicacies to tempt them?" Wilhelmina couldn't arrive at any function in town without her famous recipe. It was tradition. It was expected. She rarely went anywhere without a fresh molasses pie under a cloth in her basket.

When Mehitable had finished turning the sugar into molasses for her mother's pie, she made a batch of her own specialty, her maple, pumpkin, and oat cookies. While her cookies were baking, she stood for a moment, her hands on her hips, and asked her mother what her favorite color was.

Wilhelmina looked up from her peeling. She had moved from potatoes to carrots, made an indecisive frown, and said, "I don't have a favorite color, just like I don't have a favorite child." She winked at her daughter. "How could a mother choose? How about you, dear?"

Mehitable considered, briefly. She continued with an intensity that surprised herself, "I like red. Burgundy. The same color as my dress, I think. Now, my dear mother, how can you claim not to have favorites? What color are our dishes? What color are the curtains? What color are the table coverings? What color is your fancy dress?" Her mother's gaze followed her daughter's finger as it pointed about the house. "And look at your knitting basket. There are five different colors of yarn, and they're all green."

Her mother nodded begrudgingly as Mehitable finished her observation. "I guess you must be right. I never really noticed, but what you say is true." She looked back into Mehitable's hazel eyes, the same color as Granny's, and said, "I'm sorry."

Then they laughed. It was a silly thing to notice. It was a silly thing not to notice. It didn't deserve an apology, nor did it require forgiveness. Mehitable hugged her mother. "I can't believe I haven't noticed it sooner. Maybe you like to bring the outdoors inside so we can feel connected to nature even when we're indoors."

Her mother nodded, affirming her daughter's conclusion. She hung the pot of potatoes and carrots over the fire and began working on a pan of biscuits to go with the ham.

Mehitable's 2-year-old brother, Otto, tugged at the hem of her dress. She bent over, scooped him up onto her hip, and asked her mother if she would like a cup of tea.

Chapter 4
December 31, 1799

The next morning, Reuben was back at the store immediately after it opened. Mehitable had just finished frying some donuts. She was trying to prove another theory to Tommy: customers would buy more if the store smelled like fresh donuts. She put a donut in Reuben's hand, and asked if he would be coming to the party later that night, just as Anson came through the door. Reuben answered, "I wouldn't miss it for the world."

Tommy plucked the watch from his pocket, noting that Anson was fifteen minutes late for work. Anson watched as the boss pointed at his timepiece and shook his head from side to side. Tommy was a very understanding, likable man, and easy to work for, although he was very particular about punctuality. Mehitable put a donut in Anson's hand while Tommy and Reuben began another conversation about the business of converting rye to whiskey. Instead of thanking Mehitable, Anson walked away, mocking in a high-pitched voice, "I wouldn't miss it for the world."

It was another busy day at Tommy's bustling store, yet still it seemed to go by so slowly. When something as momentous as a sweet sixteen birthday party, or a once in a hundred years' celebration occurred, it was difficult to focus on the ordinary everyday goings on of a workday. It was finally three o'clock. Mehitable was dismayed that Anson was headed home at the same time as she was. "Don't you have to stay fifteen minutes late?" she asked.

Anson mockingly repeated what she said, in the same way he had mocked Reuben earlier. "I don't care," he added. "Let Reuben work at the still. See how he likes it. Better him than me." They walked along silently. Mehitable's thoughts tumbled in her head as she contemplated how to quickly get ready for the party and be back in town by seven o'clock. The day she had been looking forward to all year had finally arrived. Somehow, she had forgotten that Anson was walking along beside her.

Anson's stomach gamboled like a week-old colt in an open meadow. He had tried everything he could think of to get Mehitable's attention. Finally, she was walking alongside of him. What better time to ask, he thought? Anson considered clearing his throat to make sure he had her attention, but instead he just blurted it out, "Can I kiss you?"

Mehitable returned to the moment and realized that Anson had spoken to her. "Pardon me? What did you say?"

"I said, can I kiss you? In case you hadn't noticed, I've been trying to court you. I want to kiss you, then I want to—" he paused briefly, then concluded, "marry you."

Mehitable was surprised. She answered without thinking. "What is wrong with everybody? Nay, I don't want to kiss you. I don't want to marry you. I just want to have a fun party. I'm not ready to be a grown woman. Maybe I never will be. Maybe I'll just be a spinster. Anyway, we don't have anything in common, Anson Smudge. Why would you want to marry me?"

Anson's face reddened with anger. "My mother and father don't have anything in common. Women and men don't do the same things anyway. I want to marry you because you're pretty. I want to marry you because I'm a man now. I want to marry you because," he paused again, "there isn't anybody else left."

"How gallant," Mehitable chuckled. "I don't think we belong together, I'm sorry."

"You're sweet on Reuben Sanford," Anson jealously accused. "I saw you smiling at him. I saw him looking at you. He told Tommy Todd he wanted to marry you. I heard him. I wanted to put a pitchfork in him. You're going to marry Reuben Sanford. Admit it."

Mehitable stopped walking, and Anson stopped also. She repeated her initial thought. "What is wrong with everyone. I am not sweet on Reuben Sanford. I did smile at him. What is wrong with smiling? People are supposed to be nice to each other. You might think of that now and again. I'm not going to marry Reuben Sanford, and I'm not going to marry you. I just want to enjoy my birthday. Do you understand me Anson Smudge?" She turned and resumed her rapid march toward home, without waiting for a response.

Anson's frown tightened. His brow contracted. Not that she saw his expression. "So, you'll think about it then," he hollered after her. He remained several steps behind her the rest of the way home. When she turned toward her front door he stopped briefly in front of her house, still fuming. His cheeks were red, hot, and it was a good thing he was alone. He punched the fist of his right hand into the open palm of his left hand, as if he wished he was punching something. Somebody. Anybody. He spit into the snow on the side of the road before continuing toward home.

Uncharacteristically, Mehitable slammed the front door, waking Otto and startling her mother. "What's wrong," Wilhelmina asked. Then she nodded sympathetically, as Mehitable told her about her walk with Anson. "Try to put it out of your mind, dear. Sometimes boys, er… young men act strangely at that age. Let me help you get ready for the party."

Mehitable was done first. She waited while her mother finished getting ready. Mehitable's jaw dropped when she saw her mother. She had never noticed how beautiful her mother was. There she stood in an emerald green gown, surrounding mint green checked petticoats, white mitts, a white stomacher with green, floral embroidery, and a mint green neckerchief tucked in at her chest. Her hair was pinned up tightly behind her head, and a small, felt, pancake-shaped hat with emerald green ribbon surrounding the tiny top of the hat was perched on top of her head at a slight angle. She had seen her mother's dress, but she couldn't remember ever having seen her wear it. Wilhelmina held her arms out in front of her, to hold her daughter's hands. A proud tear rolled down her cheek, and she told Mehitable she looked radiant. Mehitable smiled and thought, *This is a moment to hold on to.*

Horace's cousin, Millicent, had bravely volunteered to watch the children, not just Mehitable's brothers and sisters, but Polly's brothers and sisters also. Horace sat on a plain chair on his front porch, enjoying a smoke, while Wilhelmina transferred responsibility for the children and household to the care of Cousin Millicent.

John and Anna Lewis pulled up in their large wagon-sled drawn by a matched pair of strong Appaloosas. In the wagon, Polly sat next to Aurilla on a bench behind John and Anna. John handed the reins to his wife and jumped to the ground. He helped Wilhelmina up next to Anna. Then he helped Mehitable up next to Polly and Aurilla. Horace, Perry, and John Lewis stood on the back of the sleigh. It was a dark night, but the horses knew the way, and Anna had no difficulty driving them down the well-worn road to town.

They were among the first to arrive. Mehitable wanted to greet people as they arrived at Union Academy. That way she could make sure she had a chance to visit with everyone, with at least a, "how do you do," or "lovely to see you," or "thank you for coming out tonight." The party was advertised for seven thirty. Most people arrived around eight. Anson Smudge arrived a couple of minutes after eight.

"You look pretty," he said. "Will you walk with me?" he asked, pushing his elbow into her side.

"Thank you," she said. *Better get this over with*, she thought. "Just for a minute," she added. "I have guests to visit inside."

They hadn't taken but a few steps when Anson belligerently said, "Like Reuben Sanford."

Mehitable patiently responded, "We discussed this already, Anson. Nay. Practically the whole town is inside the Academy. We should be as well."

"Who gives a hang about the rest of the town, all I care about is you," Anson pleaded.

A strange thought crossed Mehitable's mind. "Have you been drinking, Anson Smudge?" she accused.

He answered, "So what if I have. What difference does it make?"

Mehitable pardoned herself and headed toward the party. Anson stomped off toward Eagle Tavern, across the village green. At the door to Union Academy, Mehitable turned and shook her head judgmentally. When she walked through the door everyone cheered. The decorations looked stunning against the oak walls. The crunchy aromatics on the floor had been stomped and stirred by the movement of the entire village, and Mehitable thought it smelled like heaven. She felt blessed. She thought, *How lucky I am to be here at this moment, on New Year's Eve, my birthday, December 31st, 1799.*

Polly brought Mehitable a toasty cup of apple cider. They talked for a few minutes. It was fun to see all of the adults from town sitting in the small seats facing the front of a room, where normally the schoolteacher would be giving lessons. The girls talked for a few minutes, and then found themselves surrounded by a large group of adults, mostly parents and grandparents.

In a big voice, Horace asked John Lewis to tell his daddy's story. Mehitable looked at Polly, and they both shook their heads. Mehitable's father always made sure somebody was entertaining any gathered crowd. Polly's father didn't need much encouragement to tell his father's old war stories.

John began, scratching his chin between his thumb and fore-finger, contemplatively. "Aye! I still can't believe it's been two years since Father passed. He would have loved to be here, at the dawn of a new century, telling these stories himself."

John paused for a moment. Mehitable gulped hard. A faint vision of Josiah Lewis appeared right in front of John. The ghostly image inserted his thumbs in his waistband, hiked his breeches up, and stretched his arms wide, as if asking the crowd to encourage John to continue. Mehitable cleared her throat slightly and began to clap. Neighbors, friends, and family joined in, and Mehitable closed her eyes and listened, silently praying that the image of Josiah would go away.

"Of course, you might remember that Father served in the French and Indian War. That was before we were a country. That was before our town was founded. Our family lived in Connecticut at that time. Josiah was a young man then."

Mehitable opened her eyes, just a sliver. The ghost was grinning proudly, and his right hand was moving in tight circles at chest level, hoping his son would keep the story moving. Mehitable felt as if Josiah was looking directly at her, like Josiah could sense that Mehitable could see him there. A tiny squeak escaped from between her clenched teeth, and she slammed her eyes closed again.

In no great hurry, John continued, "Father liked to tell the story of how they liberated Fort Carillon from the French. It was late July, in the year 1759. Father would have been," John paused, looked up as if the answer could come to him from the heavens, made a quick calculation, and declared, "26-years-old. It would be another 5 years before I came into the world. I believe Father said there were about 400 Frenchmen occupying the fort. We were led by General Amherst, and we had a force of 11,000. They knew they couldn't hold the fort, but they hoped to have time to blow the fort to pieces before they retreated. As they marched toward the fort, Father was next to a man from Norfolk, England, a young man, maybe two years older than Father. A man with a young wife named Becky. The man's father was a viscount, which I guess is something like a duke or an earl."

Mehitable attempted to open her eyes again, and Josiah's ghost was rolling his eyes so dramatically that he was rolling his head in big circles as well. Mehitable quickly looked to a corner of the room, where two walls met the roof. She could see Josiah in the corner of her vision, but she couldn't disrespect Polly's father by keeping her eyes closed throughout his long story.

John picked up his pace a little, pleasing his father's ghost. "And wouldn't you know it, the French shot off all of their cannons from the Fort at once. Father heard the sound, looked at his friend Roger Townshend, who happened to be a lieutenant colonel, just as a cannonball blew a hole right through the middle of his belly, powerful enough to send his legs in one direction and his head and torso in another. Though he must have been killed instantly, Father said Townshend had a look of incredulity on his face, as if he was wondering how this could have happened to him."

Mehitable winced, drawing her chin toward her chest, horrified to think of Roger Townshend, and his young bride all alone back in Norfolk England. She glanced quickly at Polly's father, then looked down at her feet.

"So, before the British were able to take over the Fort, the French blew up most everything they couldn't carry, and significant portions of the fort's walls before heading north. Of course, you all know the British finally won the Seven Year War, which we knew as the French and Indian War. Then, almost sixteen years later, Father was back. The British had renamed it Fort Ticonderoga and the nearby fort at Crown Point had been named Fort Amherst."

Polly sat forward, turned, and looked intently into Mehitable's face. She stretched her eyes open wide, and Mehitable understood her friend was afraid that her father would go on all night long. In fact, John did go into seemingly endless detail about how Ethan Allen and the Green Mountain Boys captured Fort Ticonderoga, not even a month after the Revolutionary War had begun. John got sidetracked briefly, informing the young folks and reminding the old folks that Ethan Allen's brother and cousin were founders of Poultney, and Ethan himself was with them when they first set eyes upon the region. Ethan Allen was a notorious Revolutionary War hero, especially famous for capturing Fort Ticonderoga. He was also known for his irreverent countenance. Ethan Allen was a frequent visitor in Poultney in its early days.

Then John sped up and started talking with greater excitement. "Father had been stationed at the fort. Maybe some of you don't know that my mother, Molly was a messenger. Periodically she would make the long journey from town up the old military road to what used to be called Rattlesnake Hill. We know it now as Fort Independence. Then she would cross the float bridge, walking across Lake Champlain to Ticonderoga. She would deliver messages, visit with Father, then return home. 'Tis hard to believe Mother has been gone for ten years now." Then he grew quiet for a moment.

Mehitable squirmed uncomfortably. As if introduced, the ghost of Polly's grandmother appeared, right in the corner Mehitable had grown accustomed to looking off into. Molly's ghost stood, as if on a mountain with a telescoping field glass, at her eye, tilting forward, as if a couple of inches closer would make whatever she was looking at appear more clearly. Her free hand pointed in the same direction as the spyglass.

Molly's ghost fidgeted but kept her watch as John continued, "Mother was also a war hero. After our men abandoned Ticonderoga, and spilled onto the float bridge, Mother was on the top of a hill observing the retreat through her spyglass." John pulled the spyglass from the pocket of his breeches and passed it around the crowd.

"Mother made her way home quickly, sounding the alarm all along the way. Because of Mother, the villages of Castleton, Fair Haven, and the twenty families that called Poultney home, safely fled south." John told the crowd about the excitement of fleeing with his mother Molly, and his baby brother Benjamin, just ahead of General Burgoyne and the British army.

Mehitable squirmed in her seat as John went on to talk about his father's role in the Battle of Hubbardton. Mehitable's elbows were on her knees and her head was in her hands. Molly's ghost had given up the spyglass and stood with her hands on her hips, facing the crowd. Every time she looked, it seemed like both Josiah and Molly were looking directly at her.

Finally, John made quick work of completing the story. He sped through his tale of Josiah's role in the Battle of Bennington, and then Saratoga. Saratoga proved to be a turning point in the war. "Because of Father, we delayed the British at Hubbardton, and then we won at Saratoga, and because of Mother, we escaped General Burgoyne's visit to town. How's that for a short story, Horace?" John concluded.

Mehitable looked up as John mentioned her father's name, just in time to see Josiah's and Molly's ghosts disappear in a matter of seconds. She shivered, then felt a sense of relief as her father started talking to the crowd. Mehitable hadn't realized that Cousin Millicent's husband had died in the Battle of Hubbardton, and she wasn't sure why she didn't know that sooner.

Chapter 5

December 31, 1799

Horace had released control of the crowd for a while, and Mehitable remained seated, thinking. Suddenly, Mehitable realized that Polly and Aurilla had disappeared from her sides while she had been listening to John Lewis. As she was trying to decide what to do next, Reuben Sanford approached her. He touched her elbow, and she gasped slightly. Mehitable stood up and thought, *Why haven't I noticed how handsome he is?*

Reuben asked, "Would you care to walk in the evening air with me?"

Mehitable thought, *Oh dear, not again.* "Maybe for a few minutes, yes." She nodded.

Reuben complimented Mehitable's appearance. "You look lovely in Burgundy," he concluded.

Just then, Anson Smudge stepped from the front porch of the Inn at Eagle Tavern. He saw Mehitable walking with Reuben Sanford, holding on to his arm. He turned around, and stomped back inside the tavern, before Reuben and Mehitable turned the corner on the south end of the green.

Mehitable noticed another couple strolling just ahead of them. Her stomach cartwheeled as she realized it was her brother, Perry and her friend, Aurilla. *That's where she went,* Mehitable thought.

That's when Mehitable realized she had forgotten where she was, and what she was doing. Again. Reuben stopped walking, put his hand on her shoulder, drawing her closer to him. It felt exciting and reassuring at the same time. His touch was strong and comforting.

"So, what do you think, Mehitable?" he asked.

Mehitable gasped, "Oh my goodness, Reuben. I'm so sorry. I was distracted. When I saw Aurilla and my brother strolling ahead of us, my mind must have wandered. Did you ask me a question?"

Reuben laughed tolerantly. "I told you that I've been admiring you for over a year, and I wondered if there was a chance you might fall in love with me. Then I suggested we might become each other's *most beloved*."

Mehitable's jaw dropped. "I had no idea," she blurted. "Anson told me you wanted to marry me, but I never in a million years believed it." She looked at her shoes, and it occurred to her that her feet were cold. She looked back up into the expectant eyes of the handsome young man, three years older than herself, and said, "You're a very nice man, but I'm not ready. Besides, I want to marry a musical man," she said dreamily, "a man who can make the strings of a violin wail, whilst I play the virginal. I want to marry a man who can sing in a deep, bass voice, and read me Shakespeare. Maybe you should walk around the green with my friend Polly." Then she joked, "Why don't you take some singing lessons, buy a violin and marry both of us. We shall live like the two wives of Moses in the Bible."

Reuben smiled at Mehitable. "You may be only 16-years-old, but you are already an amazing woman!" Then he wasted no time following up. "Do you really think Polly is sweet on me?"

Mehitable nodded, slightly at first, then a little more vigorously. "I am sure of it." Then she smiled.

Reuben admitted, "I have to admit, I've always admired *both* of you. You're very different girls. Er. Women. Both alluring, wonderful women. I'd be honored to ask Polly to walk with me. Are you sure you wouldn't be offended if I asked her tonight?"

"Not at all," Mehitable encouraged. " 'Twas my idea!"

On the way back to the party, Reuben joked, "Now tell me how God allowed Moses to have two wives!"

When they got back to Union Academy, Polly suggested Reuben go in, she wanted to have a moment to herself outside before returning to the party. In the dark, starry, winter evening, she asked herself whether she had made the right decision. She did fancy Reuben, and he was the only man she had ever met that she could imagine a future with. She felt the beginning of a tear at the corner of her eye and quickly brushed it away. She breathed deeply and concluded, *but alas, if I'm not ready, I'm not ready.* Just then, Perry and Aurilla rounded the corner, both smiling from ear to ear. They waved at Mehitable and proceeded to begin another lap around the green. She inhaled, drawing in another breath of fresh air, opened the door, and returned to her birthday party.

Horace had gathered the crowd back together, and Reuben's father, Oliver Sanford, was just beginning to tell a story. He saw Mehitable enter and motioned her forward. She closed the door behind her and swiftly took a seat in the front row.

For many years, Oliver had kept his stories about the horrors of war to himself. The passing of President Washington half a month earlier, compounded with the passing from one century to another had put Oliver in a melancholy mood. He turned to John Lewis and said, " 'Tis time that young people learned about the sacrifices made by their parents and grandparents. If we don't tell them about the cost of freedom, they might take it for granted. We must not shield them from the unpleasantness of it all. Thank you for helping me see that and for getting us started, John." Then Oliver addressed the celebrants. "John didn't mention another big benefit from Ethan Allen's capture of Fort Ticonderoga. They didn't just capture a fort between two major waterways, they also captured 120 cannons. Cannons that allowed our young nation to win some very important early victories in our struggle for independence. The cannons from Ticonderoga allowed us to defeat the British in Boston after the Battle of Bunker Hill."

Then Oliver paused for a moment and rose to his feet. Mehitable looked at him and saw worry among the wrinkles on his face. Oliver continued, "I don't think I have talked about this in over twenty years." Oliver told the crowd about how he was captured by the British in April of 1777. The British held New York City, and from that position, they began a campaign into Connecticut that was known as the Battle of Ridgefield. Oliver had been part of the militia in Connecticut and was taken prisoner during what was called the Danbury Raid.

A tear rolled down the cheek of the 56-year-old man as he prepared to tell the town about the pain he had endured 22 years earlier. "We were taken to a place called the Livingston Sugar House on Crown Street in Manhattan. 'Twas a refinery and a warehouse—the ugliest building you ever saw. The exterior was unwelcoming. The interior was like a dungeon. It was filthy, dark, and the dead air hung there without moving." Mehitable's eyes grew wide as Oliver described a six-story building, exactly as she had seen it in her dream a few nights earlier. The scene of that nightmare repeated in her mind. Again, she saw the ghost of the man rise from his body, the ghost of the man who had been unceremoniously dumped into the shallow trench by the old death cart operator.

Oliver recounted, "We were held prisoner for over six months. Every single day was a struggle for survival. We never went outside or saw sunlight. There was no chance for exercise. There was no opportunity for washing or bathing. The drinking water was horrible. The nicest word I could use to describe the Sugar House is *squalid*. Many men starved to death. Our gums bled, and our teeth fell out, as a result of the scurvy. Our captors spoke to each other of honor but treated us worse than vermin. They added arsenic to our hardtack rations. For those of you who don't know, hardtack is a primary source of food for soldiers. 'Tis made from three-parts flour to one-part water, plus a little salt. That mixture is pressed flat, and holes are poked in at regular intervals, then baked for half an hour. It might not sound like a delicacy, but we considered ourselves lucky if we could eat *anything*, on any given day." Oliver's head drooped, and he looked at a crack in the floorboards beneath his feet. "A moldy biscuit. Raw pork. Wormy flour. Polluted water." Mehitable thought Oliver's voice sounded like he was on the verge of being overcome with emotion; like he might burst into tears and begin sobbing. After a moment, Oliver continued, "That is what we got when we were lucky enough to have food. Often, we'd be forced to go for days without anything to eat. Most men weighed less than a hundred pounds. But we learned not to complain. Even the slightest complaint was met harshly."

Oliver shivered in the warm, colorful room, and continued, "The building was cold, and damp. We had nothing to wear but the clothes we were captured in, if we were lucky enough to keep them. There were no blankets. Even as crowded as it was, there was nothing to do but shiver. To say it was cold and miserable would be a severe understatement. We were not allowed to speak with one another. If we talked, we were accused of inciting riots. Sometimes you could mutter quietly through parsed lips, but what could you say that would be worth taking the risk? Imagine the boredom. Imagine being so overcrowded you couldn't help but bump into somebody every time you moved, practically whenever you breathed. The loneliness was crushing. Our farm animals are treated like royalty in castles compared to that prison."

Oliver brought his arms tightly to his side. He pulled his shoulders in and he shuffled his feet so that there was no space between his legs, shrinking his presence as greatly as he could to illustrate what it felt like to live amongst such overcrowding. "At one time there were so many prisoners that when we lay down to sleep, we had to coordinate flipping from side to side, on command, *flip left*, or *flip right*. There was no expectation that anything would ever improve. Endless hopelessness. Every day, at least a handful of men died, many from disease, some from starvation, some from freezing, some from injuries, and I would say that some men just died from a lack of any will to go on."

Tears streamed down Mehitable's cheek. Oliver looked around the room and could see that his story was having a profound impact on everyone in the room. Mrs. Martin filled the pause by honking into a handkerchief. Betty Todd sniffled like she had been crying for hours, and Oliver's friend John Lewis looked like he had just lost his best friend. Oliver's voice caught in his throat again, yet he continued, "The boss at the prison was named Cunningham. He had an enormous, muscular slave named Richmond, who carried a whip. Cunningham liked to watch the slave whip prisoners to within an inch of their lives. Sometimes the whippings happened on the spot. Often the prisoners were taken to Cunningham's home and featured at his extravagant parties, tortured as entertainment for his guests. These prisoners rarely returned. You learned not to complain about anything, not to say a word to anyone, and not to make eye contact. The best way to survive was to become *invisible*."

Oliver's lips turned down. Still on the verge of tears he continued, "One day, my cousin, well, maybe my third or fourth cousin, Daniel was chewing on shoe leather. It had been days since we had anything to eat. Many men had taken to chewing on their clothes or boots to give their stomachs some illusion of having been fed. Daniel was standing next to me, and his son Jeremiah was standing next to him. For the crime of making eye contact, Cunningham ordered his men to move Jeremiah to the prison ship named the *Whitby*. That was just one of the prison ships anchored in the harbor off the island of Manhattan. Daniel was so devastated that he cried out, begging Cunningham to leave his boy, Jerry. I can still hear Cunningham's evil laughter. I can still see the bright white teeth of Richmond, sharing his proud smile with Cunningham. The boss always seemed to enjoy every aspect of Richmond's performance. I can still feel the wind from the flight of the whip through the air as it delivered strike after strike. I can still hear Daniel's screams, from the pain inflicted by the whip and from the devastating thought of separation from his son. It is hard to describe, and it may be hard to believe. Somehow, I almost feel like *I* can *feel* the blows. The blows of the whip on my own skin. When the whipping was over, Jerry was taken away first. Then, Daniel was taken away afterward, removed from the building with the dead. The prison employed a couple of women who sewed the dead bodies into blankets. Daniel wasn't dead yet, so he wasn't sewed into a blanket. If Daniel somehow survived, it would be a miracle. But we *never* saw *either* of them, ever again."

Mehitable sat, jaw dropped, amazed to hear Daniel Sanford's story. The ghost in her dream had a name. He must be Reuben's relative. She was glad not to see Daniel's ghost that evening, recalling the dream, and seeing the ghosts of Josiah and Molly was more than she wanted to deal with as it was.

Oliver concluded, "After the war, I sold my tanning business, packed our belongings in a wagon, and me and Phebe moved our family from Milford, Connecticut. Reuben was the last one born in Connecticut, and he was a babe in arms when we moved here." Oliver twisted his body and looked down at his son Reuben, seated behind him, to his left, and stretched his arm toward him. "We needed a new beginning and becoming a founder of this fine town was a great way to start life, anew." Mehitable clasped her hands above her heart. Finally, Oliver said, "Pardon me, Mehitable, and thank you for letting an old man monopolize a sweet young woman's birthday party for a while. It is so colorful and festive in here, and it reminds me of my wife, Phebe. I hope she is here with us in spirit tonight."

Mehitable thought, *I hope she is not. I've had quite enough of the world of spirits today.* She thought Oliver was trying to talk himself into a festive mood, instead, thinking of his wife who passed away at the age of 45, a year after the birth of their last child, made him seem even more melancholy.

It was clear that Oliver Sanford had completed his remarks. The assembled crowd stood, clapped, and cheered. Anson Smudge quietly walked through the door as the crowd was clapping and made his way to a chair at the back of the room, near the front door. Horace thanked everyone for their attention, and he thanked Oliver for his role during the War for Independence, for helping to establish the town, and for sharing his story with everyone.

Sensing a change might benefit the party spirit, Mehitable's father suggested it was time for a song. He had a table set up at the front of the room, and Mehitable's virginal sat on top of the table. Horace introduced his daughter to the crowd. She bowed and stood behind the virginal, stretching her fingers in preparation.

Reuben was standing along the wall on the right side of the room. Mehitable looked at him, smiled, winked, and nodded. Reuben smiled back. It was impossible to miss the exchange between them. From the back row, Anson fumed. As Mehitable's fingers hit the keys, the front door of Union Academy slammed shut. Mehitable jumped, missed a beat, but picked up where she left off, unaware that Anson had returned, let alone that he had left again.

As Mehitable finished her first song, Reuben spoke quietly to Polly. Moments later, she followed him out of the front door. Reuben offered her his arm. He found talking to Polly much easier than talking to Mehitable. She was far less mysterious. She looked beautiful in her bright blue gown, with blue and white floral petticoats. He was dressed in a long black coat that had served many Sanford men through the years. Reuben was the seventh child, and new clothes were a luxury even for first born children on the frontier. Even so, Reuben and Polly made an impressive couple, black and white next to blue.

Reuben had learned that a warm, direct, humorous approach worked best for him. Before they rounded the first corner, Reuben asked Polly, "What would your father say if I should ask him for your hand in marriage?"

Polly laughed and replied, "I hope he would ask you to find out what his daughter thinks of the idea first." They laughed and talked for a long while. They paused briefly along the dark, east side of the green. Polly stood on her toes, and their lips met. They kissed gently at first. Reuben held Polly closely. They kissed playfully for a few minutes before Polly backed away. She took his hand in hers and suggested that they return to the party.

They walked a few more laps of the green. Reuben told Polly about his grand plan to become an industrialist in the mountainous frontier to the northwest, the rugged land known as Macomb's Purchase. "So, what does John Lewis's daughter think? Would you wait for me to get established, and marry me when I return?"

She nodded, threw her arms around him, and they kissed once more before returning to Mehitable's birthday party. They walked through the door just as Mehitable, accompanied by her father, finished her last song. She stood proudly, smiled, and curtsied.

A few minutes later, Reuben stood at Polly's side as Polly quietly shared the news with Mehitable. Mehitable kissed her friend on her cheek, "I'm so happy for you." Mehitable smiled at Reuben, her way of letting him know she was happy for him as well. Then Polly suggested someone retrieve Aurilla. It was time to read some Shakespeare. "Is she still out there with my brother?" Mehitable inquired.

Reuben stepped out briefly, and suggested the young couple come inside for a while.

Mehitable's spirit vaulted when she saw her brother walk through the door. She had never seen a happier looking person in her whole life. She thought, *I'll never forget that look on his face. 'Tis what happiness looks like.* Then she looked at Aurilla and was shocked to see the exact same look on her face. *I guess they were meant for one another.*

The older women served desserts while Polly, Aurilla, and Mehitable prepared to read Shakespeare. Nobody declined. It was difficult to choose, and many people indulged in more than one dessert. Despite the Apple Brown Betty, Blueberry Buckle, cider donuts, pumpkin pie, pumpkin cookies, all three of Wilhelmina's Shoo-Fly Pies found a welcome home on somebody's plate.

Horace removed Mehitable's virginal from the table at the front of the room, replacing it with a wooden wash bucket. By way of introduction, Horace swept his right arm, "A cavern." Then, extending both hands in front of him, he continued, "In the middle, a boiling cauldron." He looked toward the roof above him. "Thunder. Three witches enter."

The crowd laughed. The three witches looked more like princesses.

Polly read, "Thrice the brinded cat hath mew'd."

Aurilla followed, "Trice and once the hedge-pig whined."

Mehitable projected, "Harpier cries 'tis time, 'tis time."

Polly scrounged up her best attempt at a witchy sounding voice and read: "Round about the cauldron go; in the poisoned entrails throw...."

Then all together, Polly and Mehitable read over Aurilla's shoulder the most famous lines: "Double, double toil and trouble; fire burn and cauldron bubble."

Everyone enjoyed the girls' reading and imagining the nasty ingredients in the witches' brew as they nibbled their festive, delicious desserts. The audience responded appropriately, holding their stomachs, pinching their noses, and twisting their faces at the mentions of: fillet of a fenny snake, eye of newt, toe of frog, wool of bat, tongue of dog, lizard's leg, owlet's wing, scale of dragon, tooth of wolf, witches' mummy, and baboon's blood.

As Mehitable read her lines, she thought about how crazy it all sounded the first time she had read it. It still seemed quite improbable, though the apparitions mentioned in Macbeth were beginning to seem less absurd to her. She shuddered when she read the line, "Finger of birth strangled babe...." She thought about her ongoing nightmares about dead babies and struggled to read the rest of her lines, but she managed to finish.

Aurilla completed their reading by introducing Macbeth, "Something wicked this way comes." Horace read the lines for the character of Macbeth. When the scene was finished, Macbeth and the three witches received thunderous applause, took their bows, and joined the crowd just in time for Tommy Todd to take the stage and count down the seconds to the start of a new century.

It was quickly getting late. Many of the older folks had returned home well before midnight. Fifteen minutes after kissing couples welcomed a new century, the party ended. The girls would have to return the next day to clean up after the party. Aurilla, the Lewis family, and the Munch family climbed into the sleigh and followed the steady Appaloosas home. A light, fluffy, flurry added to the late winter night scene. Horace, Wilhelmina, and Perry got out of the sleigh. Mehitable, Polly, and Aurilla had plans to sleep over at the Lewis home that evening. Perry watched until the sleigh disappeared into the dark night, already suffering the pain of separation from Aurilla.

At the Lewis home, three friends replaced their fancy dresses with their ordinary nightgowns. Mehitable brushed her long brown hair while they relived the highlights of the evening. Then they whispered girlish notions for several hours before falling asleep. One had turned sixteen, the other two had found love.

Chapter 6
January 1, 1800

I t was almost three o'clock in the morning. The party had been over for hours. The rest of the village was sound asleep. Hours of drinking hadn't mellowed Anson's rage. It had impaired his judgment. Then it went beyond that point. What had begun with a tankard of ale in Alexander Murdock's Eagle Tavern escalated throughout the evening. Mr. Murdock wisely suggested Anson call it a night just after midnight. Instead Anson walked up the road to Tommy Todd's still. As the last of the celebrants headed north up Lewis Road, Anson helped himself to two jugs of cask strength rye whiskey, sixty percent alcohol. He sat alone in the dark in front of Tommy Todd's store and lit his pipe. He thought about return-ing the whiskey. By the time he finished his pipe he had convinced himself that the pilfered jugs were fair compensation for the bother of working for the cheap merchant. He popped the cork on one of the jugs for a quick sip of the fiery whiskey before the long cold walk home. It burned his throat going down. Anson winced, rubbing his lips with the back of his hand. He replaced the cork in the jug and stumbled toward home, five miles away.

Mehitable's house was about half the distance to his own home. Anson's mood had not improved. He stood, wobbly, looking at the dark silhouette of Mehitable's house. He didn't notice that he had dropped his hat on the ground. Two jugs and a hat were too much to hold on to. He decided to take a break and stumbled forward toward Mehitable's porch. He took his pipe from his pocket and fumbled with a match. It occurred to Anson that he should burn the house down. It would serve her right. He popped the cork on a jug of whiskey for a quick nip. He still had a long way to walk before getting home. His pipe had gone out. He struck another match. Then he passed out. As he slumped, he knocked the whiskey over. The freshly lit pipe fell from his lips and met the liquid.

Anson was the first victim of the ferocious fire that rapidly engulfed the saltbox home.

There were no survivors.

John Lewis awoke later than usual. The temperature had risen above freezing. A cold rain fell, freezing when it hit the ground, making walking slippery. Outside his front door, it smelled like a fire smelled when doused with water. He had a sick feeling in the pit of his stomach. He woke his 14-year-old son, Eliada, and told him to tend to the animals.

John bundled up warmly, strapped on snowshoes, and headed down the slippery road, taking care not to fall. A quarter of a mile down the road he saw a giant pit of smoldering ashes where the Munch's saltbox home once stood. Before he could remove his snowshoes, he pitched the contents of his stomach at his feet. When he had nothing left to heave, he shuffled his snowshoes closer to the remains. The only thing he could recognize among the rubble was Anson Smudge's navy blue, tri-tip hat, a few feet away from the giant square of ash.

John's head pounded. He suffered a terrible headache despite having consumed no alcohol the night before. He made his way across the road to Horace's barn. Despite the tragedy, two pigs, a cow, five sheep, and a dozen chickens were hungry and thirsty. John made a couple trips to the creek with a wooden water bucket. He forked out a generous helping of hay to the cow and the sheep and tossed some mash to the pigs and chickens. The rooster named Dinner crowed, proclaiming that morning had arrived. John Lewis grimaced, turned his head and scratched his chin, distraught to think of how he could possibly help Mehitable make sense of such a tragedy.

Before returning home, John scouted around the property for any sign of survivors. There were no tracks. There was no sign of any survivors. He voiced his hopes, which nobody would hear. "I hope that poor family died not knowing what hit them."

When he got home, everyone was awake except for Polly, Aurilla, and Mehitable. He had cried all the way home. He walked through the door, headed straight for his chair in a dark corner of the parlor and slumped into it.

Anna knew right away that something was wrong. She brought him a cup of tea, kneeled at his side and whispered, "What's wrong?"

He shook his head. His lower lip quivered. He thought he might cry again. " 'Tis the Munch house. It has burned to the ground. There are no signs of any survivors."

Anna's hands hit her cheeks so hard she felt the sting of having slapped herself, not that she cared. "What will poor Mehitable do?"

Mehitable had just come around the corner, the first of the three young ladies to wake up that morning. Anna stood and faced her. It was dark in the corner of the parlor, yet Mehitable could see the fear in Anna's eyes. She looked at John Lewis in his chair. He looked years older than he had the night before. "What's wrong?" she begged to know.

"I don't know how to tell you this, darling," he began. Somehow, he found a way. He told her what little he knew. He only left off the part about seeing Anson's hat.

Mehitable just stood there. She couldn't make sense of the words she was hearing. She crossed her arms beneath her breasts. She shook her head back and forth. Bitter, salty tears rolled down her cheeks. In her head, she heard her father's voice singing his favorite hymn. She saw her pretty mother, all dressed up in her mint and emerald green finery. She saw her brother, Perry, lost in love. The best night of his life had also been his last. *How could it be?* Mr. Lewis must be mistaken. She saw her other brothers and sisters sitting on the floor, listening to her play the virginal. She felt the weight of her baby brother on her hip. She thought of her baby sister who always crawled into her bed at night. Suddenly she thought of Cousin Millicent. She stuttered, "No survivors?"

"I'm sorry, darling." John answered. "I really don't think so."

Desperately, Mehitable vociferated, "I have to go see. I have to go see it right now." She felt a sense of urgency, as if arriving there quickly might change the outcome of the situation.

Anna stretched her arms wide. Mehitable sobbed endlessly onto Anna's comforting bosom. Her grief was inconsolable and irrepressible. Her sobs became shrieks and eventually woke the other girls. John took Polly and Aurilla into the kitchen, giving Anna and Mehitable some space. He didn't have any choice but to tell them. He used practically the same words. A look of horror crossed Polly's face. Aurilla slumped to the floor, muttering Perry's name repeatedly. Endlessly.

John stood there surrounded by sobbing women and children. He had no idea what to do. After attempting to console them he walked slowly to the front door and stood in front of his home. It had quickly warmed up. It rarely reached fifty degrees the first week of January. His tall son Eliada stood on the porch next to him. "What can we do?" Eliada asked.

John looked deep into his son's eyes. " 'Tis not a time for doing. 'Tis a time for feeling. What can we do but wait?"

Eliada suggested, "I could get Reverend Jenney." The tepid air and a swift breeze made the ground passable.

John needed to laugh. "How did you get to be so smart, son?"

Eliada just shrugged, as if in other lifetimes, perhaps, their roles had been reversed. Then he crossed the road to hitch up the team. Eliada stopped at Tommy's store and told Tommy the news as he knew it. Tommy told Eliada that he would make sure someone cleaned up Union Academy, and not to worry about that. Tommy dumped all the cider donuts from a platter into a sack and asked Eliada to bring them back home to his family. Eliada returned home early in the afternoon with the preacher and a sack of donuts.

Mehitable could not be persuaded to remain indoors among friends. She borrowed some clothing and slowly trudged down the road toward her place, a quarter of a mile away. Her head understood the dreadful news. Her shoulders sagged as she looked at the spot where her happy home once stood, she felt an emptiness in her heart that mirrored the empty spot in the yard in front of her.

How did it happen? She knew it didn't matter. It wouldn't change a thing. Nevertheless, she couldn't stop thinking that question. She dropped to her knees on the cold ground and prayed to God, "Please help me understand. Why?" *Why* was a better question than *how*, she thought. She felt that she might cry again. Instead she looked up at where her house once stood. She got back to her feet and moved closer. She heard a distant whispering of voices. *How could that be?* She couldn't make out any words. She flashed her gaze about, looking to see where the voices were coming from. She saw a faint mass move quickly across her field of vision, then it dissipated. Anson's Revolutionary War era hat caught her eye. *What is this doing here?* she wondered. She bent over, picked up the hat, and tucked it under her arm.

The dark mass moved in and out of focus in the distance,

transparent then with visible details, but not enough so that she could tell what or whom she was looking at.

Suddenly, she felt an ice-cold breeze. Inside her borrowed jacket, she felt the tiny hairs on her arm standing straight on end. The scent of whiskey and body odor seemed to appear on the wind. The smells made her think of Anson, as if holding his hat and thinking about his behavior the day before were not enough to make her think of him.

She thought that she heard the sound of boots moving slowly across a wooden floor. *Fie! Impossible, the closest wooden floor was in the barn across the street.* She thought it sounded like the wooden floor was immediately in front of her.

Mehitable jumped, and then she screamed.

A taunting apparition appeared from a pinpoint of nothing, expanding to the size of a human immediately in front of her. It looked like his white face was plastered over a charred black interior, and his eyes glowed. Red. He pointed, cackled like a witch, and mocked her in the same voice that he had used on previous occasions, throwing her words back in her face. Anson mocked, "Have you been drinking, Anson Smudge?" At that moment, Mehitable realized that Anson had passed into the world of spirits too. She dropped his hat in shock. Like a flash, the apparition of Anson vanished. Mehitable could barely fathom the reality that her family had burned in a fire. *What could Anson possibly have to do with it? And why is his hat here?*

Standing in front of what used to be her home, Mehitable started to feel like a ghost herself. *Why am I here? Shouldn't I have been taken with the rest of my family?* It crossed her mind that she would never see any of them again, and that thought caused her tears to return.

She turned and headed for the barn. She cried harder at the sight of all the innocent animals looking back at her. Her favorite sheep lay lazily on a pile of straw. She dropped to her knees and buried her face deep in the woolen fleece of the one she called Emmeline, and she sobbed some more. She had been grateful for the comfort Anna

Lewis provided, but Emmeline felt like home. Mehitable looked up into Emmeline's big round eyes. The sheep continued to chew whatever it had in its mouth. The words *just be* popped into her mind. She lay there next to the sheep for several hours, twirling her fingers in the sheep's curly fur. Emmeline was perfect company.

After a while, she got up and gave the cow and the pigs some hay. She scratched between the pigs' ears, then she milked the cow and carried the milk down the road to the Lewis home.

The Reverend Jenney was still there, and he asked to speak with Mehitable in private. She suggested the Lewis's barn across the street, and the preacher nodded affirmation. They sat together on milking stools. Reverend Jenney took her hand and asked, "Will you pray with me?"

She nodded and dutifully said all the prayers prescribed. She punctuated his prayers with, "Amen," in all the proper places. The grief was too fresh to say her prayers with full conviction.

He asked, "Is your faith shaken?"

Mehitable answered, "Nay Father, my faith is strong. I don't understand, but I know it is not for me to comprehend. Still, I find myself asking why."

The preacher said lots of soothing words. When they were finished, the words she remembered were, "Be strong." She remembered having nodded, her promise to the preacher, and perhaps her promise to God. She would *be strong*. Somehow.

The first evidence of her strength came a few hours later when she refused to sleep in the house. John and Anna stared at Mehitable. "I will never sleep in a house again, as long as I live."

Anna pleaded, "Be reasonable, we can't let a young lady sleep outside in the middle of winter." John nodded his agreement.

Mehitable shook her head from side to side. "The preacher told me to be strong. He did not tell me to be reasonable. I will sleep in the barn."

"I can't let you sleep in our barn," John exclaimed.

Mehitable proclaimed, "I will sleep in *my* barn. May I borrow some blankets until I can make some new ones?"

After exhausting every possibility of convincing her to be rational, John insisted at least on walking her to her barn. He held an oil lamp while she brushed her hair. Her hairbrush was one of her few remaining possessions. Then she made a nest in some hay and settled into borrowed blankets next to Emmeline. John was still shaking his head back and forth in disbelief when he walked through the door of his house. "I'm sure she will come to her senses at some point. Who could imagine losing everything, all at once, overnight? Give her time. People have their own ways of grieving. I can't believe I allowed myself to be talked into letting that girl sleep outside in the wintertime."

Polly pleaded, "Can we adopt Mehitable?"

Anna agreed, " 'Tis a good idea."

John shrugged, "Mehitable is welcome here anytime. Whatever she wants or needs, she has but to ask. We will all need God's help to heal this poor young woman's broken heart."

Mehitable lay in her cold dark barn, bundled in her borrowed clothes, wrapped in borrowed blankets, her hands buried in Emmeline's soft wool. She heard the scurrying of mice, somewhere in the barn, and she felt like the mice were scurrying across her skin. If there was anything in the world she hated, it was mice. The thought of mice. The sight of mice. The mention of mice. Anything to do with mice. Unfortunately, mice were common in barns.

She lay in the dark. Sleep eluded her. She was exhausted by her emotions. Endless sobbing made her as tired as she could ever remember being. Every time she closed her eyes, she saw translucent visions from the spirit world. Mostly she saw the floating forms of her beloved family, amidst billowing smoke that swirled in the blowing air. Sometimes she saw the spiteful image of Anson Smudge.

Occasionally she saw the visions of floating piles of dead babies. The dead babies Mr. Murdock had mentioned a couple of days earlier. The twitching, dying body of Daniel Sanford being lifted onto the death cart. Her whole life the visions had chased her. Previously they had been floating, foggy clouds. Sometimes they had appeared as round spots of light randomly flitting around like butterflies in an alpine meadow. That night offered the pitch-black darkness of a moonless night, yet spirits appeared to her as identifiable individuals. *How could she look away or turn her back when the visions also came to her, even when she closed her eyes?* She held tight to Emmeline, her protector. She said her prayers. What more could she do? Every time she saw a spirit vision, she opened her eyes. It was so dark in the barn, it was hard to tell when her eyes were open or when they were closed. Eventually, ghosts or no ghosts, the need for sleep overtook her.

She woke up the next morning, well after dawn. She looked up into the faces of her friends, Polly and Aurilla. She jumped to her feet and hugged them. She hadn't had the chance to talk with either of them the day before. She tried to comfort Aurilla, understanding that she had her own kind of love for her brother. Mehitable told Aurilla that the last words she ever heard Perry say were, "This is the best day of my life." Mehitable went on to tell Aurilla that she could tell just by looking at him, that he meant it. She had never seen him look happier.

Aurilla thanked Mehitable for her kind words. "What do you do when the love of your life lasts less than twenty-four hours? Perhaps I will find love again. But enough about me." Aurilla offered her love and support to Mehitable and tried to talk her into coming to live with her at her house. Mehitable politely declined and repeated her firm resolve to never sleep in a house again.

John Lewis arrived a little while later and sent Polly and Aurilla home. He talked to Mehitable about buying her barn. He told her she could sleep in *his* barn though he still preferred that she sleep in his house. Her animals could move to the Lewis barn also. John told her that he understood she was an adult now. As she was all alone in the world, he considered her to be part of *his* family.

Mehitable finally conceded. She placed a halter on Emmeline's beautiful long face and led her down the street to John Lewis's barn. John helped her make a comfortable spot for the sheep. Then she hugged John and thanked him for his kindness.

Eliada hooked up the horses to the wagon and they returned to Mehitable's barn. Everything of value was loaded onto the sled, including Dinner and the rest of the chickens. Polly's brothers and sisters helped lead the larger animals down the road. It wasn't easy to motivate the pigs to make the move, but somehow they prodded the pigs along. John Lewis's barn was a little crowded, but it managed to accommodate the new arrivals.

Just as they finished moving the animals, Reuben Sanford arrived with a small wagon full of precious cargo, including Mehitable's virginal piano, thirty-six dried floral arrangements, and a stack of clothes. Tommy Todd's patrons had brought by anything extra that might fit a young lady, Mehitable's size. John Lewis's barn never looked more festive.

Reuben also brought news from town. Nobody had seen Anson Smudge. He hadn't returned home since New Year's Eve. He hadn't shown up at Tommy Todd's still. He had seemingly gone missing.

Mehitable proclaimed, "He didn't go missing. Anson burned down my house and he killed my family. The fire also killed him."

John Lewis's jaw dropped. "How do you know that?"

Mehitable shrugged. "I just know." She didn't tell them about having seen Anson's ghost. As bad as he had been in life, Mehitable thought Anson's *spirit* was even more sinister. She wished she didn't have to contend with it, but what could she do?

Though she would rather not have had to share her grief with the entire community, Mehitable thought she owed it to her family. She allowed Reverend Jenney to conduct a funerary service, remembering her parents, siblings, and Cousin Millicent. He said the kindest words, and everyone in town added kind words as well. She would have rather held the services outdoors. She used the money from selling the family property to John Lewis to buy markers for the cemetery on the hillside overlooking the Poultney River, just uphill from the Inn at Eagle Tavern and the village green. They were among the first markers in the young town's new cemetery. She stood on the rolling hill and tears slid down her cheeks as she stared at the names of her family on the large white slab. The names and years of everybody's birth were listed from oldest to youngest, followed by Cousin Millicent, then the phrase, *Perished in a Fire, January 1, 1800.*

After the funeral, Mehitable thanked Tommy Todd for his kindness and resigned her position at the store. She told him she just wasn't up to it anymore and encouraged him to hire Aurilla in her place.

Chapter 7

January 1800

M ehitable did her best to settle into a daily routine. Evenings were another story.

The Lewis barn was well built. It was relatively warm, even on the coldest winter days. Mehitable wondered what the sheep thought, having a *person* sleeping among them. Unflappable Emmeline seemed impervious. Mehitable thought that the sheep understood their roles as her confidants. Of course, Emmeline's sisters Augusta and Adelina were equally good listeners. She had named the sheep after three friends from a book she read at the library called *Emmeline, the Orphan of the Castle*. The book didn't have much good to say about marriage, but Mehitable liked the characters in the book anyhow, and she especially liked the sound of their names.

Mehitable was exhausted and was looking forward to a full night of sleep the first night she spent in the Lewis's barn. She nestled between the three plush ewes in their big box stall and she was plenty warm. She sighed contentedly, closed her eyes, then she felt a prickly feeling on her skin. Her eyes snapped open and her body tensed. She clenched her hands into fists and peered into the darkness. She heard a distant, moaning sound. Then she heard the chatter of people talking in words that didn't sound like any kind of language she was familiar with. That was followed by the sound of metal being slowly dragged across stone. Shovels, rakes, and hoes began to bang and clamor against the interior wooden walls of the barn. She recoiled and she placed her hand on her belly. She sweated nervously, fearing what might come next. Then everything went silent. The air felt thick. Electric. A tiny light zoomed across a long stretch of spiderweb then illuminated from the center of a web at the corner of the box stall. Just as Anson's ghost appeared in her yard the day before, he appeared outward from the tiny point of light.

Accusingly, the ghost screamed, "You thought I wouldn't find you here? It doesn't matter where you go. I'll follow. I'll hunt you down. You'll wish you had married me." The ghost tipped his head back and laughed. The laughter sounded like a cross between a growling bear and a screeching owl. Then she felt a breeze across her thighs beneath her nightgown. A moment later she felt like a cat had scratched the skin on her thighs. She screamed in dismay. Then suddenly, it was over. The ghost was gone.

Mehitable pulled her nightgown up to her waist and felt the scratches on her legs. *How is it possible? How could my legs be scratched through my nightgown?* Then she wondered if the ghost would return, or whether it was done for the night. The air no longer felt heavy. She fidgeted between the sheep. Exhausted as she was, the trauma of Anson's visit kept her from sleep for an hour and a half.

The next night, Anson's arrival was heralded with pulses of light throughout the barn and the sound of something being dragged across the floor. It sounded like a large sack of grain being dragged down a hallway. Or a dead body. Mehitable felt dizzy and her head ached. She clenched her teeth, and protectively covered her thighs with her hands to avoid getting scratched again. Instead she felt something at her ear. It felt like someone had flicked her earlobe. Reflexively, she boxed her ears and in that moment, Anson appeared, laughing.

"Did you miss me?" he said through sneering lips. Mehitable smelled the familiar scent of whiskey, dried sweat, and unwashed clothing. In the distance, she thought she heard the sound of dripping water, like the sound a leaky roof makes as water falls from the roof to the floor into a metal bucket.

Anson told Mehitable she was worthless. The barn was too good for her. She should go out and sleep in a snowbank under a tree. Mehitable's tense, frozen body could do no more than shake her head in refusal. Anson suggested she cut her wrists and watch her blood flow onto the floor as he cackled in amusement at his suggestion. Finally, Anson offered her a week's worth of peaceful sleep if she would hack off her ear. Mehitable boxed her ears a second time and shivered in fear. Moments later, Anson was suddenly gone.

When she had recovered her wits, it occurred to her that each visit was uniquely wicked, however they all seemed to last about the same duration. As if Anson had enough power or energy to torment her for only so long.

Every night she hoped that the spirit world would leave her alone. Every night Anson's ghost appeared when she closed her eyes, attempting to find sleep. More than once, she thought, *If only I had agreed to let Anson kiss me. If I had accepted his marriage offer, maybe my family would still be alive.* Despite feeling guilty about the death of her family, Mehitable never could rationalize the idea that having married Anson was truly God's plan. Nevertheless, like a recurring nightmare, most of Anson's spirit visits repeated, with variations. There was always a taunt. There was always finger wagging. There was always a threat. She didn't know whether a spirit had the power to follow through on the type of threats Anson's ghost made. The spirit made a succession of horrible suggestions. Suggestions such as: chop off your hair, slit your wrists, hack off your ear, bludgeon that baby with a carving knife. After several weeks, Mehitable concluded

Anson's ghost wanted to display anger, to terrorize her. Its fury never seemed to diminish.

Whenever she thought about it, she clenched her hands into fists, her fingernails digging painfully into the palms of her hands. She knew she needed to accept the nightly visit as part of her life, but she never got used to the feeling of dread that preceded trying to close her eyes each night, and it always took hours to fall asleep after a haunting. Some nights, Anson's ghost would appear more than once. And Anson's spirit wasn't her only visitor. She continued to see ghosts of the baby boys killed by King Herod's murderous men, 1800 years earlier. Sometimes she would see the ghosts of her family, but they never spoke to her. They were a far more welcome vision than the others. Some nights, she felt like she got hardly any sleep. Since the tragedy, it felt like a massive chore just dragging her body to a standing position each day.

Every morning, the rooster named Dinner signaled the arrival of a new day. Mehitable hated the sound of its crowing, but loved the rotten rooster, none the less. Her brother, Perry, had named the bird. It was a fine-looking specimen, mostly white with specks of brown, and the feathers around its neck had a translucent appearance, like the exotic pearls on Mrs. Martin's necklace. She couldn't help but think fondly of her brother whenever she heard or saw the rooster.

The first thing she did each morning was milk the cow. John Lewis had told her she didn't need to do it. She insisted it was a small price to pay for the use of his barn. He tried to protest, but she looked at her feet, and whispered, "It makes me feel useful." John told her he understood, and it was settled. Most mornings, she placed the milk bucket on the table just inside the house before anybody in the house was awake, and quietly closed the door behind her, returning to the barn. After she fed the animals, she liked to work at her spinning wheel until someone came across the street to invite her to breakfast. She had nothing against being inside the house during daylight hours, as long as she didn't have to sleep in the house.

John and Anna noticed that Mehitable tended to speak only when spoken to. She had been sweet, polite, and generous with welcoming, confident smiles. Since the tragedy, she no longer seemed to be a gregarious participant in conversations. She seldom had opinions. It was easy for a quiet voice to become lost among a large family, especially at mealtime. John and Anna continued to worry about their daughter's friend who lived in their barn.

Mehitable thought about telling Polly or her parents about the ghosts. She also thought about talking to Reverend Jenney about it, but she was too afraid of what he might say or do. Instead of talking to someone, she decided to say as little as possible to anyone, except for Polly and her family.

Most Sundays, Reuben Sanford came to dinner. He sat at the crowded table between Polly and Mehitable. John listened as the young man talked about his grand plan to create an industrial empire at the edge of the mountainous wilderness, west of Lake Champlain. He watched his daughter's face as she listened to Reuben talk about establishing a store, a sawmill, a still, a foundry, and building a home for his family. Reuben often quoted from his conversations with Tommy Todd, whose lead Reuben dreamed of following. Each Sunday Reuben added new thoughts to his growing plan. Sometimes John asked a question or two. The first Sunday in March, Reuben announced his intent to leave town the day after Easter. John Lewis told Reuben that he believed in him, and his dream, and he wished Reuben all the best.

True to his plan, the day after Easter, Reuben set out in search of his destiny. Few people noticed the departure of one of the small, fledgling town's promising young citizens.

The seventh child of one of the town's founding families sat on a tired old horse, carrying few possessions and meager provisions. Reuben's father, Oliver stood on the porch. Reuben's older sister Rachel stood by his side. Rachel had taken over responsibility for the household, and for raising her siblings after Reuben's mother, Phebe, passed away shortly after the birth of Althea in 1792. Oliver stepped from the porch and walked to the side of Reuben's horse. Reuben thought of his mother as he leaned down and extended his hand, matching the strength of his father's grip. Then Oliver returned to the porch to stand with Rachel and Reuben's other brothers and sisters. Their farm was productive, but not enough to support the seventh of Oliver's twelve children. He took one last look at the home of his raising and scanned the porch full of his siblings. He waved slowly, tipped his hat, nodded a final nod, turned the old brown horse and rode away without looking back.

Reuben knew he would not be the heir to his father's property in Poultney. He figured to make his own way. The world was full of promising young men. Realizing that potential was another story. He carried an axe, a shovel, and a long rifle. Outfitted as such, he set out to tame a new wilderness.

First, he had one more stop to make. Polly waited on her porch, dressed in her finest dark blue and white dress, the one she wore on New Year's Eve. Mehitable had helped Polly fix her hair and Polly stood facing into the wind, turning as the wind shifted so it wouldn't blow her hair in the wrong direction. When he thought of her, she wanted him to think of her looking her finest. Reuben arrived at the Lewis's farm in the middle of the morning. The family left Polly and Reuben alone on the porch. Reuben held Polly in his arms, whispering optimistic plans in her ear. "Will you wait for me?" he inquired. She nodded and he wiped a tear from her cheek with his thumb. "I'll be back as soon as I can," he offered. She nodded again. "I'll write every week, he promised." She kissed him gingerly, their lips barely meeting, and then she backed away.

Reuben swung up into the saddle, waved, and was gone.

After he was gone, Mehitable joined Polly on the porch. She took both of Polly's hands in her own, kissed each cheek, then hugged her melancholy friend, and assured her, "Don't worry. Everything will be okay. You'll see." Polly thanked her, then went inside to change out of her dress. Mehitable stood alone on the porch, thinking about the good-looking young man and about how his presence would be missed. Tears streamed down her face. He had wanted her first. Polly loved him more, but she had to admit, she loved him too.

The sun was shining, and Mehitable decided to go for a walk. She walked down the road to where her house used to be. Then she wandered across Lewis Creek. She found her feet following her brother's trail of snares.

She came to the place where they killed the red fox. The sling-shots they had lost lay in a quickly shrinking bank of soft, melting snow. She held Perry's slingshot over her heart as if it were a precious heirloom. She was glad to have found it. She wandered down the trail, releasing snares. Many had been triggered but stood empty. A couple of the snares barely held the rotting remains of rabbit corpses. She closed her eyes and pictured the blissful look of her brother the night he fell in love. She missed her brother and began to weep. Then she thought of Reuben, riding off into the future. She was going to miss him also.

With Reuben gone, Polly became more observant. Several times a week Polly would ask Mehitable why she looked so tired. Anson's ghost had enough power to manifest almost every day, although sometimes Mehitable would get a night's reprieve and catch up on her sleep. Usually the next day's visit was even more evil, the price of having a night off. Mehitable always attempted to shrug off Polly's inquiries by claiming that she lost sleep due to nightmares. Polly tried to get Mehitable to share her dreams with her or with Reverend Jenney. Mehitable claimed that it was her cross to bear and made Polly swear not to tell anyone. One day Polly told Mehitable that it was sometimes hard to look into her tired eyes when she knew how much Mehitable must be suffering. The topic recurred between the two friends frequently, and always went the same.

Over the next couple of years, they settled into a rhythm.

They worked furiously to create blankets, curtains, and clothing, filling Polly's hope chest and numerous other crates. Someday, Reuben would return for Polly. Polly understood that the alpine country was extremely cold. She was sure that Reuben was building their homestead somewhere near the top of an enormous mountain, and she had heard that mountain tops were very cold. She wanted to be prepared.

Reuben kept his promise. He was prolific. He wrote frequently, though he tended to use a laconic communication style. Sometimes his letters were a few sentences long. Sometimes a couple of paragraphs. Never more than a single page, but consistently, Reuben wrote a letter every week. Whenever a letter arrived, Polly and Mehitable would boil some tea and sit down together with Reuben's letters. First Polly would read his letter. Then Mehitable would read it. Then Polly would read it again. Then they discussed the letter, imagining the many details Reuben left out. Each letter repeated his question, "Will you wait for me?" and his promise. Each letter told her that he was thinking of Mehitable also. And each letter concluded with, "I long for the day we are reunited and I can hold thee in mine arms once more. Affectionately yours forever, your betrothed, Reuben."

They followed his progress through his weekly letters.

The first summer, he built a tiny cabin, cleared some land by a sizable river, and planted a crop of rye. While his crop grew, he spent the summer and fall chopping trees. He planned to quadruple his tillage the second summer. In addition to the rye crop, he had a small vegetable garden. The river was loaded with trout. He rarely had trouble finding game with his rifle. Reuben wrote, "My letters must be very dull. It seems all I do is chop down trees."

Reuben spent his second summer building a two-level barn on the side of a hill. The second story was at ground level on top of the hill, and the first story was at ground level with the bottom of the hill. Reuben made the acquaintance of three brothers who shared the last name Bump. They lived in a cabin that was a short distance up the road toward the center of the town of Jay. Reuben told the brothers about his plans to build a distillery. They offered to help him build his barn.

Mehitable had an idyllic picture of the barn in her head, and the descriptions of the mountains, rivers, and forests had captivated her imagination. As brief as Reuben's descriptions were, she could see it vividly. John Lewis's barn was adequate, but Reuben's new barn sounded marvelous. She pictured the big beautiful barn in a little meadow, set in the side of a hill near a babbling brook with tiny lambs cavorting and thousands of orange butterflies filling the air.

During the third spring, Reuben asked for Polly's thoughts before he began working on building a home for them. He did his best to build it according to her suggestions. Polly wasn't very artistic, so she described her dream home and asked Mehitable to render it on paper, both how it might look from the outside as well as how Polly imagined the rooms being laid out. Reuben made enough money the third summer to buy glass for the windows of the house. He purchased everything he needed to build his distillery and everything he needed to set up a small sawmill. He built a small building north of his barn to house the still. He built another long, narrow building to house the sawmill, south of the barn and next to the mighty river. The sawmill was powered by a waterwheel.

By the fourth summer, Reuben employed all three Bump brothers full-time. Reuben didn't have much cash, but that didn't seem to matter. The Bump boys preferred to be paid in whiskey anyhow. Polly was overjoyed when Reuben's letter arrived, telling her that he was coming home for a visit and that she should expect to see him a month before Christmas. Mehitable was looking forward to Reuben's return as well. She had missed him.

Anna, Polly, and Mehitable spent the summer making Polly a beautiful, embroidered wedding dress, though Polly and Reuben weren't officially engaged. Reuben had yet to ask John for his daughter's hand. John joked whenever he saw the ladies working on the dress, "So you'd like me to say *yes* when Reuben asks me for your hand, is that correct, Polly?"

Chapter 8
November 1803

The day before they gathered to celebrate the bounty of the summer growing season, Reuben surprised his sister, Rachel, on the porch of the home in which he had grown up. He brought her a blue Wedgwood broach featuring a woman with angel's wings holding the hands of a small child. He reclaimed his bunk in the boys' bedroom, which his brother William had grown accustomed to having all to himself, the older boys having grown and moved into houses of their own. Reuben assured William that he wouldn't be imposing very long. Rachel boiled water so that Reuben could have a warm bath. The smell of Rachel's homemade soap, using his mother's recipe, brought back childhood memories. Rachel washed Reuben's clothes and hung them to dry while he bathed. Reuben dressed in clothes borrowed from his younger brother while his own clothes dried. They enjoyed a hearty dinner and went to bed early.

The next morning, Reuben brushed his new horse and combed her mane. Reuben wet his own hair over a bowl in the kitchen and Rachel carefully combed his hair for him, showing a neat part on the right-hand side. He dressed in his own clean, dry clothes. Rachel told her brother that he looked handsome. Reuben grinned and asked, "Would you say that even if you weren't my sister?" He couldn't wait to see Polly, the girl in the frozen image in his mind. The girl who answered his letters. The girl who promised to wait for him.

Mehitable was carrying a basket of eggs across the road when Reuben rode up. He jumped off his horse, embraced her, and kissed her on the cheek. " 'Tis lovely to see you," she said. She thought of his big strong hand on her shoulder the night she had turned sixteen. Four years later, she could still feel that long lost touch.

Reuben quickly tied his horse to the porch railing, grinned widely, and gave Mehitable two quick pats on her shoulder. Then he followed her into the Lewis's home.

Anna hollered up the stairs to Polly, "Reuben is here." Anna embraced Reuben, telling him that he was far too thin. She affectionately squeezed his bicep and noticed the musculature in his arms and shoulders from chopping down hundreds of trees and erecting buildings. Polly ran down the stairs, jumped into the air and into Reuben's arms, locking her lips onto his with no regard or concern for smashed noses. Mehitable stepped a few steps backward into the dim parlor and leaned against the wall. She tilted her head, happy for Polly, and it occurred to her that she was living vicariously through her. Mostly, Mehitable didn't want a beau or a fiancé, but a very small part of her did.

John cleared his throat. He was sitting in his chair in the darkest corner of the parlor, but the sound was unmistakable. Reuben helped guide Polly's feet to a safe landing on the floor, his hands wrapped around her waist.

An hour later, everyone was sitting around the crowded table, having cleaned their plates. Everyone, that is, except for Reuben. They had peppered him with questions. He hardly had a chance to stick a fork into his pile of mashed potatoes. He recounted the long version of his story. They had heard bits and pieces from Polly through the years. Reuben told his story slowly that night, adding every detail he could think to add.

Reuben was aware that John was listening attentively to every word. There was a lot of interest and plenty of laughter as Reuben described his employees, the Bump brothers. Mehitable asked a couple of questions about them, and Reuben went into great detail about the family. Otis was the oldest. Lester was one year younger, and Dudley was two years younger. They looked like identical triplets and seemed to share one personality. The good news was that the boys were strong, dutiful, obedient, steady, consistent, reliable workers. They didn't mind being paid irregularly and they didn't mind being paid in whiskey rather than cash. They couldn't read. They couldn't write. They were lacking in the manners department. They were short, a little pudgy, and had blond hair, so light it looked like corn silk in early August. Reuben asked Anna if she would permit him to share details, considering the children had finished eating. Anna nodded consent and Reuben told the Lewis family about the Bump boys' penchant for burping, farting, and making offensive sounds with their hands under their armpits. "Otis, Lester, and Dudley were a community unto themselves," Reuben joked. "Fact is, I couldn't have built a barn, a house, a still, and a sawmill without them." Reuben forgot to tell the Lewis family about Lester's wife.

John nodded, clearly understanding that Reuben's success came from his own hard work and also from his leadership. He left with an axe, a shovel, and a rifle. He returned as a young man of substance and prospects. John put a stop to Reuben's questioners, allowing him to clean his plate. Despite the cold food, Reuben claimed that it was the best meal he had feasted on in years. The curious eyes of spectators didn't keep Reuben from gormandizing until his plate was clean.

John suggested that Reuben walk with him while Anna, Polly, and Mehitable cleaned up. They sauntered slowly north up Lewis Road. Reuben thought, *I should feel nervous, asking a man for his daughter's hand in marriage. Especially his oldest daughter.* Quite the contrary, Reuben felt comfortable in John's presence. It started with the short preamble, "I guess you know all about my interest in your daughter, Polly." The question rolled off his tongue quite easily.

The older man stopped walking and extended his hand, "Welcome to the family, son. I can't think of a better man to marry my daughter." They wandered half a mile further up the road before turning around. Dessert was ready and Mehitable's peppermint tea was boiling in the fireplace. John hushed the room as he walked through the doorway. With everyone's attention focused on him, and complete silence except for the crackle of a log burning at the hearth, John began, "I have an announcement to make. Aye," he said, stretching the word out as long as he could, " 'Tis official. Mr. Reuben Sanford has asked me for my daughter's hand in marriage." He turned to face Reuben. "Which one did you say you want?" 16-year-old Azubah covered her eyes in embarrassment. Mehitable laughed loudly. John pointed at his youngest daughter, baby Hannah, cradled in the crook of her mother's arm, and continued, "I hope not that one." Polly's open hand found her forehead, and Mehitable shook her head and smiled at John's teasing while he paused briefly before continuing. " 'Tis my honor to announce the official engagement of Reuben Sanford and Polly Lewis." The family hooted, hollered, stomped, and clapped.

Polly and Reuben enjoyed an intimate unchaperoned hour-long visit on the porch after dinner. Mehitable helped Anna serve the family chocolate cake and milk. Then she delivered a dessert tray to Polly and Reuben on the porch, forcing a small cough as she opened the door with her backside. Mehitable's words conveyed her genuine pleasure regarding their engagement, but she did not linger long. She wished them a goodnight and concluded, "I shall see you anon." Mehitable hurried across the yard to the barn.

Shortly afterward, Reuben climbed into his saddle and rode off into the night. Polly hurried into the barn to find Mehitable. It was very unusual for them to visit together in the barn. Usually, they visited in the Lewis's kitchen or parlor instead. Polly was bursting with joy and preferred to share her emotions with her friend rather than her family.

Mehitable had dressed for bed but was sitting on her chair, knitting. When she saw Polly, she set her work down and stood to welcome her. Polly sat beside her and they talked for half an hour, revisiting the evening and repeating the most memorable moments of the day.

When Mehitable thought that Polly had finished, she looked up into the rafters of the barn for a moment, then looked back at Polly. "I have been wanting to talk to you about something for quite some time." Polly sat back, nodded, and waited for Mehitable to continue. Mehitable turned her chair so she could face Polly at less of an angle. She swiped her wrist behind her head, sending her hair down her back, looked into Polly's eyes and said, "I don't want to be an imposition, and I know that newly married couples need their space. Your family always makes me feel included and I treasure them. 'Tis just… I wondered… do you think I could move with you and Reuben to the frontier? I've fallen in love with the idea of living in the mountains and the barn sounds like a palace, suitable for royalty. What's more, I don't think I could stand to lose you, on top of everyone else I've lost from my life." Tears streamed down Mehitable's freckled cheeks as she talked.

Polly nodded vigorously, raised her eyebrows in sympathy and agreement. "I should like that very much," Polly answered. "I shall discuss it with Reuben as soon as I can."

When Polly left, Mehitable fretted. She worried that Reuben might not think it was a good idea.

Then the wight appeared, as it did most evenings. Anson was furious. Whatever was happening, whatever Mehitable was thinking, Anson always seemed to know something about it. That night, she crossed her arms, crossed her legs, and focused on trying to portray a blank expression. It was a new approach for her. She tried to clear her mind of all thoughts, fears, and concerns. This seemed to make the ghost angrier. Anson threatened to harm Polly and Reuben if she went with them to their new home on the frontier. Mehitable told herself that she didn't care what the ghost thought or said. She needed to move. She needed a change, and she was ready to go.

Reuben visited again, early the next afternoon. Mehitable was in the barn, and Polly met Reuben on the porch. After an amorous greeting, they sat together, side by side on a bench in the chilly late autumn air. Polly turned to Reuben and told him she had a matter to discuss. She told him that Mehitable wanted to move with them to the mountains. "She's hardly any trouble, she'll stay in the barn, and she'll be company for me while you and your Bumps are busy with business."

Reuben laughed and readily agreed. He thought about the joke that Mehitable had made on that fateful New Year's Eve about marrying both Polly and Mehitable but decided not to mention that joke to Polly. Reuben thought Mehitable was mesmerizing, but he was completely in love with Polly. He would have agreed to most anything to make her happy.

Polly and Reuben hurried to the barn together. Such news couldn't wait. Polly talked while Reuben nodded. Mehitable clasped her hands together, pulled them under her chin, and cried tears of joy. She told them that she couldn't find words to express what it meant to her, and that she could hardly wait until it was moving day.

Then Polly put her lips to Mehitable's ear and asked her for a favor.

John had been gone all day. Polly's mother was taking a nap with the baby. Mehitable had no idea where the rest of Polly's brothers and sisters were. She was distraught with the position her friends had put her in. The newly betrothed couple couldn't keep themselves separated, and Mehitable had the unfortunate job of standing watch over the outhouse. Mehitable feared that Polly's parents or one of the children would need to use the outhouse, and she had no words at the ready. How would she send them away? She wished that Reuben and Polly made less noise and hoped that they wouldn't take their passions too far. All at once, it made Mehitable glad, struck her fancy, and nauseated her to think that her favorite friend had found a love so strong it could flourish even in such an abhorrent setting as a privy.

A month later, on Christmas day, Reuben and Polly met in Mehitable's old barn down the road. They were gone a very long time. After they made love in the abandoned loft, Reuben told Polly he should go. "As long as I am here, I don't think we can bear to be separated. I need to get back to my place," and quickly corrected himself. "Our place up north. I will return before Saint Valentine's Day."

Polly agreed, "I hate to admit it, but you are right. We could get caught or I could get pregnant. We shouldn't be taking so many chances. Just imagine what Reverend Jenney would say," her forehead wrinkled with worry and she frowned.

Reuben reassured Polly, telling her not to fret. He kissed her goodbye in Mehitable's old barn and they walked back to the Lewis's home, hand in hand. He climbed up into the saddle and rode off with a wave. Polly was excited to think that the next time she saw him they would be married and she would be leaving her childhood home.

Polly found Mehitable in the barn at her spinning wheel. Polly told her that Reuben had just returned to the mountains. They sat down for a while and Polly told Mehitable about their time together in Mehitable's old barn, sparing no details about their activities in the loft. The girls talked about how happy they would be in their new home.

Mehitable thought perhaps she could leave the ghosts behind. The years hadn't made her existence any easier. She longed for a good, full night's sleep and a fresh start.

That night, alone in the Lewis's barn, Mehitable wished that Reuben and Polly had waited until their wedding night to be together. She said her prayers, as she always did, and then she prayed extra hard, asking God to forgive her friends.

When Mehitable closed her eyes, she saw the ghost of a dead baby. Not like her other visions. Not piles of dead babies. She saw a vivid floating image of a chubby, newborn baby boy. The ghost giggled, cooed, and looked happy, but Mehitable still found the vision upsetting. *What can it mean?* Then Anson appeared, pointing his finger at her, mocking her. "See, he didn't want you. You should have married me." In a high-pitched voice, he laughed, cackling, like one of Shakespeare's witches.

The next day, Mehitable told Polly, "I think you are pregnant."

Polly brushed her off. "Of course I'm not pregnant. How could you possibly know anyway?" As she thought about it a little more, she became more concerned. "What if I am?" Polly could tell by the look on Mehitable's face that Mehitable wasn't sure of the answer.

"I guess, maybe we can conceal it," was the best Mehitable could offer.

A week later, Mehitable stood in the cemetery beside her family's marker. It was the first time she had returned to the cemetery since the funeral, four years earlier. She had dreaded going to the cemetery and had to force herself to look upon the words carved into the stone. Though she felt a sense of loss every day, New Year's Day was always particularly hard for her. The painful memories cascaded around her like snow dropping from heavily laden branches on a sunny winter morning. She brushed the tears from her cheeks with a wet mitten and inhaled. She was glad that she visited the cemetery after all. Soon she would move away with Polly and Reuben, and she might never return to Poultney again. Other than the fact that her toes were cold, she realized that the visit to the cemetery was quite peaceful.

As she began to leave the cemetery, something caught the corner of her eye. It was a man. Not just a man, but a soldier. She walked slowly toward the road and cast her vision to the ground in front of her, where she planned to place her feet. Even with her eyes diverted, she was able to watch the man whose path she was certain to cross. She couldn't remember ever having seen a soldier before.

As she got closer, her pulse quickened. He was an imposing figure of a man. The closer she got, the more intriguing he looked.

Every couple of steps he stopped to look off into the woods or turned to look back down the road behind him. He put his fingers in his mouth and sent a shrill whistle trumpeting down the intervale below. Then he put his hands to his cheeks and called out, "Pendennis!"

Mehitable walked slowly toward him. Normally she would have walked briskly but she tarried along because she was fascinated. She felt drawn to him. He had a certain magnetism, though he seemed somewhat distracted. She wondered if he was looking for a child, or perhaps a dog.

The man looked to be in his mid to late twenties. He was tall, significantly taller than most men, even taller than Reuben. His shoulders were broad and his waist was narrow. Instead of a red coat or a blue coat, like the soldiers she had heard of, the man wore a dark green jacket with bright gold buttons that matched the tassels that dangled from epaulets at his shoulders. He wore a tricorne, beaver skin hat with a cockade that resembled a chamomile flower. His waistcoat was tight, like his jacket and matched the color of his snug breeches. His neatly tied white cravat and ruffled jabot adorned his neck and chest. His tall black riding boots looked immaculate. Mehitable had never seen such a well-dressed man. She was working up the courage to politely say, "How do you do?" when the man began to fade. She gulped and hurried her pace. The air smelled strangely of woodsmoke, horse manure, and pomander, that intoxicating scent of an orange spiked with rare and exotic cloves. It had not crossed her mind that the man was a spirit. She wondered at the strength of his presence.

She chastised herself for getting all out of sorts over a dead man. Yet she couldn't resist stopping and turning to look when she heard his voice again, calling. "Pendennis!" When she turned, he stood at attention and stared straight into her eyes. Then he removed his hat, bowed deeply, sweeping his long arm dramatically behind him before returning his hat to his head. Mehitable turned and hurried away as quickly as she could.

Finally, when she could only hear his call far off in the distance, she turned to look one final time. He appeared as a tiny green dot surrounded by white snow on the top of the hill. Despite his flamboyance and the fact that he was dead, she couldn't help having romantic thoughts about him. Thoughts she hadn't entertained about living men or boys, except Reuben, briefly and occasionally before sending those thoughts from her mind. As she hurried up Lewis Road that afternoon, she compared the man to Reuben. He was a bit taller, more muscular, and his facial features looked strong and boyish at the same time.

She tried to put the man out of her mind, but she couldn't shake a feeling of sadness over his loss, and she felt a desperate need to know what or for whom he was searching.

Half a mile from the Lewis farm, Polly's 14-year-old brother Albert appeared beside her on the road. He had been out alone, hunting for small game. When he saw her, he ran, smiling and holding a magnificent ring-necked pheasant. He proudly turned the bird in his hands, showing her the condition of the plump bird and the foot long tailfeathers that seemed to double the size of the bird. The bird's coloring was so exotic, it was hard to believe such a creature was real. The black, brown, and tan spotting on his body were spectacular enough. At the neck, the bird sported a white band at the base, then shiny green and blue colors proceeding up his neck. A large red feature encircled its round eyes, like the waddle on a chicken, only it fully circled the pheasant's eyes. It was a gaudy bird, and it made Mehitable think of the well-dressed man she had seen. She corrected her thoughts, well-dressed ghost.

Mehitable told Albert that she was certain he would become a hunter, which seemed to damper his enthusiasm. His face tightened, and he insisted, "I am a farmer. I am going to build my own farm. I'm going to follow Polly and Reuben to the mountains, and build a farm of my own, you shall see!"

She quickly agreed, "Aye, of course. Yet you are mighty good at hunting too."

His good cheer quickly returned and he agreed, "Indeed!" He held the bird up once more, so they could both take another look at it.

Albert reminded Mehitable of her brother, Perry. Sometimes, talking to Albert made Mehitable feel a little sad. Most of the time, she enjoyed his company. Albert cheerfully chattered the rest of the way home, while Mehitable's distracted thoughts returned to the captivating man in the green coat.

By the time February rolled around, Polly was weeks late and was beginning to think Mehitable was right. Throughout January, the excitement of getting married, and the worry about being pregnant occupied Polly's time and attention. Fortunately, she had not experienced morning sickness, but she did seem to be gaining some weight. Her wedding dress fit her perfectly at Christmas. By the first of February, it was snug. Polly and Mehitable worried that it would be tight by Saint Valentine's Day. After that, she could wear loose fitting, homemade dresses prior to the big move.

Mehitable shook her head and furrowed her brow with wonder at how Polly could be so nonchalant. Of course, she believed that Reuben would return for Polly, but what if he did not? She shuddered at the thought of poor Polly having to endure the shame of carrying and bearing a child without the presence of the child's father. The only one who ever spoke of sex out of marriage was Reverend Jenney, and it was always spoken amidst his fiery rhetoric about sins of all sorts. Yet even in their small town, Mehitable was not naïve. She knew it happened more frequently than anyone cared to admit, particularly among engaged couples. She shook her head and wished that Polly and Reuben could have waited.

Anna had suspicions about what was happening but kept them to herself. Polly had asked for her mother's help preparing the things she would need in her new home. They made a list, and Anna made several trips to Tommy Todd's store to add things to Polly's collection of belongings. Anna said, "Ultimately, whatever you don't have, you'll have to find a way to do without. You'll figure it out."

Reuben returned several days before Valentine's Day. It was a snowy winter, and Reuben had to walk the whole way home, on snowshoes, staying at inns where he could find them, and begging board in a farmer's barn when he couldn't. He spent a couple of hours at the Lewis's home on his way to his father's house. Polly was glad to see him. She had worried that he wouldn't be able to make it home through the deep snow. They walked together, hand in hand. She whispered her concern about being pregnant. "How sure are you?" Reuben asked.

Polly laughed. "About one hundred and ten percent sure."

Reuben swooped her up in his arms. Polly was even more relieved to know that Reuben wasn't angry. They finished their walk. Reuben strapped on his snowshoes again, kissed her once more, and said, "I'll see you at noon on Thursday."

Polly said, "Don't be late. I can't wait." She watched as Reuben disappeared onto the horizon.

The Lewis Family and the Sanford Family welcomed friends and neighbors at the meeting house on the village green at noon on Thursday, Valentine's Day, 1804. Polly wore a dark purple dress, bright white petticoats, and a borrowed string of pearls around her neck. Her dark, shiny hair was neatly tacked up behind her head. Her bangs were twisted into loops and pasted onto her forehead. Her head was covered with a veil. Mehitable stood in her burgundy dress, the only fancy dress she owned. Reuben wore a plain, black great coat, common tan colored trousers, and white, knee-high stockings. Reuben's brother stood beside him.

After Polly and Reuben married, they lived in the Lewis's house for two months as they waited for winter to end and prepared for their big move. They occupied a tiny, makeshift room in the unfinished attic, which required climbing a ladder through a rectangular hole in the ceiling. Anna proclaimed, "Love will find a way." Many afternoons the young couple carried a picnic basket down to Mehitable's old barn, preferring to make themselves comfortable there together, when they wished to be alone.

Chapter 9
April 1804

As moving day approached, Reuben became concerned. It looked like Polly intended to bring half the household with her into the wilderness. It looked like Mehitable planned to bring half the contents of the Lewis's barn. John offered the team of Appaloosas and his big wagon. Even so, Reuben didn't think everything could make the trip. There were several challenging waterways, and tricky, steep mountain passes.

Mehitable's possessions consisted of a hairbrush, her burgundy dress, the virginal, some sheet music, a spinning wheel, her carding paddles, and a big sack of clothing the town had given her, plus three sheep, the rooster, and six chickens in a box made of strong twigs between thick boards. Polly had considerably more possessions, packed into her hope chest, her mother's hope chest, and numerous wooden crates of assorted sizes. Reuben promised he would find a cow closer to their destination. Looking at the assembled possessions, Reuben shook his head and worried aloud that it would take months to get there.

They set out at noon on April 14th, exactly four years to the day after Reuben initially set off to find his fortunes. Anna sobbed like a baby and tears rolled down John's face as well. Polly was their first-born child, and the first to grow up and move away. It was a scene they would need to get used to facing. Polly's brother, Albert, hollered to Reuben, "Save some land for me up there."

Eliada shouted, "Me too!"

Reuben and Polly sat on the bench in the wagon, side by side, riding off into their future. Mehitable followed the carriage, leading her three sheep, Emmeline, Augusta, and Adelina.

The first town they came to was the town of Skenesborough. It was situated on the southernmost tip of Lake Champlain. It was an easy trip along an established road. Reuben parked the wagon along the side of the road, on the outskirts of town, just to the north of it. Polly set up their bedding just under the wagon.

Mehitable set off to gather kindling and firewood. She crossed a meadow, went over a hill, and followed a small game trail into the woods. At the edge of the woods, she heard footsteps behind her. When she turned to look, no one was there. She had a feeling in the pit of her stomach that someone was watching her. She thought she heard a twig break behind her. She wondered if someone darted behind a tree whenever she turned to look. She turned to look again, faster than before. She quickly grabbed a few branches and dragged them from the woods toward the meadow. She hated the thought of returning empty-handed.

At the edge of the woods she saw a man leaning against a tree. He was wearing a dirty, ripped, blue uniform. *Another soldier*, Mehitable thought, *how strange*. Her blood raced through her veins. She thought of the soldier in the green coat she had seen in Poultney, months earlier.

She had no choice but to pass directly by the soldier at the edge of the woods. His head was tilted forward. Most of his face was blocked by his hat. As Mehitable moved slowly, dragging the branches toward the meadow, she got more and more anxious. The closer and closer she got, the less the man looked like a man, and the more nebulous he looked. He appeared a little hazy, not like a person should look. Fear struck her chest as it occurred to her that he might be another ghost soldier. She moved faster, dropped one of her branches and continued without it. She decided she would pretend she couldn't see him. She tried not to look directly at him. He tilted his head slightly. She was almost upon him, twelve feet from the path to the tree he stood under. In the corner of her vision, she saw an eye. A bright green eye. He was watching her. Even in her haste, she noticed his skin was pocked with angry red blemishes, oozing ugly yellow puss. She felt a breeze which carried a foul odor, vastly different from the pleasant smells she associated with the ghost in the green coat. When she had made it into the meadow, she looked back behind her. The man's body had shifted. Instead of facing into the woods, he was facing her in the meadow. At that moment, the man realized she could see him. He hollered after her. "Hey! Hey, you can see me, can't you." She gasped, hurried along even faster, and dropped another branch. She moved swiftly across the meadow and was gasping for air when she reached the wagon. Her face was covered with sweat.

Polly exclaimed, "What's wrong?"

"I got scared," Mehitable said, looking away from Polly. "I don't know what came over me," she evaded. Polly raised an eyebrow. Then she hurried to make a small fire to heat water for tea. It was a cool, early spring evening, and they enjoyed the heat from the fire. Camping conditions that time of year were not ideal, and they planned to sleep fully dressed under their heaviest blankets. Mehitable suggested that she could share her warm sheep friends with her human friends.

As the sun set, Mehitable periodically peered off into the darkness. She felt feverish and sweaty, though her skin had dried. She felt like someone was tugging at her coat, and she still felt like she was being watched. A couple of times she strained her eyes looking at a distant tree, just barely in her line of sight. She thought she saw movement around the base of that tree. She was convinced it was the man she had seen earlier, at the edge of the woods.

When they all lay down for the evening, they huddled together among the three sheep. It took a while to get the sheep settled under the wagon, particularly because Emmeline started licking Mehitable's face. One lick led to another, Mehitable got the giggles, the giggles proved to be contagious, and all three of them giggled while Emmeline licked the dried salt-sweat from Mehitable's face. The odd feeling had set Mehitable off, and the joy of laughing, in and of itself, made her happy. When Emmeline was finished, Mehitable thought about how long it had been since she had laughed like that. She couldn't remember having laughed with reckless abandon since Anson had burned down her home and killed her family.

They packed up quickly, first thing in the morning, traveling north along the western shore of Lake Champlain. Mehitable had discovered that the sheep would follow the wagon if she tied them to it, which left her free to walk without having to lead the animals. They set a slow and steady pace, walking sixteen miles from dawn to dusk.

As Mehitable walked, hour after hour, her mind often wandered. She thought about her frequent nightly hauntings. The visits had been growing in frequency, duration, and intensity. She was glad that Anson's ghost hadn't come to her while she and her friends had slept under the wagon. A comforting thought came to her. *What if Anson's ghost remains in John Lewis's barn?* On the other hand, the pock-marked stranger at the edge of the woods was unsettling. *Have I traded one ghost for another?* She couldn't shake the feeling of being followed. Often, when she turned to look behind, she thought she saw a fast-moving shadowy blur, ducking for cover. One time when she turned to look behind her, wondering if someone might be there, she was sure that she saw the ghost from Skenesborough and he wasn't alone. Walking alongside him was the tall dapper ghost in the dark green coat. She had not seen him since New Year's Day. She was certain they were following her. *But why? Why does my pulse quicken when I think of this handsome spirit and why does he make eyes at me?* For some reason, it gladdened Mehitable to think of the man in the green coat.

That evening they made camp along a tiny creek with a nice view of Lake Champlain. Reuben gathered wood for their tiny fire. It was unseasonably mild. They were camped high and dry. Mehitable enjoyed another refreshing night of sleep under the wagon. In the morning, as they were packing everything back into the wagon, Polly placed a hand on Mehitable's shoulder and peered into her friend's face. At first Mehitable thought she was trying to lock their sight, eye to eye, then she realized that Polly was looking beneath her eyes. "What," Mehitable questioned and exclaimed at the same time.

Polly laughed, and said, "I don't know what it is. I haven't seen you look like this in years. You look happy. You don't look worried, and I can't find those bags under your eyes."

Mehitable playfully shoved her friend, "Oh stop it," she laughed. "It must be the mountain air agrees with me."

Sometimes Polly walked hand in hand with Reuben. Sometimes she walked side by side next to Mehitable. Often when they passed through a meadow, they'd all walk together. Thirteen miles went by quickly. An early start and a steady pace allowed them to reach their camping spot hours before dark. Mehitable enjoyed the feeling of an easy-going day until the last hour. Then, a growing sense of dread began to overwhelm her. She felt her innards tighten, a cringing feeling in her gut. In the distance, she heard tiny popping sounds. She thought of the sound of icicles crashing from a roof, only it was a bright, clear sunny day. Mehitable thought she could see gray smoky wisps drifting through the air. Sometimes she felt a speeding rush of wind zipping by her ear or along her cheek. The closer they got, the more she thought the pops and wisps resembled musket fire. She waited for Polly or Reuben to notice, but they never did. They walked along happily, as if everything was right in the world. Finally, Mehitable asked, "Where do we camp tonight?" She held her left forearm against her stomach, just beneath her ribs. The pressure eased the pain in her stomach.

Excitedly, Reuben answered, "Didn't I tell you? Tonight, we will camp near Fort Ticonderoga." Reuben was eager to show them an important site in their country's struggle for freedom, just a generation earlier. He looked into Mehitable's face and asked, "What's wrong? You don't look too good."

Mehitable quickly answered, "It's nothing. Just a little belly ache. I'm sure a hot cup of tea and a biscuit will make me feel better." That prescription seemed to work for Polly. She was enduring the foot travel and pregnancy, no worse for the extra exercise, but periodically her stomach became a little unsettled. Reuben suggested with a smile that Mehitable was having sympathy pains. "Aye, I'm sure," Mehitable agreed with a smirk.

They crested a small hill and the road curved slightly to the right. On the left there was a stump where a tree once stood. Mehitable jumped and gasped in surprise. She saw a young man sitting on a stump to their left. Just like the man she had seen near Skenesborough and the man in the green coat, this man wore a uniform. He was bent slightly at the waist. His hair fell over his forehead, and he had a sad frown on his lips. Looking at him made Mehitable think of a dog with his tail between his legs. The man held his hat in his hand, and he looked at her. She felt an overwhelming sense of desperation. The man's eyes followed them as they approached, and then he watched as they departed. As before, she couldn't help but look back at the man. It finally struck her that the poor young man looked hopelessly lost and depleted.

They made camp just above the spot where La Chute River spilled into Lake Champlain, near the foot of Mount Defiance. They parked their wagon, settled the animals, and gathered wood for an evening fire. Then Reuben suggested they make a hike up the hill. " 'Tis not far," Reuben promised, fully aware that Polly and Mehitable had been walking for days. Neither woman protested, and they scrambled up the 900-foot hill that bore a mountain's name.

When they reached the summit, Reuben put his arm across Polly's shoulders and pointed toward the star shaped fort at the edge of Lake Champlain, a short distance below. Mehitable sat cross-legged, fifteen feet from her friends, but within hearing range. Polly and Mehitable listened attentively as Reuben told the history of Fort Ticonderoga.

For Mehitable, history seemed to come alive. All around her, she saw tiny flashes of light and heard the constant pop of musket fire. There were smudges of smoke from all of the gun blasts. She could see the walls of the fort like she was standing right in front of it. Mehitable lost her sense of time. One moment it seemed to speed by quickly, like each minute was a second, then it seemed like time passed so slowly that she could see bullets slicing through the air and the moment of impact as they pelted the bodies of the fighting men. Mehitable saw Josiah Lewis, Polly's grandfather, as a younger man, loading his musket, firing, and then reloading. When the smoke cleared, she saw many rows of dead bodies, hundreds of the white uniformed bodies of the French soldiers, almost three times as many dead bodies compared to the British and American fighting men. Mehitable felt like her own spirit was arcing through the air toward a young man, barely more than a boy, weeping over the body of a fallen friend. *Perhaps he is a brother*, she thought. A tear rolled down her cheek, and she wished she could hug the poor young man and bring him some comfort. When Reuben was done telling them about the role Fort Ticonderoga had played in the French and

Indian War, and then in the War for Independence, they hiked back down the mountain.

They enjoyed a hearty meal cooked over a small campfire and settled in for the night. The next day would bring another long day of travel. Just as Mehitable was about to fall asleep, she saw another military man. He wasn't young like the man on the stump, and he wasn't older, like the man at the edge of the woods. He wore a British uniform. Mehitable thought that he looked to be 30-years-old. She saw him stand up to survey the French lines and then she saw a French cannonball strike him in the belly. His head and torso flew off in one direction and his legs dropped in place beneath him. Mehitable screamed in shock at the sight, making her friends jump, just as they were beginning to drift off to sleep. Mehitable apologized, blaming a sharp rock on the ground, beneath her blanket. Over and over, Mehitable saw and felt the cannonball blow through the soldier's belly until finally, after midnight, the vision stopped. She remembered the story of that man which Reuben's father had told at her birthday party.

Mehitable fell asleep and dreamed about a tall, handsome man in a green uniform taking over the fort. She realized that it was Ethan Allen and his Green Mountain Boys. In her dream, Ethan Allen and Benedict Arnold bickered with each other. It was clear that they didn't like each other at all. She also saw Ethan Allen and his men drinking and celebrating at the fort after they captured it.

At three in the morning, she heard a voice in her ear. She saw the British in their redcoats following the Americans over the float bridge that connected Fort Ticonderoga to what was dubiously called Mount Independence, directly across the lake on the Vermont side. She recognized Polly's grandmother, Molly Cole and watched as she sounded the alarm. Mehitable felt a breeze along her arm. Molly was running, and carrying her toddler, Benjamin. Polly's father, John was about 12-years-old. He hurried along behind his mother. Word was carried from town to town, and all the residents of Fair Haven and Poultney fled miles to the south. Then her vision advanced to the Battle of Hubbardton. After heavy fighting, she watched as the Americans evaporated into the woods.

It seemed to Mehitable that she had just closed her eyes and drifted off to sleep when her friends began to stir. The rooster crowed from his box at the back of the wagon. Mehitable rose to add logs to the fire. She yawned and thought about what a long day it would be. She recalled her dream of Ethan Allen and Benedict Arnold, then she suddenly realized that Ethan was the ghost that she had encountered at the cemetery in Poultney. She wondered why he was following her, and why he had appeared in her dream. She was ready to get away from Mount Defiance, Mount Independence, and the ghosts of Fort Ticonderoga.

They hiked thirteen miles the next day and camped after crossing Grove Creek where they enjoyed a view of Bulwaga Bay and Lake Champlain a few miles to the east. Mehitable was the first one to sleep, having left the drama from Fort Ticonderoga behind. If there were any distressed spirits attached to nearby Fort Amherst at Crown Point, they left Mehitable in peace.

Another early morning followed. They completed a grueling seventeen-mile hike which was made more challenging by the increasing elevations. They reached Elizabethtown a couple of hours before dark. A kind farmer named Dalton Weeks allowed them to camp out in his front yard. Reuben had spent the night in Farmer Weeks's yard on previous occasions and had formed a friendship with the man. His wife had passed, and his children had grown. Reuben introduced Polly and Mehitable, then the conversation turned to politics, the Louisiana Purchase, and farm prices. Dalton turned his kitchen over to Polly. He seemed to enjoy the full, home-cooked meal as much as they did. After dinner, Dalton insisted they spend the night indoors. Reuben began to accept, but saw Mehitable standing behind Dalton, vigorously shaking her head. "That's very kind of you, but we are enjoying camping and we have our routine down to a system."

"Suit yourself," Farmer Weeks exclaimed. He slapped Reuben on the back, and laughed heartily. Mehitable tilted her head and wondered what the man was thinking. When Mr. Weeks jabbed Reuben in the side, she was certain that the man thought Reuben was a polygamist and she made a point to inform him that she was a friend of the family, and her hands on her hips clearly conveyed her displeasure at his inference.

Then, off to the side, Mehitable saw the faint, transparent image of a diminutive woman standing on the landing of a steep staircase. She had jet black hair pulled tight and it sat on the very top of her head in a ball. Both hands rested on a large round decorative ball that adorned the staircase. Mehitable felt like the woman was surveying them and supervising their visit. She had the strange feeling that the woman was glad that they were there.

Mehitable asked Dalton about his wife. Dalton told them how he missed his wife Francine, who had passed five years earlier. He leaned forward, and with his open hand at the side of his mouth, Dalton said confidentially, "Sometimes after dinner, when it is really quiet, I almost think I can hear her whispering in my ear."

Mehitable glanced toward the landing on the stairway. Dalton's confession seemed to please Francine immensely.

In the morning, Mehitable and Polly treated Dalton to a big breakfast and left him with a large supply of baked goods, enough to last him several days. In the kitchen, and at the dining room table, Mehitable had a clear view of the landing on the stairway. Francine was ever present. Mehitable wondered if her spirit ever moved from that exact spot. Francine tipped her head back and Mehitable thought it looked like the ghost was smelling Polly's cinnamon pastries. She tried not to stare. Usually she looked away whenever she saw spirits.

There was something about Francine's approval that kept drawing Mehitable's gaze back to the landing on Farmer Weeks's staircase.

After breakfast Reuben shared the news with Polly and Mehitable. He had purchased a 2-year-old milk cow from Farmer Weeks. She was a fine bi-colored Jersey cow with friendly eyes and long black eyelashes. Her fur was soft, and she seemed to enjoy the attention as the women rubbed her neck. Her coloring consisted of approximately one-third white spots, which looked like islands on a sea of brownish-orange, approximately the same color as pumpkin pie.

"Pray, Mr. Weeks, what is this cow's name," Mehitable asked.

Dalton thought a moment, and said, "Aye, yes. Well, I'm not going to tell you that. You should name her yourself." Dalton looked pleased with himself, like he had just done them a big favor.

It was late morning before they left Elizabethtown. The terrain was tough and steep, slow going up and then down. The cow wasn't accustomed to long walks. Reuben suggested they make camp at Otis Brook, about five miles south of Jay. They camped in a tiny clearing along the heavily wooded creek. Mehitable fell asleep to the rhythmic sounds of flowing water and the cow chewing its cud.

In the morning after packing everything back into the wagon, Mehitable stood by the creek with her right arm resting comfortably at the small of her back. She exhaled contentedly. That spot was so tranquil and unspoiled. Mehitable thought to lock the image of it in her mind. She heard Reuben hitch the horses to the wagon, then she heard him tell Polly that they should reach their new home by the end of the day. Mehitable took a deep breath and turned to follow the wagon. *I'm going to miss the traveling*, she thought. Before that trip, Mehitable had spent her entire life in the same place, never having left the town she was born in.

Chapter 10
April 1804

"Almost there," Reuben kept repeating. Finally, it was true. For the previous couple of hours Mehitable and Polly were amazed by the stunning natural beauty of the enormous mountain, and they seemed to be getting closer and closer to it. Reuben kept looking at them to see if they loved the view as much as he did. Mehitable looked at Reuben, tilted her head curiously, and thought, *I wonder if Moses behaved like this when he led his people, finally, into the promised land.* Mehitable had seen so many places that looked like fine locations, she wondered how those spots were passed by. She would have been happy to build a life on the banks of Otis Brook. They had been headed downhill for a while, mercifully, and then Reuben gestured proudly with his right arm.

Polly gasped when she saw it. It was a beautiful plank home with lots of windows. A large barn stood a short distance from the house and stood between the sawmill and the still that Reuben described in his letters. Several hitching posts stood near the barn. Reuben tied the team to one and helped Mehitable tie the sheep to another. Then he scooped up Polly and carried her across the threshold of the house he had built just for her.

Mehitable clasped her hands in front of her and twisted her shoulders from side to side. She was curious to see the inside of the house, but she could wait. She was always keen to recognize those moments when Polly and Reuben required privacy. For a fraction of a second, she pictured Reuben carrying *her* into the new house instead of Polly and admonished herself for having such a thought.

She wandered through the wide barn doorway. There was a large loft above, half-full of hay. There were several large box stalls. Reuben's tall black mare occupied one of the stalls. Her name, Lucy was carved into one of the planks of her stall. Mehitable thought of the song her father used to sing while she played. She thought of the sad words, "My Lucy alas is no more, is no..., ...no more, my Lucy alas is no more," and a tear rolled down her cheek.

The rest of the stalls in the barn were clean, new, and empty. Mehitable felt a sense of optimism. Surely such a grand barn offered the promise of a fantastic potential. She walked along the stalls until she came to the last one. Her mouth dropped open in surprise. Emmeline. Augusta. Adelina. She unclasped her hands and brought them to her chin. She thought, *You can really tell someone cares for you when they go out of their way to care about something you love.*

In the middle of the box stall stood a little three-legged milking stool. There was something on the stool, wrapped in a thick blanket, and there was a paper placard with Mehitable's name on it. She set the placard aside and untied the twine from the blanket. Inside were four leather bound books. The cover read, *The Complete Dramatic Works of William Shakespeare.* She opened the cover of the first volume, and read, "Boston: Printed by Munroe & Francis, 1802." There was a small piece of paper set inside the cover that said, "For Mehitable Munch, with love, from Reuben and Polly Sanford, April 1804," in Reuben's handwriting. Tears streamed down her face, and she felt the burning, salty brine at the back of her mouth. She knew she was hard to love. She deeply appreciated her friends and loved them both. She opened another volume, randomly flipping to

Ophelia, and then it hit her. That was the perfect name for the new cow. Ophelia.

At the end of the stall she saw two tiny doorknobs. It looked like kitchen cabinets. She wondered, *Why would someone place kitchen cabinets inside a sheep's stall?* Another placard inside read, "Mehitable's Wardrobe."

Outside the stall she noticed a chair and three tables. She wandered over to investigate. One table was labeled, "Mehitable's Virginal." The second said, "Mehitable's Desk." The last table was very short, and had a placard that read, "Mehitable's Spinning Wheel." There were several wooden crates. She laughed when she read the sign above them that said, "Mehitable's Treasure." She knew she would spend much of her time in that barn, at those tables, and in that stall. She dropped to her knees and said a prayer. She prayed that she would know peace and tranquility in her new home.

At the opposite end of the barn, Mehitable came to a hole in the floor, and a hatch that had been folded open. A ladder led from the top to the lower level. Mehitable climbed down the ladder. In one corner on the lower floor there was a stall, completely enclosed, only the planks were separated by narrow gaps, allowing air to pass through the stall. The words, "Dinner and Mehitable's Hens" was carved into one of the planks. There were several stalls next to the chicken coop suitable for pigs, goats, or sheep. Across the aisle was a row of stalls suitable for horses or cows. She noticed another placard sticking out between a couple of boards in the stall nearest the big door on the lower level. The paper read, "Mehitable's Cow."

She wondered what little surprises Polly was discovering inside her new home. She clapped her hand to her mouth. She tried to erase the thought that came to her mind.

Mehitable felt honored, cherished, and loved. Polly's husband had gone out of his way to include her, to make her feel welcome. She wandered out the lower door, around the barn, and untied

Ophelia from the back of the wagon. She led the cow to her new home. Ophelia celebrated her homecoming by stretching her neck, grabbing a clump of hay and chewing contentedly as if she had been born there. Next, Mehitable untied the box of chickens from the wagon. It was heavy, but she managed to haul them to their new coop. They flapped their wings and ran around, glad to have plenty of space to run around in after days of confinement. She carried the rest of her possessions into the barn, and unpacked them, placing each one in their properly labeled places. She saved the virginal for last. It was heavy, but she had carried it before. It had been carefully wrapped in many protective layers. She took a deep breath, lifted, and carefully lugged it to its own table in the barn and unwrapped it.

It occurred to Mehitable that she hadn't played for a while. She stretched her fingers, then she started tapping on the keys. Emmeline looked up at her, then returned to her snack. Mehitable thought her music sounded rich and full in the big, open, airy barn. She played several songs, then she wandered back to the wagon. Since leaving the Lewis's home in Vermont, she had started to feel like her old self again, almost reclaiming the personality she had prior to the tragedy.

Mehitable found a shovel and dug several small holes. Then she got the bucket from the wagon and planted the pineys, peppermint, and lemongrass clumps that she had brought with her. She hoped they would adjust to the alpine climate.

Then she climbed up on the back of the wagon, swung her legs lazily, and gazed out at the pine trees which contrasted with birch trees in the foreground. She stared at the enormous mountain above, and listened to the noisy river, busily hurrying from one distant place to another. She felt carefree, like a child rather than a woman.

Mehitable was just thinking about the pleasant absence of people when she saw three men approaching, walking slowly up the road, if you could call it a road. The closer they got, the more detail she made out. They all looked nearly the same. She saw their hair and knew at once that they were the Bump boys that Reuben had described. They looked like they had been working very hard, all day long, and it looked like none of them had gotten a fresh change of clothes in far too long.

She could hear them from far away. Perhaps they didn't know how well sound could travel down a country hillside. "What is that? It's a wagon. Do you see somebody sitting on the back of it? Yes, I sure do. I think it's a lass. A lassie? Which lass do you reckon? The wife? Maybe it's the friend. I say she's mine. I reckon it's up to her. She can take her pick, far as I'm concerned. Remember, boss said be polite around the ladies. Yeah, that means nothing more than aye, ma'am. Nay, ma'am. Have a nice day. Reckon she can hear us from here?" Mehitable couldn't make one out from another, they all sounded the same. By the time they reached the back of the wagon they were completely silent. Normally, since the tragic fire four years earlier, Mehitable was quite reserved around strangers. Something about those men made Mehitable feel like she was talking to children. She always felt comfortable among children.

Mehitable remained seated on the back of the wagon, and said, "Good afternoon, men. My name is Mehitable. I am Reuben's wife's best friend. How do you do?"

Like a well-practiced church choir, the men said, "Howdy, ma'am." They looked at each other, pleased with themselves for having gotten their line right, and not messing up.

"What are your names," Mehitable asked.

"Otis."

"Lester, here."

"You can call me Dudley."

Mehitable asked, "Are you triplets? How can I tell you apart?"

Otis giggled, and kept his thought to himself. "I'll wink at you with my left eye."

Dudley said, "I'll wink at you with my right eye."

Lester concluded, "I'll blink at you."

Mehitable replied, "Oh, I see. Are you allowed to wink at all the girls?"

They giggled and looked at each other. Dudley let out an enormous fart, and they all laughed. "I don't think we're allowed to talk anymore."

Finally, Reuben and Polly appeared at the doorway of the house. They looked disheveled. Mehitable smiled at her friends as they walked toward the wagon. Reuben raised an eyebrow, and asked, "You've met Otis, Lester, and Dudley?"

Mehitable smiled, winked at the Bumps and said, "Aye, they are most charming young men," causing the trio to giggle and jab each other with their elbows.

Reuben nodded, put his arm around his wife's shoulder, and introduced her to the boys.

" 'Tis a pleasure to meet you," Polly said nicely.

Lester held up his index finger, then his middle finger, then his ring finger. Lester was the only one with a ring on his finger. "Howdy, ma'am," another perfect performance. They giggled again. Lester said, "Have a nice day." And they were off.

Polly looked at Reuben, and Reuben shrugged. "They work hard, and they don't ask for much."

Mehitable said, "Reuben, I want to thank you for your kindness. You didn't need to let me come along, but you did. I know I'm not an ordinary woman, and I appreciate your understanding. What you did in the barn makes me feel loved and appreciated. You have no idea what it means to me."

Reuben bowed, "You're welcome, milady. 'Twas my pleasure. And the Shakespeare was Polly's idea." Reuben offered to show Polly around the barn and gestured for Mehitable to join them. Then Reuben asked Polly to show Mehitable around the house, leaving the ladies alone for a while.

They walked through the front door. A few feet inside, a wide staircase led upstairs to the second floor. Polly led Mehitable to the right. They passed through a dining room with a large rectangular table surrounded by ten chairs. Polly pointed out a large china cabinet with cupboard doors and drawers beneath, and glassed-in shelves above. Beyond the dining room was a large, spacious kitchen, dominated by a ten-foot wide stone hearth, with a built-in oven. Inside the fireplace was a large crane with three hooks. Chunky brass andirons sat on the floor of the hearth, and matching cookware hung above them, including a cauldron, a kettle, a cookpot, and a skillet. Next to the fireplace was a sturdy wooden bench with a high back. Firewood was stacked beneath the seat of the bench. Mehitable thought the bench looked like an inviting spot to warm feet on a cold day. A plain door at the back of the kitchen opened into a long, narrow pantry. A doorway in the kitchen opened to a path that led to the barn. Polly told Mehitable that she was pleased with the windows in the house and the windows in the kitchen in particular.

Polly showed Mehitable back through the dining room, past the stairway into a large parlor with a small fireplace. There were three doors at the back of the parlor. The first led to a study with a large desk. The second door led to a guest bedroom. The third door led to a small sewing room with a small bed, and a secret doorway that connected through the pantry behind the staircase to the kitchen.

Then they made their way up the staircase. To the left was a large bedroom and a nursery. To the right were two large bedrooms and each held four small beds. Mehitable asked Polly, "Do you anticipate having lots of company, or are you planning a large family?"

Polly shrugged, rubbed her growing belly, and suggested, "I guess we'll be ready for either."

They went back down the stairs to the parlor. There was a small fireplace, five inviting chairs, a settee, a small bookshelf, and a small round table covered with a cloth. They sat in chairs on either side of the round table. Mehitable's eyes were drawn to the mantle. Polly's grandmother's spyglass stood alone on the shelf. Polly noticed Mehitable's gaze, and said, " 'Tis the only thing I've unpacked. I've got some decorating to do."

Mehitable reached across the small table, put her hand on Polly's shoulder, and said, " 'Tis a lovely house. Every room is beautiful, and full of possibilities. You'll make this fine house into a wonderful home, Polly."

Polly talked about her decorating plans. Curtains were her priority. Polly had brought curtains that she and her mother had made before they left Poultney. After that, she hoped to cover the plain white plaster with decorative wallpaper. After a few minutes, Polly suggested they best get to the kitchen and see what they could do about dinner.

The contents of the kitchen cupboards were sparse. Mehitable built up the fire in the hearth, and Polly prepared beans, bacon, and biscuits. Ironically, they had the same dinner as the Bumps. The difference was that the Bumps had the same dinner every day, and often had beans for breakfast and lunch as well. Reuben told Polly and Mehitable that Lester Bump's wife referred to feeding her husband and his brothers as "slopping the pigs."

In the barn, Reuben had a safe stone box built into the wall near the sheep stall. Because hay and straw are so flammable, the barn was not a good place for fireplaces, candles, or oil lamps. The stone box made for a safe place to house a little oil lamp, so that Mehitable would be able to see in the dark barn at night.

Mehitable had been looking forward to sleeping in the large comfortable barn. She made a nest among her sheep sisters and prepared for a good night's sleep.

Her first night in the new barn was a living hell. As soon as she closed her eyes, the ghost of Anson returned. She opened her eyes quickly, but he was still there. Mehitable gasped. Anson was angry, angrier than usual. He wagged his finger at her. "You thought you could escape me. Ha! You'll never escape me. Look at this place. *He* made this for *you*? He's supposed to be married to your best friend." Mehitable blinked. Open, closed, open, closed. She tried to look away, but Anson's ghost moved to wherever she looked. Finally, she looked at the tip of her nose, crossing her eyes. She still heard Anson's ghost rant. She didn't know what else to do. She figured if the ghost could physically hurt her, it would have done so previously. Eventually, the ghost said, "I'll see you in hell. Someday," and he was gone. For the night.

She had a tight grip on a fist full of sheep fur in each of her hands. With Anson gone, she relaxed her grip. She had hoped to be sleeping already, but instead she lay awake, wondering. How could Anson have followed her? Why hadn't she seen Anson's ghost when they were traveling? She wondered why she always asked such impossible questions. She tried to close her eyes again. To her dismay, the floating ghost of a dead baby returned. Eventually, Mehitable was able to blink away the baby ghost. She closed her eyes again. Finally, no ghosts. Just as she was about to drift off to sleep, she heard a scurrying sound. The scurrying sound of mice. She thought it sounded like dozens of mice. At four in the morning, the need for sleep overwhelmed her distaste for ghosts and mice, and she fell asleep.

Mehitable slept soundly for an hour and a half. She was glad that the chickens were a bit further away in the new barn, but Dinner was a noisy rooster. She dragged herself from her cozy nest the second time she heard the rooster crow. She fetched her milk bucket and sat on her new milking stool next to Ophelia. She was so tired, she fell asleep sitting there, her head resting against the cow's hind leg. Dinner woke her again, and she finished milking. She delivered the milk to the kitchen. Polly and Reuben were having a cup of tea.

Mehitable stood in the kitchen for a few minutes. She watched Polly separate the milk from the cream and fill the new churn that sat on the counter. She handed the churn to Reuben, who looked surprised to have the butter churn appear in his hands. Polly began mixing ingredients for some biscuits. Reuben looked at Mehitable. Mehitable shrugged. Reuben began churning the butter, and Mehitable excused herself.

After a hearty breakfast, Reuben set out to work in the fields. Together, Reuben and the Bumps prepared the soil for seeds. Reuben was hoping for a big crop of rye so he could distill lots of whiskey. With the proceeds from the sale of whiskey, Reuben hoped to build a foundry.

Mehitable spent the day in the barn setting dozens of figure-four traps. She gathered rocks, whittled twigs, and propped them up against the walls of the barn. Maybe she couldn't stop the ghosts, and maybe she couldn't stop the sound of scurrying rodents, but she would try to fight back. She thought of her brother, Perry. She owed her knowledge of trapping to him.

Despite being tired, Mehitable enjoyed her first full day of life in the barn. She took an hour to visit with Polly, who was busy placing curtains in her windows. Then Mehitable returned to the barn and did some spinning. She was running low on wool, and the sheep were getting quite bushy. She had brought her father's sheep sheers with her from Vermont, and she had seen the sheering done many times before. She had never seen a woman sheer a sheep, even so she resolved to give it a try, and she prayed for a peaceful night's sleep. She thought, *I will be happy in this place, if only I can get some sleep.* She fantasized about using Perry's slingshot on the rooster, then she chided herself for thinking such a thought. She said her prayers and closed her eyes. Her prayers were not answered that night.

Chapter 11
May 1804

Mehitable got almost four hours of sleep, better than the night before. Still, she trudged her way through her morning chores. She apologized to Dinner for wishing him harm, and she thanked Ophelia for a bucket of milk. Mehitable delivered the milk pail to the kitchen. Polly got the churn ready for Reuben, but when she turned to hand it to him, he was gone. Polly looked at Mehitable, and Mehitable raised an eyebrow. Mehitable excused herself, wondering who was going to win the butter wars. Clearly, Polly did not intend to churn the butter.

She returned to the barn to check on her traps. Perry had taught her well. Six traps had been tripped. Four of them had flattened mice beneath them. She got a sack, made a face, and picked up a flattened mouse by the very end of the tail, dropping it into her sack. Then she bagged the other three. She reset the traps, retrieved Perry's sling-shot from the box Reuben had labeled, "Mehitable's Treasure," and headed down the road to explore. She found a spot where a deep, dark cliff fell away from the side of the road. She dumped the dead mice from her sack onto the ground. One at a time, she loaded them into the slingshot and sent them flying into the ravine. She wondered why she found flinging dead mice so satisfying. Maybe it was just her way of *fighting back*. She thought about having touched the tiny mice tails and shuddered. She didn't know why the thought of mice repulsed her so. Just the sight of a mouse tail in her trap made her squeamish.

She wandered a little farther down the road and found a good spot to tiptoe into the edge of the mighty, swollen river. She removed her shoes and socks and stood with just her feet in the icy water, chilled by the melting snow on the mountain above her. A beam of sunshine found its way through the dense woods that surrounded the river, and Mehitable enjoyed the warmth of it on her cheeks. She watched as swarms of black flies flew around the surface of the river. A large, spotted fish with a pink belly jumped from beneath the water, twisted its body, and returned to the river. Mehitable slapped her face, picked another black fly from her ear, and thought, *That big ol' fish can have all these dastardly insects.* Then she thought about trying her luck at fishing. She set that thought aside. She had a big job to do.

Back at the barn, Mehitable thought about all the things she would need. Each year she had watched as her father sheered the sheep. She had also seen Polly's brother, Eliada, and her father do that job. It occurred to her that she could ask Reuben to shear the sheep for her. Then she thought of all the plowing and planting ahead of him that spring, and all the butter he would have to churn. She giggled and steeled her resolve. She would do it herself.

She held the shears in her hands. She looked at them closely, felt their weight, and flipped them over, amazed at how they seemed to spring back to open after they had been squeezed shut. The blades of the shears were really nothing more than knives. They had been manufactured by Burgon & Ball in Sheffield, England, carried across the ocean by one of her ancestors, and now they sat in her hands. John Lewis had told Mehitable that one of the causes of the Revolutionary War had been England's prohibition against the colonies' production and export of wool. Mehitable shook her head and recalled Reuben's father, Oliver, telling them about the price the nation had paid to become free.

Heavy shears or not, it was time to get to work. Mehitable decided to start with Emmeline. Emmeline was older and had a few years of experience with the process. Mehitable rolled Emmeline over on to her back while humming songs familiar to both of them. With a short rope, Mehitable tied three of Emmeline's legs together. The sheep went limp, like she had gone into a coma.

She sat for a moment, looked at her favorite sheep, and felt her heart skip a beat. "I'll be very careful," Mehitable promised. She sat on her milking stool and wrestled the heavy sheep into position so that it looked like it was sitting on its tail, like a person sitting on the ground. Emmeline rested against Mehitable's legs and lay her long black head on Mehitable's lap.

Her hands burrowed to a good starting point on the sheep's chest. She separated the wool until she got close to the skin and made a tentative first snip. Emmeline rested silently and pliant against her legs. Complete trust. She clipped as close to the skin of the sheep as she could so that the fleece would remain connected as a solid mass. Snip by snip, she revealed the naked sheep beneath the wool. Emmeline didn't move a muscle as Mehitable spun her around. First she thought about how men twirled ladies around while dancing. Then she thought about peeling apples. It was fun to try to remove the skin of an apple with a knife, leaving the entire skin in one long, connected spiral. As she snipped away, she couldn't decide whether shearing sheep was more like dancing or peeling apples. Emmeline patiently allowed Mehitable to move her as needed, so that Mehitable could get to every inch of the sheep's body. Mehitable didn't stay seated on the stool very long. She discovered it wasn't work that could be done from a sitting position. Sometimes she sat on the ground, but mostly she stood, bent at the waist. There was plenty of squatting required to complete the task.

She worked slowly. An experienced sheep shearer could have done the job in forty-five minutes. It took her two hours. When she finished, she untied Emmeline. Emmeline remained on the ground, looked at Mehitable, not realizing she had been freed. She helped the sheep to her feet, and Emmeline took off running, twisting, and darting from one end of the stall to the other. She thought that the sheep looked relieved to be free of the heavy wool which had kept her warm during the cold winter, and celebrated by jumping and playing, as if she were a lamb once again.

She took a little break before she started in on the next sheep. She thought about when she was a little girl, watching her father shear the sheep. She felt sorry for the sheep, as her father snipped quickly, almost recklessly, she thought. Horace flopped them around with his strong hands and arms as if they were ragdolls. She turned her head sideways, then her thoughts returned to her work. She took a deep breath and put Emmeline's fleece in a large sack. Emmeline's younger sisters weren't as relaxed. It took more effort and time to separate them from their dense wool. Shearing the three sheep took Mehitable most of the day, but she was proud of the work she had done.

After Mehitable had put away the shears, the rope, the milking stool, and the bags of fleece, she stood in front of the stall looking at the sheep. They looked back at her. She thought they looked so small, tiny fractions of their former selves. She couldn't resist spending a few minutes sitting among them, running her hands along their velvety, wrinkly coats. Her right hand and wrist hurt from squeezing the big shears.

Soon it would be dark. It was time to milk the cow again. Reuben returned home shortly before Mehitable arrived in the kitchen with a fresh pail of milk. He walked through the door and found the butter churn sitting at his place at the dinner table. Polly didn't speak to him, or look at him, until he began churning the butter. He had just about finished when Mehitable walked through the door carrying another bucket of milk. Polly had her back to them. Mehitable made eye contact with Reuben and raised her eyebrows inquisitively. She handed Polly the bucket and grinned at her friend. *Perhaps*, thought Mehitable, *the butter war was over.*

The next morning, after breakfast, and after churning the butter, Reuben hitched up the horses he had borrowed from his father-in-law. He had promised to return the Appaloosas as soon as the fields were prepared and planted. Reuben hugged Mehitable and shared a long embrace with Polly. Then he tied the big, black mare to the back of the wagon, and set out for the Lewis's farm. Polly and Mehitable had sent him with lots of biscuits and cookies. He would not go hungry on his trip.

Reuben had left Polly and Mehitable in the care of the Bump brothers. While he was away, the Bumps were asked to construct strong fences around the barn so that Mehitable could let the animals out during the daytime.

Early one afternoon, a couple of days later, Mehitable and Polly were working together in the small vegetable garden near the path that was gradually becoming a well-traveled road. It was early yet, but they thought they would take a chance on sowing some seeds for the earlier crops, mostly peas and beans. Something caught Mehitable's eye. She saw a large woman waddling down the road, carrying something. Mehitable and Polly looked at each other, then they heard the woman hollering, "Lester! Lester Bump! Where are you?"

Polly spoke quietly to Mehitable, as if the woman could hear her from way up the road, "What is she carrying?"

Mehitable answered, "It looks like some kind of stick. Poor Lester."

The woman moved quickly, despite her size. She was obviously in a hurry and it wasn't long before she was standing at the edge of the little vegetable garden. She gave voice to polite greetings, using appropriate words, but they came across as gruff rather than cordial.

She said, "Good afternoon. How do you do? My name is Coriander. You must be my new neighbors," looking down at Polly and Mehitable, who were considerably shorter. The Bump boys saw Coriander in the front yard and abandoned their fence making, arriving at the edge of the garden just as Polly and Mehitable concluded introducing themselves.

Polly asked Coriander which one of the boys belonged to her. Coriander responded with a bemused, "Harrumph." She stood there with one hand on her hip, waved the pastry rolling-stick she held in her hand at the three men, and said, "I don't have any idea. Who can tell them apart? I just go with whichever one blinks." The three of them giggled naughtily, and they all began blinking. Coriander stood there shaking her head from side to side, and asked her neighbors, "See what I have to put up with? I married the one named Lester, but I ended up getting all three of these dunderheads."

Just then, a wave of pain overtook Coriander Bump. She dropped her stick, planted both feet on the ground, and stood with a hand on each hip. She closed her eyes tightly, and she breathed rapidly, inhaling and exhaling for half a minute, until the labor pain subsided. Then she continued, "So, you see, one of these boys is about to become a daddy."

Coriander pivoted, looked at the small garden, shook her head from side to side, and said, "What are you doing planting already? 'Tis too soon." She offered several other criticisms, including the opinion that the garden was too close to the road. She concluded her thoughts about the garden with her customary *harrumph* before another wave of labor pains overtook her.

Finally, Lester stepped forward, offered his arm to his wife, and asked if they could help her get home.

Coriander tilted her head back, looked down her nose at Lester, and barked, "There's no time for that. It was all I could do to get here. Unless someone has a better idea, I'll plant this baby right here in this God forsaken vegetable patch."

Mehitable and Polly looked at each other in amazement. Then another wave of pain overtook the woman. Finally, Polly took over, instructing the boys to guide Coriander into her home. Polly sent Lester to retrieve the woman's nightgown and house coat, checking quickly with Coriander to see if there were any other comforting items she'd like to have brought back. Otis and Dudley helped Coriander into the house. Then Polly sent them back to their work at the fences. Mehitable boiled water. Polly helped Coriander remove her apron and her enormous dress, then she helped Coriander onto the bed. She offered her a blanket, then she asked her if she would like a cup of water. Another pain wracked Coriander, who was again clutching her pastry stick as Polly hurried to the kitchen.

Mehitable could tell Polly was distraught. "What are we going to do?" Polly asked.

Mehitable responded, "What else can we do?" She saw her friend rubbing her own expanded belly, and she saw a distant, fearful look on Polly's face. Mehitable took Polly's hand, and said, "We will get through this." Mehitable told Polly to sit down and rest, then she took the cup of water to Coriander. Mehitable had been present for many human births, and many births in the barn as well.

The pains were coming very quickly. Mehitable wiped the sweat from Coriander's brow and asked, "How long have you been in labor, dear?" The woman told her that she had started to have the pains the day before. She had planned to give birth all by herself, but as the day went along, she thought better of that plan and hurried to find her husband. Less than an hour after arriving at Polly's and Reuben's house, Coriander gave birth to a big, healthy, baby boy.

Polly was grateful that it was over quickly. Coriander's final scream made her shudder in horror with the realization that she would be facing a similar experience, and soon. She sat at her dining room table, elbows on the surface, head in her hands. Polly was excited to be having a baby but was fearful about the birthing process. She was grateful that Mehitable was tending to her houseguest.

Coriander tried to enlist the help of her husband and his brothers to get her home that day. Polly insisted that she and the baby stay at her home for the night.

When the house was quiet, Mehitable slipped out to the barn. It was well after dark. She was tired, and she prayed a restful sleep would find her fast. Instead, Anson came to her, wagging his finger angrily, telling her she would never know the joys of motherhood. She should never put her filthy hands on other mothers' children. She should stay in the barn, with the animals, where she belonged. She should sleep with pigs instead of sheep. Every time she felt she was about to fall asleep again, Anson returned, repeating his foul tempered messages. He was louder each time. His appearance was always accompanied by the smell of tobacco, whiskey, and the smell of dried sweat after days of not bathing. Sleep finally claimed Mehitable at two-thirty in the morning.

By sunrise, Coriander was her usual self. She refused assistance getting to the table. She greeted her hostess with the words, "Top of the morning to you, ma'am." Coriander's polite words sounded more like a barked order than a polite greeting. She sat down to a breakfast cooked by others. She sat looking from side to side, a little lost. Coriander was accustomed to serving meals, not having food set before her. She was grateful, though she boldly suggested that the tea was too strong, the biscuits were too dry, the bacon wasn't crunchy enough, and the eggs needed salt. Coriander questioned why Polly had hung curtains on the windows. She couldn't see the point. Why go to the effort of putting in windows only to cover them up?

Before breakfast was over, Coriander was asking why Mehitable slept in the barn with the dirty farm animals. Polly gingerly answered for Mehitable, trying to explain in as few words as possible, the tragic events which led to Mehitable's fear of sleeping indoors. Mehitable placed her fork on her dish, suddenly finished with her breakfast, and stared at the remaining food on her plate. She felt the intense gaze of their judgmental neighbor boring into the top of her head, and then she heard the *harrumph* that ended the discussion and ended breakfast. Coriander wiped her lips on the sleeve of her housecoat. Then she politely excused herself. "Pardon me, sisters," The words were proper, but Mehitable thought they sounded more like a barking dog than a woman who would refer to her friends as sisters.

Shortly thereafter, Coriander had changed into her homespun dress and apron, packed her belongings in a sack, and handed them to her brother-in-law, Dudley. Lester carried the baby and Otis escorted Coriander.

Polly and Mehitable sat for a while over tea after the Bump family had left, commiserating over the horror and wonder of the birthing process. Then they discussed their neighbors. The Bumps were nothing like the neighbors they had known in Vermont. Polly wondered at Coriander's ability to be polite and insulting at the same time. Mehitable took a sip of her tea and stared at her thumbnail. She told herself she didn't care what Coriander thought. She compared her sheep to the Bump brothers and felt better about her situation. Truly, she didn't mind the company of Otis, Lester, and Dudley. *Hopefully*, she thought, *Coriander will not visit often.*

That evening, Mehitable saw the dead baby ghost again. She looked closely. It didn't look anything like the little baby that Coriander had unceremoniously named Bacon Bump.

Chapter 12
May 1804

Reuben made good time in both directions, six days to the Lewis's farm and five days back. On his way through the tiny new town of Elizabethtown, Reuben stopped again at the farm where he had purchased Ophelia. He always enjoyed visiting with Farmer Weeks. Reuben purchased a fine young Merino ram, and Mr. Weeks gave Reuben a freshly weaned kitten. Reuben thought of the rows of figure four traps in the barn and thought the kitten would be very useful. A busy barn full of many sheep had always been part of Reuben's overall plan. Reuben unbuttoned his shirt and tucked the fluffy kitten inside. It squirmed a little, tickling his belly. He carefully climbed into the saddle, and Farmer Weeks passed him the long rope tied to the young ram. Reuben arrived home well after dark, riding slowly, trying not to disturb the kitten. It drenched his shirt with urine just as he was riding up to his house.

Mehitable was in the barn, brushing her hair. It was her one remaining vanity. Her hair always shined and glistened as a result of her dutiful attentiveness. She loved the feel of it gliding through her fingers, even smoother and softer than the sheep's wool as she fed it into her spinning wheel. She stood up as Reuben approached, dropping her brush to the floor. He didn't come into the barn that often, and never at night. Her jaw dropped as he started unbuttoning his shirt, baring his chest. She didn't know what to think. She didn't know what to do. Her heart began to race. Then Reuben pulled a small black kitten from within his shirt. Mehitable cradled the kitten in her hand, and Reuben re-buttoned his shirt. Reuben said, "I have another surprise for you. Follow me."

Outside the barn, Mehitable saw Reuben's horse tied to a rail, then she noticed the young ram tied to another rail. She gasped and kissed Reuben on the cheek, then she led the ram around the barn to the lower entrance and settled him into his stall while Reuben tended to his horse. The little ram was a rare, Merino breed of sheep, not yet common in North America. She named the ram Jester, another animal name to make her think of Shakespearian plays. Mehitable slowly welcomed the new sheep to the barn, bringing him water, hay, and murmuring comforting words into his ear, all the while holding the kitten, before she returned to the upper level of the barn.

Reuben had hastily tended to his horse. Mehitable checked to make sure that he had given her water and hay before returning to her carding. She set the kitten down on the floor, sat on her chair, and pondered. She admonished herself for letting her thoughts run away from her. She had been shocked to think that Reuben would make an inappropriate advance, and yet she readily jumped to an improper assumption when he appeared unexpectedly and began unbuttoning his shirt. Perhaps, she acknowledged to herself, it was because of her own inappropriate thoughts, thoughts about her and Reuben together, that caused her to think the worst. She always kept those thoughts at bay, squelching them before they developed into anything significant. She knew she would never act on them, and she resolved to chase those thoughts from her mind whenever they flashed into her consciousness, and she warned herself to keep a little more physical distance between herself and Reuben.

Not waiting for Mehitable to begin trying to fall asleep, Anson appeared earlier than usual, laughing and taunting, "How could you think he would want *you*. You aren't nothing but a common farm animal anyway. You should just run away into the wild woods. They don't want you here. You don't belong. They make fun of you when you're not around." Anson's dastardly ghost had increasingly suggested that Mehitable harm herself. Sometimes the power of suggestion caused her to doubt her friends, though they never treated her with anything but kindness. She tried to remind herself not to take advice from the evil spirit.

As summer progressed, and while Reuben waited for the crops to mature, he kept the Bumps busy making endless mazes of fencing, increasing the protected grazing range of the farm animals. Reuben busied himself inside the barn, crafting furniture for the nursery. As he sawed wood, whittled dowels, drilled holes, and sanded surfaces, he listened to Mehitable hum while she worked at making yarn. Sometimes he enjoyed listening to her sing while she played the virginal for an otherwise apathetic audience of barnyard animals. Sometimes she read aloud to the sheep. They enjoyed the comforting sound of her voice. Reuben thought her voice sounded soothing, even when she was reading from Shakespeare's darkest tragedies. He often found himself sanding to the rhythm of her songs, or to the cadence of the iambic pentameter in the playwright's verses.

Sometimes Polly would step out into the barn in the evening while Reuben was working, and she would sit watching him work while listening to Mehitable in the distance. The evenings were growing cooler, and the leaves were beginning to change. It would be their first autumn together in the mountains.

One Sunday evening in late September, Polly sat in a chair in the barn watching Reuben build a dresser for the nursery. She sat and thought. She had noticed that Mehitable seemed tired. She had noticed that the deep dark circles beneath her friend's eyes had returned. Yet Mehitable always seemed to be happy and content. Polly knew that she still grieved for her lost family, and she doubted that Mehitable would ever return to sleeping in a house as her father had suggested would someday come to pass, and Polly was certain there was something Mehitable kept to herself, that she didn't share with anyone. Polly wished she could absorb her friend's burdens, whatever they might be. It was getting late, and she wasn't feeling very well. She wasn't sure what it was, but she felt a pain in her abdomen. She struggled to rise from her chair. It wouldn't be long before she would be a mother. She still dreaded the idea of giving birth. On the other hand, she was terribly tired of being pregnant. She affectionately patted Reuben on the shoulder. He said, "I'll head inside in a few minutes."

Overnight Polly managed to sleep, on and off, between the pains, which remained far apart. After she realized the pain waxed and waned, she knew what it was. She thought about the date, the 27th of September. She did some figuring, and worried. Was it too soon? What could she do? She focused on relaxing and tried to sleep as much as possible. She was aware that it could be a long day and that she should conserve her energy.

When Reuben awoke next to her, she told him that the labor pains had begun overnight. He kissed her gently then jumped from bed to bring the embers in the hearth to life. He hung the pot from a hook over the fire, and then helped Polly up from the bed. Next, he escorted her to the outhouse. It was a trip she made quite frequently, the longer her pregnancy went on.

They arrived back in the kitchen just as Mehitable was delivering the milk pail. Reuben blurted, "The baby is on its way." Polly nodded behind him, confirming the news. Mehitable hugged Reuben quickly, then she hugged Polly. They helped Polly into a chair, and Mehitable and Reuben hurried around tending to breakfast.

Polly had managed to quietly endure her pain during the night. As morning progressed, the pains came more frequently, and Polly was less and less able to get through them silently. Reuben had sent his crew to work without him. It was time to harvest the fields. It was a clear day, and Reuben hoped they would get a lot of the grain in. Every time Polly whimpered in pain, Reuben grimaced. His pacing made Mehitable nervous. Finally, she suggested that Reuben help his men in the fields. She told him he didn't belong in the house while the baby was being born anyway. She pressed his hat into his chest, insistently, opened the door for him, and told him not to worry.

Mehitable hummed soothingly as she put her friend to bed and got ready for what was to come. She had no idea what to expect. Would the baby come quickly? Would it be a long, slow, painful delivery? No two birthings went the same. Mehitable yawned, breathed deeply, then resumed her happy humming. She prayed to herself, nothing else to do anyway.

By the middle of the afternoon it was inevitable. Mehitable reassured her friend frequently, telling her she could endure, letting her know that she was praying for her, and constantly reapplying a moist cloth to her forehead. Mostly she just held Polly's hand and hummed.

Finally, just after dark, the baby came. Polly cradled him in her arm, looked closely into his face, and declared that the boy's name was Reuben. Just like his father.

He looked healthy, but he wouldn't nurse. Polly tried tirelessly to feed him. Nothing seemed to work. He took no interest in nursing. Failing to get him to breastfeed, they tried to get Ophelia's milk into him. Whatever went down seemed to come back up. For days they tried everything they could think of, yet nothing seemed to work. Reuben galloped to Elizabethtown in search of a doctor, since there was no doctor settled in town. By the time Reuben returned with the doctor, it was too late.

The baby was born on Monday and took his last breath on Friday. Mehitable now understood why she had seen his ghost at Polly and Reuben's wedding. She felt guilty for not telling Polly about the feeling of dread she had at seeing a vision of a baby ghost. If she had warned them, maybe something could have been done to prevent his death. Though she couldn't reasonably think of what they might have done, she still felt like she had let Polly and Reuben down. Then she wondered about the vision of the little girl she had been seeing. Mehitable tried to be a comfort to her friend, but had difficulty finding sufficient words to console her. She hoped that her presence by Polly's side was enough. Often, Polly would catch her in tears, and they'd end up sobbing together. Mehitable couldn't understand why she felt that baby was in some small part her own, and she felt a distant yearning for a baby of her own someday. Someday when evil spirits were no longer part of her long nights.

With the wood left over from building the nursery furniture, Reuben built a tiny box. It was just the perfect size for the baby's coffin. Reuben found it hard to see through his watery eyes, but somehow it came together. When it was finished, Reuben wondered why he bothered sanding the coffin, but he couldn't stop himself from doing so. That evening he put his tiny son in the box with a small blanket, and a tiny wooden toy wagon he had made for him. Later, he lay on his back in bed, and Polly sobbed on his chest half the night before finally falling asleep.

The next morning, they buried the boy in the front yard. Reuben shoveled dirt over the coffin and then he placed a large rock directly on top of the temporary grave. Reuben promised they would move him to a suitable cemetery as soon as a cemetery could be established. They each said a few words, and Reuben concluded by promising, "Someday we'll make a stone for you, son, and we'll bury you properly." Reuben, Polly, and Mehitable wandered down to the river. Along the way they collected wildflowers and colorful leaves. They spent the afternoon sitting on rocks in the middle of the river, dropping flowers and leaves in the water, and watching them float downstream. Words felt futile. They were silent. The noisy river did all the talking.

On the way back to the house, Polly looked at Mehitable and said, "If the baby had been born a girl, I was going to name her Wilhelmina, after your mother." More tears ran down their faces, and the friends embraced.

Mehitable cupped Polly's cheek in her hand and said, "I am so honored, honored beyond comprehension, but if you have a baby girl, please give that baby her *own* name."

Polly distracted herself from thinking about the loss of her baby by decorating the house. She talked endlessly about wallpaper. Without knowing what existed, she made plans for each room. With measurements carefully noted on a piece of paper, Polly and Reuben took a long trip to Plattsburgh by carriage.

Preprinted wallpaper was very expensive. Plain wallpaper was more affordable. They hung the plain wallpaper in the bedrooms upstairs. Polly picked out several stencils, and with the ink and brushes she bought, she planned to decorate the second story.

For the dining room, Polly chose a green floral paper. Songbirds perched on the branches of blueberry bushes surrounded by nasturtium vines. The green spaces and the white spaces were well balanced. The green made Mehitable think of her mother.

In the dining room they hung blue and white wallpaper with a repeating pattern of Chinese koi fish, lily pads, and blue dots that represented bubbles.

They chose a red wallpaper with a large scene of a family of deer at the river for Reuben's study. The color was deep, rich, and the scene was so realistic, Reuben couldn't wait to hang the paper.

For the guest room they picked green and white paper with interlocking antlers repeating endlessly throughout the room. The drawing of the antlers was thin and dainty, and the green was a pale green. Mehitable told Polly she thought the effect was neither too masculine nor too feminine.

Polly asked Mehitable which paper she favored the most. Mehitable thought about her answer, like it was an important thing to consider. She loved the red color. The green birds on branches were calming in some way. The blue fish in the parlor made her feel like she had traveled to an exotic land. "The blue, I suppose," she said.

When the papering job was finished, Polly brought the leftover blue pieces to the barn and helped Mehitable line her cupboards with it. Mehitable hugged Polly appreciatively. Then they began work on stenciling the upstairs bedrooms. It was painstakingly detailed work and consumed their free time for the better part of a year. Reuben and Polly's bedroom was stenciled with a purple trellised grape vine pattern. The pattern in the nursery was blue rabbits on a rolling hillside. Pink roses and black bears decorated the other two rooms.

On another September evening, two years later, Polly gave birth to a baby girl. She named the baby Perlina. The image of Reuben standing proudly over Polly's shoulder while Polly held Perlina was so endearing, Mehitable froze that moment in her memory, like a fine painting on a wealthy person's wall. Mehitable thought that Perlina's arrival filled Polly's heart with joy, finally lessening the pain of losing baby Reuben. Yet nagging doubt dampened Mehitable's happiness for her friend. She couldn't overcome the feeling that something was wrong and she couldn't figure out why she felt that way. It reminded her of the feeling she had before baby Reuben was born, only it wasn't exactly the same.

Polly had labored for over two days. It was such a difficult labor that Polly frequently worried she wouldn't survive it. She knew that women often died at childbirth, especially in remote frontier towns. A couple of hours before the baby came, Polly asked Mehitable to get a sheet of paper. Polly wrote a letter to Reuben. The pains came quickly. She was worn out. She wasn't sure that her words made sense. So, she kept her thoughts brief. Polly told Reuben that she loved him, she wanted him to be happy, and that it would please her greatly if he would marry Mehitable after she was gone. She folded up the letter and asked Mehitable to give it to Reuben if she didn't make it. Then she insisted that Mehitable promise to marry Reuben if she perished during delivery.

Mehitable had loved Reuben for years. Not in the same way as Polly, but there was a tender quality to the relationship that Mehitable and Reuben shared. She had been attracted to Reuben as a girl, but she knew she didn't want to build a life with any man when she was younger. She no longer felt like she had at sixteen. She felt a strong calling to be a mother, though she still wasn't in a hurry to attract a man just to have a man. She would not encourage or accept suitors or matchmakers, but despite what she'd always told Reuben about the kind of man she was waiting for, *he* always was exactly the sort of man she would hope for. Mehitable had to make that promise in order to calm Polly, for her peace of mind near the end of her difficult pregnancy. She said, "I'm sure it won't come to that, dear, but aye, if that is your wish and his, I shall promise." It was an easy promise to make and she was glad her friend didn't ask her to promise that she would sleep in the house, because married or not, she had no intention of changing her position on that.

Mehitable could understand how weak Polly must feel. She felt weary herself and wondered if she had the strength to attend Polly's pregnancy. With very few exceptions, the nightly visits of the evil arsonist had continued. Unabated. Mehitable endured as best she could. It was getting harder and harder for her to cover up her suffering. Aside from looking unrested, she yawned her way through every day. She often had difficulty maintaining pleasant conversations with her friend over tea. Many days it was all she could do to trudge her way from dawn to dark.

For months, Polly had begged Mehitable, suggesting she would sleep better in the house. Failing that, Polly reasoned that they could build her a bed in the barn. Mehitable insisted that her sleeplessness was merely a result of perpetual grieving. *Time heals all wounds except for a broken heart.*

Baby Perlina took to breastfeeding instantly. They were relieved not to be faced with whatever malady had claimed baby Reuben. Mehitable settled mother and daughter in for some well-deserved rest and retired to the barn, where Reuben was waiting for news. Mehitable hugged him quickly and congratulated him on the birth of a healthy baby girl. She held her finger up to her lips and told him to go in quietly. Mother and daughter were fast asleep.

When Reuben was gone, Mehitable brushed her hair. After a hundred and fifty strokes with her brush, she piled it up under her nightcap and strolled through the barn door to look at the stars. She climbed up into the wagon parked just outside of the barn, stretched her body out behind the bench in the wagon, and lay there watching the stars twinkle. She closed her eyes and drifted peacefully off to sleep. It was the deepest, most satisfying sleep she could remember having experienced in years. She awoke to the crowing of the rooster, smiling from ear to ear. She thanked God for the simple blessing of a peaceful night of sleep.

Mehitable tended to the chores in the barn and then took care of the housework. She insisted Polly relax, rest, and recover. In the afternoon, while Polly napped, Mehitable held Perlina, rocking her in her arms, quietly singing her a song. She looked at her tiny, precious face, and wondered why it looked so familiar to her.

A great night's sleep was followed by a busy day. That night, Mehitable prepared for sleep as usual. As she made herself comfortable among the sheep she jumped violently, scaring the animals. It felt like the static electricity that occurred on the driest days, only a hundred times more shocking. Anson appeared, floating menacingly above her. He was angrier than usual. He told her she had no business being in the house with Polly and Reuben. He told her to keep her hands off that baby. He told her she should just walk away and lose herself in the forest or simply cut herself and let her blood flow freely from her veins.

Mehitable lay there, shaking. Her teeth chattered with fear. *What was the use of having one night of peace if the next night was all the worse for it?* Eventually, the spirit of her nemesis evaporated. A couple of hours later, she had almost found sleep, when another familiar vision appeared. It was the little girl she had seen before. Her face appeared more clearly than it had in the past. Mehitable gasped. She looked just like baby Perlina, as a toddler rather than as a baby. Tears streamed down Mehitable's face, and then she sobbed uncontrollably.

Chapter 13
September 1806

When morning came, Mehitable had managed less than two hours of sleep. After she trudged through the chores and took care of her friends, she set off down the road. She crossed the river and followed a path deep into the woods. The path grew steep, and she continued to follow it. It felt good to be away from the barn and the house. It was nice to leave duties and chores behind as well. Before she realized it, she had reached a fair elevation. She could see Reuben Sanford's place along the river, way below. In addition to the Bumps, the little neighborhood had come to include three more families.

She walked further up the path until she was standing on a big rock beside the path, overlooking a deep gorge below. The river rushed furiously through the canyon. The intense water pressure over the course of thousands of years had drilled perfect circular holes in the solid rock.

The flow of the water was mesmerizing. Mehitable felt the rhythm and the power of the flow of the water drawing her spirit toward it. She felt herself leaning. Then she leaned a little further. She blinked and she felt the presence of Anson Smudge behind her. Her feet slipped and she started to fall. Her fingers found a prominent crack in the rock. Anson's spirit was rarely present in her life during the day, but that day was an exception. He screamed at her, "Let go. Be free. Nobody wants you anyway."

Mehitable's blood rushed through her veins like the mighty river, hundreds of yards below. *How easy*, she thought, *would it be to just let go?* Then she got mad. She summoned all the strength she could muster, and dragged her body up onto the rock, then she rolled onto the path. She curled into a ball and cried. *Life is hard, I miss my family, but I must go on. My friends need me. I'm here to serve God's purpose, not mine. Pray, God, do please help me persevere. Why must I suffer the devil alone?* She had come to refer to the ghost of Anson Smudge as the *devil*.

In the back of Mehitable's head she thought she heard a voice say, "What makes you think you are alone? I am here with you, child." She wondered if the voice belonged to Granny or some other spirit.

After the terror of nearly plunging into the gorge had passed, Mehitable took in a deep breath, then exhaled. She inhaled the scent of cedar, took in the sight of the trees just beginning to show their fall colors, and headed back down the path she had followed.

That night the devil tormented, "Why are you still here?" Mehitable was too exhausted to remain awake, ghost or no ghost. It was fitful sleep, but better than the two hours she had gotten the night before.

The next morning, Polly was back in the kitchen, making breakfast. Perlina had been awake before dawn, had nursed, and gone back to sleep. Reuben and Polly were talking quietly, trying not to awaken Perlina. Most mornings, Mehitable joined them for breakfast before returning to finish the chores in the barn.

Polly buttered a biscuit, then looked up at her friend and said, "Mehitable?" Polly waited until she acknowledged the question in her voice. Looking into Mehitable's eyes, Polly continued, "Reuben and I have been talking. We think you should have a husband. Will you let us help you find one?"

Mehitable merely shook her head, looked down at her hands on her lap, and repeated the lines she said the night she turned sixteen. "I want to marry a musical man. A man who can make the strings of a violin wail, whilst I play the virginal. I want to marry a man who can sing in a deep, bass voice, and read me Shakespeare." Then she added a few new lines. "Besides, what man would want to sleep in a barn." She looked up at Polly and concluded, "That probably limits the field to Otis and Dudley."

Polly accused, "You have no intention of welcoming a suitor, do you?"

Mehitable shook her head, confirming Polly's statement.

Exasperated, Polly exclaimed, *"Any* man would be lucky to have *you."* Reuben nodded, agreeing with Polly. He had met many men who preferred the barn to the house and said so.

After dinner, as Mehitable was preparing to go, Polly warned her that she would continue to pester her until Mehitable came to her senses. Mehitable took the butter churn with her to the barn, shaking her head from side to side as she went. An amused look crossed her face as she realized that *she* was the one that had lost the butter wars.

Every time Mehitable held Perlina, she recalled the image of the ghost that looked just like the baby. She kept the vision to herself, cried a lot, and continued to sleep very little. Every day she prayed she was wrong.

Mehitable was a long way from home on a cool mid-May after-noon. Normally she was very good at retracing her steps, but she had wandered recklessly. It had gotten colder, and it had started to rain. She crouched under a tall tree, shivering. She wondered, *Who cares if*

I live or die anyway? It occurred to her to give in to hyperthermia and let herself freeze to death. Her demon wanted nothing more than for doubt to consume her. It wasn't in her nature to give in and give up, but the ongoing presence of evil in her life had built to a point where it was tougher and tougher to take. She reminded herself of her friends and the role that she played in their lives. Even with the villain's voice in her head, she reaffirmed her resolve to continue. *Shall I give in? No, I can not. I must not. I will not. Instead, I shall be more pertinacious and find a way to survive this like I survive everything else.*

Mehitable looked for any place to take cover. Eventually she found a cave-like structure that seemed to appear in the hillside, just when she needed it most. It was dry. It was out of the elements. It was dark and dusty, but it would do. It appeared to have been made from stacked slabs of rock, perfectly pieced together to provide a safe shelter. It looked like it had been built a long time ago, and Mehitable wondered about the people that occupied it.

She sparked a fire with the flint that she carried in the pocket of the breeches she had borrowed from Eliada in Vermont, the day after the fire. She made herself comfortable and fell asleep on the floor of the cave hut. She woke up in the middle of the night and gathered some twigs and branches from outside the cave. The fire roared back to prominence and heat bounced around the stone enclosure like the inside of Reuben's brick oven. She was safe, comfortable, and dry.

She figured that morning was still several hours away and decided to go back to sleep, but as the wood in her fire caught, the flames cast light within the cave. She saw several drawings on the walls and got up to examine them more closely. One drawing depicted three large spirals that met in a continuous line, and she thought that it resembled a clover leaf. She tried to trace the line with her eyes, but it was dark, and she kept losing her place. Then she used her finger to slowly trace the line from spiral to spiral. When she finished, she felt the magic power of the image, and had the sense of being connected to the vast infinite world of the earth, sky, moon, and stars.

Then she jumped at the sight of a man in the cave with her. He apologized to her without speaking. Usually she had the sense that spirits were talking to her as they would have in life, but this one didn't need the pretense of moving ghostly lips. He turned his head and made expressions as he thought his words into her head. She felt herself thinking her own words back to him. He appeared to her as a strong but slender older man. His name appeared in her head and she said it out loud, *Wanders Far.* He nodded as if he hadn't heard his name said aloud in a very long time. He had a burst of white hair that sprung from the top of his head near the back. She had a sense that his soul was ancient, highly evolved, and purposeful about what he wanted to share with her.

He told her about a man named Conchobar who had crossed a great ocean from a land very far away, over twelve hundred years ago. He arrived alone and the old man's people took him in. Conchobar married one of their women, and together with their sons, they built the stone cave that Mehitable had found that night. The spiral symbol was Conchobar's spirit power. Then the old man conveyed that he and his grandson had discovered the cave hundreds of years later. He wasn't sure why, but someone had filled in and covered it up, erasing its existence. In addition to the spiral symbol on the wall, the man's grandson had found a shiny medallion with that symbol on it in the cave. The old man's ghost looked in Mehitable's eyes and passed the thought to her that one day she would find that medallion, and she must wear it around her neck. "When you find that medallion, you shall remember this night. We shall meet again, but next time, my spirit might not appear as it does today." Then he was gone. She thought about the intensity of his gaze as they had communicated wordlessly and she thought she would recognize his eyes, regardless of what form he might take.

She lay down on the floor of the cave next to the fire and slept peacefully until dawn. In the morning, she walked from the cave into a small clearing just outside of it. From there she saw a perfectly straight path through the woods. The path led directly to the familiar river, and the road that followed the path of the river took her home.

Reuben and Polly had all the neighbors out looking for her. When she hadn't returned the evening before, they had worried. Mehitable apologized profusely and promised to be more careful in the future. It was the first time she had become lost in the woods.

One late winter's morning the following year, Mehitable was feeling restless. It seemed to snow every day, and she had been feeling snowbound. She strapped on her snowshoes and headed out into the woods. It was an unseasonably mild, overcast day that grew darker with every step that she took. It became so dark that it felt like dusk instead of the middle of the day. She slowed her pace and took tentative steps. Something didn't seem right. Just beyond the last house in town, she gazed at the silhouette of a tall stand of pine trees by the river, barely visible through the dense gray fog. Suddenly, an imposing figure with bright red glowing eyes sailed across the vast distance, growing in size and striking terror in her chest as it rapidly approached. She turned quickly, and hurried home as fast as she could. She fell a few times and quickly stood back up. She didn't know if the snowshoes made her faster or slowed her pace, but she was too afraid to stop and take them off. All the way home, a howling wind blew fiercely behind her. When she reached Polly and Reuben's house, she heard a scream so loud that it reverberated throughout her entire body. She felt completely surrounded by the sound, and its echo lingered long after the scream had ended. She inhaled deeply and a protective feeling grew within her. She turned to face whatever it was, her jaw set in anger. Suddenly, the wind subsided, and the energy retreated from the direction she had run. Her erstwhile fear returned, and her anger waned. She quickly stepped out of her snowshoes and ran into Polly's kitchen.

Polly was on the floor, wailing. Perlina lay in her arms, her tiny limbs akimbo. Her skin was a saturated blue. Polly looked up at Mehitable. Words were not necessary, but Polly told Mehitable through her tears that she couldn't understand what had gone wrong. Perlina had been such a strong, healthy toddler. Polly had put her down for a nap half an hour earlier, then she had gone to check on her, and something seemed wrong. Perlina was gone.

Mehitable took Perlina's body from Polly and placed it back in her crib. She helped Polly to her feet and held her in her arms while Polly sobbed inconsolably. Polly had been so happy, having recently realized that she was pregnant a third time. When she was able to speak, Polly told Mehitable that she was scared to have more babies. She said she worried that they would keep dying. Mehitable put her hands on the side of her friend's barely bulging belly and promised, "You will *not* lose *this* baby."

Polly retorted, "How could you possibly know that?"

Mehitable had a distant look on her face, swayed from side to side, and answered, "I just know, and that's all I can tell you."

Unconvinced, Polly asked Mehitable if she would hold her while she cried. They climbed into Polly's bed and Mehitable held her friend in her arms, quietly humming until Polly fell asleep. Mehitable thought about Polly's grueling labor, bringing Perlina into the world, and then she thought about Polly's gut-wrenching grief, mourning the loss of her second child. She thought about the premonitions she had had about Perlina, concluding that she had done the right thing in keeping them to herself.

Suddenly, the bed started shaking. Mehitable had read about earthquakes and wondered if they were having one. The bed continued to shake and then she heard grunting from under the bed, like the sound of hungry piglets. In her ear, Mehitable heard the whisper of a familiar voice, barely audible, "Get out."

Through it all, Polly slept soundly. Mehitable got out of bed, tucked the blankets in around her friend, and went to the barn.

The next day was a bleak winter day. Spring seemed far away. It didn't seem there was anything in the world to look forward to. Mehitable sat on her chair and mindlessly knitted. She was happy to have her hands occupied. She tried not to think about anything and evidently succeeded. Hours later she looked down at the pile beside her chair and realized that she had created a nice warm scarf. The only problem was, it was thirty feet long. She set her knitting down, shaking her head, admonishing herself while she milked the cow and tended the animals before she went into the house to help her grieving friends prepare dinner.

That night during his regular visit, Anson's spirit suggested that Mehitable was bad luck. Anson told Mehitable that her friends would be better off when she joined him in the afterlife. "We shall be together forever," Anson promised, and concluded, "and I can't wait for you to arrive." Mehitable heard his wicked laughter as his spirit essence dissolved. She wished the lingering scent of dirty, sweaty armpits and stale whiskey would disappear more quickly.

As the snow melted and the air warmed up, Mehitable began wandering farther and farther from home each day. She was happy exploring in the woods. She enjoyed fishing in the mighty river. She took to setting up snares and it pleased her to think of Perry.

She imagined he would be proud of her, to see the success she was achieving with the traps. Just the way he had shown her.

Mehitable was equally as happy to put one creature in her sack as another. Her friends were wise not to ask what creatures she had baked into her meat pastry pies or stirred into her stews. One day, Otis and Dudley had been spying on her when they saw her catching frogs. Another day, their new neighbor, Mrs. Bull had watched in horror as Mehitable butchered squirrels on a stump in the front yard.

Polly and Reuben's third child arrived on the 18th of September 1808. Mehitable again tended the delivery. Fortunately for Polly and Mehitable, it was a much speedier labor than Polly's previous pregnancy. Polly desperately wanted to name the new baby Perlina. Mehitable convinced Polly that the new baby should have its own, unique name. Polly finally settled on Eliza Bucklin Sanford as the name for her new baby girl.

It was early in the evening, after dinner, and Polly had just put Eliza down to sleep. Reuben was away making a delivery. Polly made apple fritters, put on water to make tea, and set out to the barn to ask Mehitable to join her for a late-night snack.

It had been a rainy day. Mehitable spent most of the day contentedly working on carding, then spinning, then weaving. She had just removed a large, triangular shawl from her loom. Except for three small stripes of tan, the shawl was a deep burgundy. She held the shawl in her outstretched arms, assessing the quality of her work. Suddenly, she took a chill. The temperature seemed to plummet. Mehitable thought it felt like the windy force of a January blizzard rather than a calm September evening.

Then the familiar apparition appeared, as if blown in earlier than expected, by the wind. It wasn't bedtime. Stubbornly, it would not leave. She tried to wait it out. She tried to look away. She tried to close her eyes. She listened to his latest diatribe. She breathed deeply, and exhaled slowly, wondering, *Will you ever go away and leave me alone?* She had never dared to address the ghost. Sometimes, it had occurred to her afterward, but in the moment, overcome by fear, she always froze.

That evening, she could take no more of it. She started yelling, "I have had it." She turned to face the presence directly, "Why must you torment me? I never did anything to you. You were a selfish greedy bastard boy. You turned into a jealous, drunken son of a bitch. You burned my house. You killed my family. Now you are an evil spirit." She swung the new shawl over her shoulders, planted her feet firmly on the ground, bent her arms and balled up her fists as if she might attempt to have a fistfight with the apparition. "Go to hell, where you belong, Anson Smudge. And stay there," she shrieked.

Polly had entered the barn just as Mehitable began yelling at the ghost. She stood well behind her friend and witnessed Mehitable's rant. She leaned forward in amazement and her mouth hung open.

The ghost didn't argue. The apparition's visage drooped. Finally, the other-worldly bully had met its match. The ghost of Anson Smudge quickly shrunk, then disappeared into a pin-sized dot. Mehitable saw a small flash of light and heard a popping sound.

Polly saw the light and heard the pop as well but did not see the ghost. She stood, breathlessly squeaked, and tried to form words.

Mehitable swung around furiously, her eyes open wide in rage, expecting to see Anson Smudge. Polly stood there, astonished, with her hair blown wild by the sudden gust of wind that had gathered while she crossed from the house to the barn. Polly stammered, finally forming a question, "What has happened?"

Mehitable spun around, bent at her waist, protectively, still prepared to battle. Her tormenter was gone.

Mehitable concluded her new shawl was magic. She crossed her hands at her chest and stroked the heavy fabric. She felt powerful with it draped over her shoulders. She wondered how a garment could repel spirits.

Fully certain that the evil spirit had left the barn, Mehitable stretched her arms wide, drawing Polly into a protective hug. Mehitable had meant to reassure her friend who had looked frightened. Instead, Mehitable began to whimper, then sobbed loudly, held Polly tightly, and let years of terror go all at once.

Polly reassured her, "There, there, now. 'Tis alright. I'm here now. Everything will be fine." When Mehitable's sobbing finally subsided, Polly suggested, "Come on inside for some tea and fritters, and tell me all about it."

Polly's kitchen was inviting. It smelled like apple pie. Polly poured two cups of tea and brought Mehitable a fritter on a small dish. Then she sat down and waited, staring directly at Mehitable until she was compelled to begin speaking.

Mehitable started slowly, tentatively at first. She told Polly about the sweet sixteen party on New Year's Eve, eight years earlier, as if Polly hadn't been there. She told about having seen the ghost of Anson Smudge on New Year's Day. She described the years of sleepless nights she had endured silently, until all at once, she had just exploded in rage.

Supportively, Polly asked, "What took you so long?" Then she shivered and continued to ask Mehitable question after question. Finally, she asked, "Why didn't you tell me?"

Mehitable laughed explosively. "I didn't want to frighten you, and I didn't want to burden you. Your family has done so much for me." Tears streamed down her face, and she concluded, "I guess I did frighten you, and now I've awakened the baby."

Polly stood and patted Mehitable's shoulder on the way to pick up Eliza. She placed the baby in Mehitable's arms and sat back down at the table. "Won't you sleep in the house now? I'm sure you'll be safe from ghosts in here."

Mehitable vigorously shook her head. "Nay. No, I can't. I must not. I won't. There's more that you should know." Mehitable went on to explain that it wasn't just the ghost of Anson Smudge. She told Polly about the vague apparitions she had tried so hard to avoid seeing as a little girl. "My life is full of the spirits of departed people. Mostly they just float around, as if they would like to tell me something."

The baby began to fuss, and Mehitable passed her to Polly. Eliza nursed while Polly changed the subject. Mehitable nibbled at the edges of her fritter and emptied her cup of tea. Then she kissed her friend on the cheek, thanking her and telling her how much better she felt. In fact, better than she had felt in years.

That shawl became her most precious possession. She memorized everything she could about how she had made it. The wool. The process. The pattern. The colors. Her sheep protectors. As she prepared for bed, she looked at Emmeline. Emmeline looked back at her, unblinkingly. Mehitable curled up in a ball, took a deep breath, and instantly fell asleep.

The next morning, Mehitable woke up just before the rooster. She jumped to her feet, feeling refreshed. She swept her brush through her hair, packed it under a bonnet, and changed from her nightgown to her work clothes. She draped her pretty new shawl over her plain dress and sped through her chores. She had a busy day planned.

For the past week she had been collecting lye from a large barrel in the lower floor of the barn. It dripped from a hole at the bottom of the barrel, into another barrel. The top barrel had been filled with cold ashes from Polly's hearth, and layered with twigs and straw, especially near the hole at the bottom, to keep it from getting clogged. Each day she poured water into the top of the first barrel.

She built a fire in the pit outside. A large, three-legged spider pot hung from a beam above. The beam was affixed between two thick posts in the ground, buried well to the side of the fire pit. She thought the pot looked like a witch's cauldron. She brought small buckets full of ashen infused water from the barrel in the barn and filled the spider pot until it was mostly full. Then she stirred the pot with a wooden paddle that looked like an oar. When the mixture reached the right consistency, she spread the logs in the fire pit below, so she could reduce the heat. Then she melted pork fat from the pigs Reuben had butchered several days earlier. She slowly poured the melted pork fat into the spider pot with the lye. She held her breath as a white cloud of rancid smelling gas billowed from the pot. Then she jumped away for a minute or two. She tried to get used to the smell. It was the same every year. She thought it smelled like she imagined a decomposing skunk would smell. Then she returned to the pot and stirred with the oar. It seemed to take forever as the long, slow process of emulsification transformed the horrible contents of the pot into soap. Finally, the liquid congealed into a pudding like consistency, and then solidified further. She had a bag of dried pcppermint leaves and rosemary needles which she had mashed into a powder with a mortar and pestle. She added the powder to the mixture with a little bit of salt and stirred the globby mess some more. Then she scooped the soft soap into another bucket. Back in the barn, she filled a dozen topless boxes with the soap. The boxes were the shape and size of bricks. She covered the soap molds with cloth and left them to set.

She took a little bit of the remaining soap down to the river. She looked around her to make sure she was alone. Then she removed her clothes. Her toes passed through a brittle leather loop, which she could see had been attached to a spectacular spiral medallion. She picked up the ancient necklace and the leather crumbled in her hand. She traced the design with the tip of her finger, then she held the medallion in the palm of her hand. She felt a tremendous surge of power and energy, and a fantastic sense of well-being. She thought of the night she had spent in the cave, and the old soul, Wanders Far, who foretold her discovery of the ancient medallion. The design was embossed on the coin shaped object in three raised spirals and the background was white, like plaster. The continuous line was just like the drawing on the wall of the cave. The silver colored back was smooth and shiny. The necklace had the heft of a rock, a little less heavy, but just as rigid. She placed the medallion on top of her clothes and thought about how she would make it into a necklace again.

Then she covered her body with the sticky soap that smelled of rosemary and peppermint. She slathered it into her hair. Then she gasped for air as she jumped into the frigid water. She laughed joyfully as she washed the smell of death from her body. Under the water, she twirled her head around, running her fingers through her hair until the slippery soap had been carried away by the current. Finally, she washed her clothes and dressed in a fresh, plain dress she had brought with her.

It had been a hard day's work, but she felt happy to be clean. Sometimes soap making went well, sometimes it went poorly. She was glad it was a good soap day.

Chapter 14
September 1808

The next morning, a young rooster crowed. It wasn't a full-throated screech. Mehitable woke up slowly after another great night's sleep. She stretched and again heard the awkward crow. Mornings always began with an awful, ear-splitting scream, as Dinner the rooster alerted hens, humans, and every other species that night was over and the day had begun.

Mehitable quickly slipped out of her nightgown and into her work clothes. She climbed down the ladder with her milk pail, set it by the cow and opened the door to the chicken coop. She felt her stomach drop when she saw the valiant rooster laying on his side, motionless. She picked him up by his yellow feet. He wasn't yet stiff, and his body wasn't cold. She removed him from the coop and grabbed a shovel. A dead chicken was a common sight for an experienced farmer. Dinner was different. She couldn't help but think of her brother Perry whenever she heard Dinner crow. She chided herself for her foolishness, but it made her happy to think that Perry had left a little piece of himself behind. She did the math in her head and realized that Dinner had lived an extraordinarily long life. Usually chickens lived only five to eight years. Dinner was over nine years old when he died. She punched the shovel into the earth of the front lawn, not far from the vegetable garden.

That night as she was brushing her hair, Mehitable heard a familiar sound. It was a voice she hadn't heard in a very long time. She turned, mid-stroke, with her brush in her hair. Cold shivers jumped to the surface of her skin, arms, legs, and everywhere. She didn't see anything. She didn't hear anything, there was only dense silence. The kind of quiet that captured Mehitable's attention. It was the kind of quiet that let her know something extraordinary was about to happen. It was as if the spirit world was gathering strength from the air before materializing in a way that was visible to living humans.

A figure appeared just a few feet from her. The air seemed to shake and shimmer, like a billion mirrors on strings, moving slowly. Mehitable sat on her stool, astonished. After years of facing the violent arrival of Anson Smudge, whatever was happening before her eyes that night felt different, very different.

As the mirrors stopped shaking, Perry's ghost became visible to Mehitable, and she suddenly placed the familiar whisper she had heard a minute earlier. He looked the same as he had on the last day of his life. Mehitable's eyes grew wide with wonder, and she stammered, "Perry!"

Then the ghost spoke to her. "Remember, I told you if I ever died, I would come back and haunt you?"

Mehitable felt foolish, preparing to converse with a ghost. She thought of the words Polly had said to her not long before, and repeated them. "What took you so long?"

Perry replied, "It takes a lot of energy to become visible when you are a ghost. There was a powerful force that blocked us from coming through. We were warned that you would be harmed if we ever tried to communicate with you, but we were able to watch over you from far, far away. I don't know exactly how to describe it any better than that."

Mehitable asked, "Who is *us* and who is *we*?"

"Oh," Perry answered. "All of us, Mother, Father, and all us kids. Granny too."

Mehitable's brow furrowed, and she said angrily, "So you know Anson Smudge burned down our house and killed you all?"

"Aye," Perry confirmed, "and I know how you feel about Anson, but that isn't even the worst part of it. It wasn't really Anson's fault. He was possessed by another ghost, and by a demon. So, it is no wonder he did what he did. He was a naughty boy, a bad man, and an evil spirit all rolled up into one."

Mehitable was exasperated. "How can you make excuses for him," she blurted. Mehitable rolled her eyes back into her head, and thought, *I should be making the most of this moment. Being able to talk with Perry is nothing short of a miracle. 'Tis ordinary to argue with a brother, unless he's a ghost. What if I never have the chance to speak with him again?* Her cheeks sagged into a sad frown.

Perry said, "You'll see. You have a gift, you know. Granny told you that you had a gift, but you didn't know what she meant. You proved it the other night. You are proving it again now. If you didn't have this gift, I couldn't talk to you. You must embrace this gift and make it your life's work. It is how you can best serve God." Perry paused for a moment so that Mehitable could hear his message before he continued. "You need to listen, and I might not have much time to tell you this. You have separated the boy, the man, and the demon. Your spirit is very powerful. But the boy, the man, and the demon all remain. It is critical that you deal with all three of them. The boy and the man will be easy, they're just confused. You must listen to them, then help them by speaking to them from your heart. From your soul. To deal with the demon you will need to use your mind, body, and soul. Pile salt in every corner of this barn. Form perfect cone-shaped piles. You need to purify the air by burning sage. Do this every day. Burn it in a bowl and fan the smoke into the air. Repeat Granny's prayer, over and over until you defeat it, a thousand times in a row if you must. A thousand times. 'Tis a strong and powerful demon. Be strong and confident. If it senses your fear it grows stronger. Tell it to go to Jesus. Sing hymns. Think positive thoughts. You can do it, I know you can." Perry's voice grew faint. "Our spirits can't be free until you do this. I believe in you, Mehitable."

Perry's ghost blurred. His energy was subsiding. Before he vanished completely, he said sweetly, "Thank you for giving Aurilla the fox fur. And thanks for taking such good care of Dinner the Rooster. I can't tell you how much that means to me."

Mehitable whispered, "I love you, Perry," as his ghost disappeared in a sparkly shimmer. She added, "Pray, please don't go," but it was too late. He was gone.

She started brushing her hair again, slowly at first, and then quickly, mirroring the determination she felt as she contemplated her brother's request for help. Scared or not, she would have to face her fears bravely, like she had when she told Anson's ghost where to go. She thought about what Perry had told her: *the boy, the man, and the demon.*

After Mehitable brushed her hair she took out some paper and wrote down what Perry had told her. She wanted to make sure she didn't forget any of it. Then she went to sleep and enjoyed a night free of dreams. In the morning, Mehitable tended the chores quickly, had breakfast with Polly, and set out to collect wild sage in the meadows. It sounded like she would need a lot of it, so she pulled a wagon behind her and filled several large sacks. She returned home in time for lunch with Polly and held Eliza for a few minutes before heading back to the barn.

Mehitable made a tiny funnel with a piece of paper and carefully poured salt into the paper. In all four corners of the barn, on both floors, Mehitable poured perfectly symmetrical, tiny cone shaped piles of salt. Two of the corners were in stalls occupied by livestock. After she poured the piles, she covered the salt piles with crates and piled rocks on top to prevent the animals from moving them. She thought, *I hope I can get rid of this demon before anybody sees all the crazy things I'm doing in this barn.* Mehitable oversaw the barn so well, Reuben rarely came into the barn except when he needed Lucy, his horse, and even then, Lucy's stall was close to the barn door.

After the salt, she got to work on the sage. She twisted several stalks together, folded them over in the middle, and then she tied them together with twine. It took hours to prepare the stalks, and she finished just in time for afternoon chores. Mehitable fed the animals, collected the eggs, and milked the cow. While she milked the cow she ran through the list in her head. Mountains of salt. Positive thoughts. Repetition of prayers. Strength in the face of evil, even when it is hard. Rub mint. Burn sage.

Reuben returned home just before dinner. He had left a week earlier, with a wagon full of cask-strength, rye whiskey, and he had returned with provisions to carry them through the winter. Mehitable had just finished milking and was carrying the pail up to the house just as Reuben drove up. Mehitable ran the pail into the house, then ran back out to meet Reuben, right behind Polly. She thought of Tommy Todd's store, back in Vermont. In addition to the more useful items, Reuben brought Polly a large bag of oranges and a small bottle of perfume. Then he handed Mehitable a set of three books, *Select Fables*, by R. Dodsley, printed in 1807.

Mehitable stood there by the wagon, flipped open the first book, landing randomly on page 67. At the top of the page it said ANCIENT FABLES. There was a drawing of a castle in the background, with a river or a moat in the foreground, and at the left edge was a tree. There was a rooster in the tree, and a fox at the foot of the tree. A label under the picture said, *The Cock and the Fox*, shown in italics.

She started reading the text:

An experienced old Cock was settling himself to roost upon a high bough, when a Fox appeared under the tree. I come, said the artful hypocrite, to acquaint you in the name of all my brethren, that a general peace is concluded between your whole family and ours. Descend immediately, I beseech you, that we may mutually embrace upon so joyful and unexpected an event. My good friend, replied the Cock, nothing could be more agreeable to me than this news: and to hear it from you increases my satisfaction. But I perceive two hounds at a distance coming this way, who are probably dispatched as couriers with the treaty; as they run very swiftly, and will certainly be here in a few minutes, I will wait their arrival, that we may all four embrace together....

Mehitable's reading was interrupted by Polly's announcement that dinner was almost ready. She closed the book, grinning over thoughts of the fable, and glad that the rooster had gotten the best of the fox. The fox made her think of the demon. She stroked her shoulder through the fabric of her new shawl and looked toward the heavens. She should have asked Perry about the power of her shawl with respect to the demon. Then she closed her eyes and prayed to God that she would be strong enough to defeat the evil demon spirit when the time came.

Reuben stopped Polly before she darted back indoors. He said, "Come see what else I have in the wagon." Reuben and Polly had worked together on the words. The marble slab had a line drawn down the middle. On the left hand-side it said: INFANT *son of* Reuben & Polly C. Sanford. DIED, Sept 27 1804, Aged 4ds.

Chiseled on the right-hand side were the words: PERLINA, *daut of* R&P.C. SANFORD, DIED, Mar 12 1808, At 1 yr & 6 mo. Polly looked at the stone and twisted up her face. Tears slid down her cheeks and she hugged her husband. They both needed the final formal recognition that the stone provided.

Mehitable took care of the horses and Reuben went inside to wash up for dinner. After dinner, Mehitable returned to the barn. It was well after dark. She hadn't expected Reuben to return that day. The black cat that she had named Bosley followed her everywhere she went, begging for attention. He had become precious to her, and she could rarely deny him when he sought attention. *There is much to do. Tonight, Bosley, you will have to wait.* She quickly fixed a small fire in the brick kiln behind the barn. Then she placed the clump of sage into the flame. When it was smoldering, she placed it in her porcelain bowl and walked into the dark barn. Mehitable dutifully fanned the hearty scented sage smoke into every corner of the barn, above each cone of salt. For good measure, she waved the smoke everywhere in the barn that she could walk to. When the bundle stopped burning, Mehitable went back to the kiln and re-lit it. The last part she purified was the sheep stall where she slept, and the belongings in her workspace.

Outside, the wind howled. Pebbles, dirt, and twigs pelted the walls outside the barn. Inside, shovels, hoes, pitchforks, and axes banged and clattered against the walls. Mehitable thought it seemed like the barn might physically implode from the strength of the sudden squalls.

She screamed when she saw the demon. She almost dropped the smoldering sage bundle. It was horrible to look upon, and it seemed to appear just after she had purified her spinning wheel. She gasped for air, her heart raced, her blood seemed to boil, and the barn smelled like a swamp. Bosley's back arched, his fur prickled, and he hissed. Then she remembered her instructions. She remembered that her family was depending on her. She recalled how she stood up to Anson's ghost a few days earlier. She placed the bowl of sage on her table and stood before the bellowing demon.

Mehitable took a deep breath and said Granny's prayer, three times, slowly. "God indeed is my savior; I am confident and unafraid. My strength and courage is the Lord, and he has been my savior."

The demon roared, "I am not impressed with worthless words. Dithering prattle. You are worthless." In a deep, ominous voice, it threatened, "I will destroy you."

Mehitable felt large cold hands touching the skin on her arms. She barked at the demon, "I am not afraid." She watched as the demon's long fingernails slowly scratched her from elbows to wrists. Beads of blood raised on the surface of Mehitable's arms in long, thin, parallel trails.

"Good beats evil," Mehitable screamed. She felt the demon's hand grasp her elbow tightly. She looked down at the massive claw where it touched her. She felt a burning sensation on her forearms. She felt light-headed and out of breath. She focused on short sentences, talking slowly, and breathing between sentence fragments. "Go to Jesus. Behold the Lamb of God who takes away the sin of the world. Go to Jesus, now," she commanded.

The demon let go of her arm and circled around behind her. She felt like she was being bitten on the back of her thighs.

Mehitable said the Lord's Prayer. "Our Father who art in heaven, hallowed be thy name. Thy kingdom come. Thy will be done, on earth as it is in heaven. Give us this day our daily bread. And forgive our trespasses, as we forgive those who trespass against us. And lead us not into temptation, but deliver us from evil. For thine is the kingdom, and the power, and the glory, for ever and ever. Amen." Even as she said the words, she felt exhausted. A dark, foreboding feeling began to overwhelm her.

Menacingly, the demon growled through bared teeth, "Are you through yet?"

Mehitable repeated the demon's words back to her, the way Anson had done to her so many times, "Are you through yet?" Then she picked back up where she had left off. "Deliver us from evil. Go to Jesus. *Now*," she commanded. Then she repeated Granny's prayer. Dark clouds of thick smoke spilled from the ground around the perimeter of the barn. Mehitable felt a deepening sense of sadness accompanied by a sharp pain in her head.

She watched as the demon furiously flew around the barn, quickly to the farthest spot, then as fast as it could toward her. She closed her eyes and sang at the top of her lungs, "Amazing Grace, how sweet thou art...." The demon flew between her legs. She felt the cold wind in its wake on her skin.

When she finished singing, the demon laughed. It was an evil, oppressive laugh. The tiny hairs on Mehitable's body stood on end. She lied to the demon, "I am not afraid. Go to Jesus. You are not welcome here." Then she repeated Granny's prayer five times.

The demon continued to scream at her, inches in front of her face. Mehitable screamed back, over and over, repeating those words, the words that she was promised were magic words. She heard Perry's ghostly voice in her head, warning she might need to say the prayer a thousand times. Triumphantly, She proclaimed, "You lose. I win. Good triumphs over evil."

The demon said meaner and meaner, scarier things, but Mehitable couldn't help but notice that it seemed to be shrinking, right before her very eyes. It threatened torture. Rape. It told her that she would shiver in fear. It promised that it would rip her to shreds and leave her lifeless. The demon growled, "Your friends are no longer safe. I shall destroy them all. They shall suffer agonizing deaths. 'Twill be your fault." Mehitable steeled her resolve, raised her voice slightly, and fell into a rhythm of determined repetition. It was a time for doing, not thinking or feeling. She had been told what to do and she would not let down the spirits of her beloved family.

She had been yelling at the demon for almost two hours. Her legs were tired. She felt herself sweating everywhere, but at the same time she felt herself getting stronger and stronger. Her throat felt sore, but she felt stronger each time she repeated Granny's prayer. She noticed every time that she said, "Go to Jesus," the demon shrank a little more. Mehitable changed her pattern and repeated, "Go to Jesus. Good beats evil," over and over, dozens of times.

At that point, the demon had shrunk from what Mehitable thought was twenty feet tall to less than a foot tall. Mehitable sat down on her rocking chair, as if calm and relaxed, returned to Granny's Prayer, "God indeed is my savior; I am confident and unafraid." She crossed her arms, symbolically. "My strength and courage is the Lord, and he has been my savior." As she chanted, she watched the demon's arms and legs stretch, like yarn extruding from her spinning wheel, each limb toward a salted corner of the barn. Mehitable repeated Isaiah 12:2, over and over until the demon exploded from its core outward, and nothing more remained.

Mehitable was exhausted. She wanted to collapse into her nest among the sheep. Emmeline looked at her with her usual aloof stare. In the distance, Jester the ram blatted loudly. The adolescent rooster answered with its loudest crow yet, though it was unusual for roosters to crow at that time of day. Bosley curled up among the yarn in the knitting basket and went to sleep.

Mehitable took a deep breath, picked up the bowl of sage, and returned again to the brick kiln. She brought the little fire back to flames again, and lit the sage bundle a third time. She toured both floors of the barn one final time before she was ready to seek sleep. When she was done, she made sure the fire in the kiln was extinguished, and the sage bundle also. She knew how dangerous fire was.

After she changed into her nightgown, Mehitable sat in her rocking chair for a moment to collect her thoughts. She felt the air around her change again, and she pulled her magic shawl over her shoulder. Then she smiled as Perry's soul shimmered back into her presence.

He said, "You did it. Now rest. Mother, Father, and Granny are so proud of you. Sleep now. You have a busy day tomorrow."

Mehitable blew her brother a kiss and Perry disappeared in a shimmer. Then she curled up with her three sheep sisters and slept through the night. She slept so soundly that she didn't hear the cracking voice of the adolescent rooster. She didn't hear the cow bellowing, hoping to be milked. She missed breakfast. Finally, Reuben shook her sleeping body. "Wake up Mehitable. It's morning. We've got to get to the cemetery."

Mehitable jumped to her feet and looked for her milk bucket.

"I took care of that this morning," Reuben smiled, "and methinks Ophelia doth protest too much. I must not have the right touch." Reuben grabbed a shovel from the wall and headed out into the front yard.

Mehitable quickly changed from her nightgown, splashed some water on her face, passed her brush through her hair and headed for the barn door. Then she stopped, dead in her tracks, went back to her table, and kneeled. She put her hands together and prayed.

Reuben rolled away the rock that stood above the graves of his son and daughter. He lifted the tiny coffins to the back of the wagon. Reuben stood looking at the boxes for ten minutes. He placed his left hand on the smaller box, and his right hand on the larger one. Mehitable walked up behind Reuben and put her hand on his right shoulder. "Their souls are at peace," she reassured him.

Reuben turned and said, "I don't understand why, but I feel the need to open the boxes and look upon their faces, just once more."

Mehitable nodded, "I know you do, but let them rest in peace." She cocked her head slightly and gazed off into the distance. Then she said, "They want you to remember them as they were, and they ask you not to look now upon their remains." She looked back into Reuben's face and said, "They have sent their sister, Eliza, to heal your hearts and mend your souls." Mehitable raised her eyebrows and had a look of wonder on her face. The dead had just spoken to her. Not evil spirits, but the kind, gentle, innocent souls of babies. Yet they communicated in fully developed thoughts.

Reuben thanked Mehitable and wiped a tear from the corner of her eye with his handkerchief. He didn't appear to be at all surprised that Mehitable had given him a message from his children, from the other side. He just interpreted her words as sympathetic. Reuben fetched Polly who was dressed in her church clothes. He helped her up to the bench in the wagon and then climbed up beside her.

Mehitable followed the wagon on foot. A short distance down the road, she turned and looked behind her. She gasped at the sight of two rows of ghosts, barely visible, but she could make out some of them. She saw the ghosts of her family, and her heart skipped a beat. She saw the ghost of Anson Smudge, and he didn't look the slightest bit intimidating. Instead of appearing as a young man, Mehitable noticed he appeared like he did at about 10 years of age. In addition, she saw many ghosts of men in military uniforms including the man in the green coat, and others she did not know. She quickly counted three dozen, but there could have been hundreds more behind those. She quickened her pace toward the cemetery. The ghosts moved slowly in the full light of day as they followed her through the open gate.

The entire trip to Hayes Cemetery was less than a quarter of a mile. Reuben dug the holes and set the stone. Then they each said a few words. Mehitable began singing. Polly and Reuben joined in and they sang a few songs together surrounded by the brilliant colors provided by maples and birches. Autumn was at the peak of its brilliance. Mehitable looked at the stone tablet. She thought the line down the middle made the two sides look like pages in a book. She sent a thought to the heavens, *Yes, little ones, this stone is a great comfort to your parents. You will not be forgotten.* But Mehitable could see that they had not yet crossed.

When they left the cemetery that afternoon, many of the ghosts remained behind. She noticed that the ghosts of her family, the ghost of Anson Smudge, and several of the men in military uniforms had followed her back home. Those ghosts kept a respectable distance from her, but she was aware of their presence.

Later that day, back in the barn, Mehitable went right to work making a series of shawls, all different sizes, but each using the same colors and pattern. She made one for Polly and another one for Eliza. Mehitable insisted that the shawl be wrapped at the canopy of her crib. She made tiny shawls for her sheep, chiding herself for dressing sheep in wool. She draped shawls over the framework at both entrances to the barn and convinced Polly to let her do the same inside the house. Mehitable was certain the shawls protected her from evil spirits, and the fact that the demon never returned seemed proof enough to her.

Mehitable felt grateful for the exodus of evil from her life. Though the malcontent from the other side left her alone, her connection to the dead increased. Tiny Reuben and Perlina were just the beginning. Everywhere she went, the spirits of the departed stepped forward. Sometimes Mehitable went to the little cemetery just to commune with them or to watch them commune with each other. Even when she experienced them near bedtime, Mehitable was able to drift off to sleep comfortably. She thought, *You must know sleeplessness to fully appreciate the exquisite refreshing respite of a good night's sleep.*

Chapter 15

September 1808

The next evening after dinner, Mehitable was rocking in her chair, knitting a wool sweater, and thinking about the demon. She glanced at her spinning wheel and shook her head to think that an evil spirit would choose such an object in which to make its home. Before she took up the knitting needles, Mehitable had taken the time to spread the smoke of sage throughout the barn again. She breathed deeply and held her breath for a moment, enjoying the fragrance. She set her knitting in her lap for a moment and flipped the shawl from her shoulders with her thumbs.

Before she could return to her knitting, the ghost of an older man, dressed like a British soldier, appeared slowly from the far end of the barn. He had his hat in his hand. He had a carefully trimmed, white beard. It looked like he had an angry red scar circling his neck, and he carried his chin abnormally high, as if he was looking toward the heavens, or perhaps he suffered from a lack of range of motion. Mehitable frowned. She didn't feel threatened by the ghost. The ghost's slow approach gave her plenty of time to be conscious of her thoughts and feelings. *Perhaps I am getting used to this.* When the ghost had finally reached her, Mehitable asked gently, "Pray, how can I help you, and what is your name?"

He looked like an old man, but Mehitable thought that his voice sounded like a boy at the age of thirteen, cracking back and forth between the voice of a boy and the voice of the future man. The ghost answered, "Cunningham, madam." After each short sentence he paused, like he wished he didn't have to continue. Like he felt ashamed. He continued, "William Cunningham. Captain William Cunningham, ma'am, and I was the British provost marshal for New York. I was the commander of the military prisons during the War."

Mehitable softly encouraged, "Please, go on."

Cunningham said, "Yes, ma'am. Well, the sad truth is, I was a bad man. Not just a bad man, I was evil." Cunningham turned a quarter turn away from Mehitable, so that he wouldn't have to face her directly. If he could have looked at the floor, he would have. He went on, "I don't know how it happened. I was a good boy. I studied hard, did my lessons, learned Latin, and excelled at my figures. Old folks seemed to favor me. I just wanted to make my parents proud. Inside, I always felt anxious. I felt like I was never good enough. I don't think I wanted to become a man. I think I just wanted to remain a schoolboy. I hate to utter the words in front of a young woman, but I am ashamed to admit that I became an evil, murderous, sadistic man. I hated anything that wasn't British, and I especially hated Americans. I treated them with contempt. To feel British is to feel superior, so I sought power and rank. On my last day in America, I fought with an old woman who, together with her husband, owned a tavern. I tried to enforce an ordinance that restricted her from flying the American flag. I galloped up to her with the most vicious intent. The very sight of that flag vexed me. And who was this old woman who thought she could whack me across the side of the face with her broom? How humiliating to be whacked by a woman with a broom. She must not have known that I was responsible for killing thousands of Americans, and I didn't just kill them, I saw to it that they were tortured in the most obscene, unscrupulous ways. Pardon me, ma'am. Oh, what you must think of me. It makes it hard for me to continue. In the years that followed, I never forgot the tenacious old lady who fought so bravely for her right to display that flag."

Mehitable asked, "Do you still wish you could have stayed a boy? That you had never become a man?"

Cunningham answered, "That I do, ma'am. I wish I could explain what happened to me. What got into me. Now that I have died, I don't feel like the man I became was the person I really was. I don't even know if what I'm saying makes any sense." Cunningham turned slightly back toward Mehitable, opening himself up for the possibility that she had some wisdom on the matter, and praying that she did.

She sympathetically offered a contemplative utterance. She placed her thumb under her chin and curved her forefinger around the front of her chin, pensively, and asked, "What happened to your neck, Mister Cunningham?"

"Well," he began, evasively, "after a lifetime of craving the finest things, and worshiping the supremacy of the British way of life over the colonial ways, I had a hard time returning to Britain after the war. Everywhere I went, the story of how I was beaten by an old woman turned me into a joke. I suffered to make ends meet. I forged documents and stole money. I, the master of prisons, found myself in debtor's prison, and on August 10th of 1791, I was hanged. To think, I was hanged for forgery, and never punished for murdering men and ruining families." Cunningham was quiet for almost half a minute before he asked, "Do you think a man can make confession after his death? Does it have to be before his death? Can God forgive *anything*? Is it possible for a pretty young woman to hear that confession instead of a professionally trained and ordained man of the cloth?"

Mehitable thought the inquiry sounded like an earnest young boy asking a schoolgirl to walk home from school with him. Without thought, Mehitable answered, "I do. I don't know how. I don't know why, but I do. I am not an authority on such matters. I just know you can't *stay* here. You must go into the world of spirits, Billy. May I call you that?"

Cunningham grinned, "Aye, I'd like that. My mother called me Billy when I was a child." Cunningham nodded freely. His neck no longer seemed stuck in the position left by the hangman's noose. His gray hair transformed into a dirty blond mop atop his head, and his cheeks appeared to absorb his beard, leaving his cheeks clean, clear, and unwrinkled. His presence seemed to illuminate, brighter and brighter, until light completely filled the darkest corners of the big barn. Then it faded back to blackness, and Mehitable sat beside her tiny oil lamp, rocking contentedly in her chair.

Mehitable said a short prayer, asking God to have mercy on Cunningham's soul. Then she asked for peace on behalf of all the tortured souls who suffered at Livingston's Sugar House, the other Revolutionary War prisons, and the prison boats in New York's harbor. She thought of Reuben's 64-year-old father. She prayed that he, and all the men who served in the War for Independence, would know peace and comfort as well. The world was full of pain, suffering, and injustice, but for just a moment, Mehitable felt like the peace, joy, comfort, and kindness had won out. She set the unfinished sweater in her basket and picked up her hairbrush. The familiar motion of the bristles through the strands of her hair always calmed her thoughts. Even so, she wondered if Cunningham's body was occupied by an evil demon spirit in adolescence, like Anson Smudge—the boy, the man, and the demon. Were they three separate things, or all combined? Mehitable twisted a strand of her hair, lost in thought. Whether she had solved a mystery or not, there was nothing more to do about it that day. It was time for sleep. She realized that she craved it.

The next morning, as Mehitable was saying her prayers from her milking stool, petting Ophelia's soft, pumpkin colored belly, it dawned on her that her great purpose in life was to help troubled souls find their way, from life and death to the tranquil universe occupied by spirits. She recalled the light that had enveloped Cunningham. If she could help Cunningham make that transformation, Mehitable thought, it should be possible for anyone. She didn't just feel her calling in an intangible way, Mehitable felt like it was thoroughly visible to her. Then another thought popped into her head. Ophelia bellowed as Mehitable increased the speed and grip of her hands on Ophelia's teats. Streams of milk became white jets, pinging the sides of the metal milk bucket. Mehitable was thinking of Polly's grandparents, and the story her father had told about Josiah and Molly Cole Lewis.

Mehitable hurried into the kitchen with the pail full of milk, grabbed a handful of bacon, politely asking, "May I?" She ate quickly without sitting at the table. Polly was making thick flapjacks, but paused briefly when Mehitable asked, "Pray, might I borrow your grandmother's spyglass?"

The artifact stood on a shelf in the parlor. It was never touched or thought of, except when Polly dusted the house with a damp cloth, usually twice a week. "Of course you can, let me get it for you," Polly allowed. While Polly was in the living room, wiping the spyglass with a cloth, out of habit, before bringing it back to the kitchen, Mehitable flipped the cake in the pan.

Mehitable kissed her friend on the cheek and was gone. She didn't even hear her friend call after her, "What about breakfast?" Mehitable hurried to Hayes cemetery. She placed one hand on the top of baby Reuben and Perlina's gravestone, and she held Molly's spyglass in her other hand. After a couple of minutes with her eyes closed, Mehitable walked slowly from the cemetery down the path along the river that she had followed two years earlier when she was lost. She followed the gradual incline up several hundred feet until she saw the tiny settlement beneath her in the distance nearby. Mehitable didn't go all the way to the spot where she had almost fallen over the edge, but to a safe and comfortable spot that afforded a nice view.

She had forgotten to wear her bonnet in her haste that morning, and her hair flew freely in the breeze as she stood on the hill between the town and the mountain. Mehitable held the spyglass in her outstretched arm, at eye level for a woman slightly taller than herself. The ghost of Molly Cole Lewis appeared on the hillside, in the light of day, and put her eye up to the spyglass. She looked down at Reuben Sanford's place below, and saw Polly come out of the front door holding baby Eliza. Polly sat on a chair on the porch, looked up and down the street to make sure that the Bump brothers were nowhere in sight, and began to nurse the baby.

Mehitable spoke slowly and softly, "That is Eliza Bucklin Sanford, your great-granddaughter, and your granddaughter Polly. This is a small town they are helping to establish, just like you and Josiah founded the town of Poultney. Our new nation is strong and getting stronger, thanks to our war heroes, like you and Josiah. I want to thank you for your sacrifice. Your descendants are populating this great new country. You can be proud of what you did." Then she added, "But you can't stay here. You should find heaven. Before you go, there is one more thing you can do to help your family." The ghost of Josiah appeared at Molly's side. "You need to take these babies with you."

Molly Cole's ghost answered, "We understand."

Josiah added, "Say no more."

Mehitable made the motion of passing a baby to Molly so she

could carry the baby's spirit with her. Baby Reuben appeared in the crook of Molly's arm.

Josiah bent down and took little Perlina's hand. Perlina said, "Tell Mother and Father I love them. I love you too, Ma-humble."

Mehitable whispered into the breeze, "I will, honey. I will." Then she used Molly's spyglass and looked out in every direction from the top of that hill. If there was a more beautiful setting on God's earth, she couldn't imagine it.

Mehitable returned home early in the afternoon. Polly had baked scones and had water on for tea. "Sit down, let's talk," Polly invited. "You dash in, then you dash out again, it doesn't seem like we've had much time to visit lately. Tell me, what's going on?" Polly's hands grabbed the edge of the table firmly. "Ever since that ghost in the barn, things have been very *strange* around here." She stretched out the word strange like it was an empty cave, one that needed exploring, but one that she was afraid to step foot into.

"Are you sure you want to hear this," Mehitable asked, shaking her head. "You'll need to listen with an open mind. And you must promise not to tell. 'Tis my secret, to share with others when and how I see fit, if at all."

Polly's eyebrows moved closer together, she pulled her shoulders tightly into her torso, and nodded agreement. A couple of weeks had passed since Polly had witnessed Mehitable's supernatural battle against evil in the barn.

Mehitable could tell that her friend was scared. "I have to warn you, some of what I'm going to tell you is very disturbing, but don't be troubled. Everything is fine now, and we are all safer than we have ever been." Mehitable told Polly about her visit with Perry's ghost, and how she had cleansed the barn. She told the story about how she battled the demon, as if it had occurred a millennium earlier. Then she took Polly's hands in her own and told her about crossing her grandparents and her babies. "Josiah and Molly have been watching over you all these years. When you felt weak, they were there to help you feel stronger. Now they have helped Reuben, Junior and Perlina find their way to God. Perlina told me to tell you and Reuben that she loves you very much."

Polly's face looked gray. It was as if the flow of blood within her body had been cut off. Her jaw dropped, and she said, " 'Twas the most amazing feeling. I was sitting on the porch feeding Eliza. The air was completely still. Then a breeze appeared from out of nowhere. It was as if every tiny hair on my body stood straight out, especially the ones on the back of my neck. I felt like a child's tiny hand had grabbed onto my forearm." Polly placed two fingers on her left arm, in the exact spot she had mentioned. "Then I felt lips on my cheek." Polly's eyes grew wide, understanding that Perlina had visited her before passing into the world of spirits. She stroked the skin on her cheek with the tip of her right index finger, looked at Mehitable and said, "Praise the Lord. My baby is safe at last."

Mehitable nodded, reassuring, "Isn't it amazing?" She reached into her pocket and pulled out Molly's spyglass. She gave the relic back to her friend, and said, "I bet you never expected this spyglass held the spirit of your grandparents within it."

Polly stretched her lips in an upside-down semi-circle on her face and held out both of her arms. She asked, "Is that how all of this works?"

Mehitable laughed, tossed her head so that her hair landed on her back, and said, "Don't ask me! I'm still learning all of this myself."

Polly took Mehitable's hands back into her own, looked her square in the face and said, "Please don't stop. You can help people, whether they know it, or whether they like it, you can help them." Polly looked at their hands, together in the middle of her dining room table, then looked back up at Mehitable and said, "I love you, Ma-humble."

Mehitable tilted her head slightly and shook her head in amazement. "I love you too, Polly."

Chapter 16

September 1808

After dinner, Mehitable returned to her wheel. She hadn't used it since her experience with the demonic. Her foot pumped up and down as the thick thread passed through the wheel, and the fine thread passed through her finger before landing in a basket on the floor near her feet. She thought about how the demon must have gathered energy from the wheel, like the way a waterwheel channels energy, using the flow of water to grind grain into a powder. Then she saw movement from the corner of her eye. She slowed the speed of her foot and looked off into the barn. An adolescent boy sheepishly appeared from the darkness.

Mehitable stood up, moved to her rocking chair and sat waiting. Bosley, the black cat jumped into her lap and Mehitable gently rubbed his cheeks. When the boy was close enough, Mehitable said lovingly, "Hello, Anson." Mehitable thought she sounded like his mother rather than his former classmate.

Anson kicked at the floor, like he was on the path between school and home and felt the urge to send a tiny pebble flying into the brush along the path. He stammered, "I'm so sorry." He paused, and then he said her name tentatively, "Mehitable."

Quietly, she said, "Me too. *Now* I know that you were a lonely boy in school. You didn't have a friend. I didn't notice. I didn't pay attention. I should have been your friend." Mehitable looked at the cat in her lap. Bosley had just begun to purr loudly. "I would have liked that, Anson."

"You are so kind," Anson said, "and all I ever did to you was just be mean. Mean and spiteful, hateful, and worse." His voice trailed off. A moment later, he added, "I don't know what got into me."

Mehitable whispered warmly, "I think I do Anson." Mehitable picked up Bosley and placed him on the floor. She stood up and went to the large box labeled, "Mehitable's Treasure," and retrieved Anson's tricorne hat, wondering why she had saved it in the first place. At that moment, she wondered if Anson's ghost had attached itself to his hat. Anson placed one hand on top of the other at the center of his chest. Mehitable thought he was pleased that she had kept his hat. Her eyes began to well up with tears.

She sniffled and then continued, "I know it is hard to understand, but I think that a very troubled spirit grabbed hold of your soul at just the wrong moment. Then *that* spirit fed a demon." She mourned the loss of the life that Anson could have lived. She was overcome and speechless for a minute as her emotions overpowered her. Tears streamed down her face, and she felt the briny taste at the back of her mouth. "It wasn't really *you* who burned my house and killed my family. You *must* forgive yourself." She paused for a deep breath before continuing, "*I* forgive you, Anson Smudge. I hope your spirit will find a happier path to travel in a future lifetime."

Mehitable hadn't seen tears on the face of a ghost before. She couldn't remember having ever made eye contact with Anson, intentionally. They shared a long gaze. Regardless of intentions, their souls were linked together throughout time, just as they would have been if they had been married, though they were not meant to be married in *that* lifetime. Anson's lips moved and he made a sour face like he had just taken a sip of vinegar and he meekly said, "I am not worthy."

"You are," Mehitable reassured. "You *truly* are." She nodded and smiled, and it occurred to Mehitable that she had gone from motherly to grandmotherly in an instant. *I'm too young to feel like this*, she thought. "Then she said, 'tis time for you to join the spirits, Anson. Everything will be all right." Mehitable had no idea where the words that followed came from. She didn't think them before she said them. "I have prepared you for what comes next."

Before Mehitable's eyes she saw Anson rapidly mature from the boy he was at adolescence into the man he would have been if it hadn't been for Cunningham and the demonic. She saw the life he would have led, playing out before her. She saw the woman that would have been his wife, and the children whose souls he would have helped guide into adulthood. That woman wasn't anyone Mehitable recognized. *There is someone for everyone*, Mehitable thought. *Everyone but me, I guess.* She blinked at the water in her eyes, then the bright light from within him transported Anson into the spirit world.

A ferocious wind howled outside the barn. It was a cold, late December evening. It was a little too early for bed, but Mehitable had brushed her hair and changed into her nightgown. She relaxed in her rocking chair. Her shawl kept her shoulders warm, and Bosley had settled in for a nap on her lap. Gently, Granny's ghost appeared from thin air across from Mehitable, complete with her own rocking chair. Mehitable didn't move. She didn't want to disturb the sleeping cat, but she was happy to finally see Granny again. She had begun to think that Granny had joined the spirit world.

"You are a powerful woman," Granny told Mehitable. "I knew you could do it. I couldn't have done that at your age, but I knew *you* could. She squeezed her ghostly face into a proud, radiant smile that glowed." Granny's ghost began rocking in her translucent chair.

Mehitable said, "You have no idea how I have missed you, Granny." Mehitable began to rock, mirroring the pace Granny set.

"I have been right here with you, wherever you went, sweetie."

Sadly, Mehitable said, "I wish you could have told me more, Granny. I wish you could have explained. There was so much I needed to know. I was *so* lost. Sometimes, I still feel that way."

Granny shook her head as she rocked, "Nay, Mehitable. I couldn't have told you more. You had to find out for yourself. You must never feel lost. All you will ever need exists within you already. You'll see. I'm proud of you, Mehitable."

Mehitable smiled. "I love you, Granny." Then she paused. There was another emotion she needed to express. *How do I tell this woman she should move on? She who knows more of such matters than I. She can't remain here endlessly, can she?* She decided to just ask, "Can you stay with me Granny, or must you cross into the world of spirits, like everyone else?"

Granny chuckled, "You're getting good at this, Mehitable. I think you understand exactly how all of this works now! And I, of all spirits, know not to linger. 'Tis time for me to go, but first we have one thing left to do. We can do it together. Something long overdue. Eighteen hundred years overdue, I'm afraid."

Seeing Granny made Mehitable feel like a young girl again. Mehitable recalled how she used to hide beneath the folds of Granny's long skirts, bit her lip, and in a quaking voice, she said, "That sounds scary, ominous even."

"Don't worry, sweetie," Granny assured her. She hesitated to add, "I hate to disturb a sleeping cat, but could you play a hymn on the virginal?"

Bosley was quick to forgive the interruption in his nap. He went back to sleep in the warmth Mehitable left on the rocking chair after she stood up. She wondered how long it had been since she had played the virginal. She moved the chair from her desk table to the table that it sat on. She opened the front, exposing the keys, then she opened the top, so that the keys could sing into the air. She stood back quickly in surprise. A milky white, ghostly cloud appeared from within the instrument. She looked at Granny, who smiled and nodded back at her. The cloud expanded, wider and wider. She saw hundreds of tiny ghost babies in the cloud, just as she had seen them so many years earlier, except that now she could clearly see their tiny baby faces. Mehitable gasped, "Herod's babies."

Indignantly, Granny corrected, "They are *not* Herod's babies. They are the babies killed on Herod's command. They are *God's* children."

Mehitable nodded. "I understand."

Granny asked, "Do you know what today is, Mehitable?"

Mehitable thought, and then suddenly realized. It was Holy Innocents Day. She hadn't recognized or celebrated it since the tragedy.

Granny asked, "Will you play us a song?"

Mehitable sang while she played "Antioch." Granny preferred to call the song "Joy to the World." At the end, Mehitable sang the fourth verse twice:

He rules the world with truth and grace,
And makes the nations prove
The glories of his righteousness
And wonders of his love.

Granny said, "That was lovely, Mehitable." Then she asked, "Would you remove your necklace, hold it over the oil lamp, and swing it back and forth? Now before we go, I want to tell you how proud I am of you. You have mastered your gift. I will see you again when you join the world of spirits, someday when you are an old granny yourself."

Mehitable thought, *I'm a strange old maid with no prospects, out in the middle of nowhere, alone in the world. It doesn't seem likely I'll ever become an old granny.*

She hummed the song again while the medallion swung back and forth, like a pendulum. The shiny side refracted light from the oil lamp in tiny pinpoint sized spots around the barn. Slowly, Granny stood from her rocker, walked a short distance, turned around and faced Mehitable, then she bent her arms, held her hands out in front of her, palms up, and looked up toward the heavens. A cloud of cooing ghost babies was drawn into Granny's embrace. "Keep humming dear, don't stop until we are gone," Granny said. Ten minutes later, Granny and the baby boys had crossed into heaven. Mehitable wondered if others could see the intensely bright light that came from the barn during the transformations she attended to, or if that was another thing that only she could witness. Then she recalled that Polly had seen something when she separated Anson, Cunningham, and the demonic.

She sat and rocked for a while. As long as she thought about it, she couldn't come up with any other description for it. Crossing over hundreds, thousands, or however many spirits there were, all at one time, eighteen hundred years after they were murdered, seemed nothing short of a miracle to her. She would never forget Granny anyway, and she would certainly never forget what they had accomplished together that night.

Mehitable walked out into the barnyard and gazed into the night sky. She put her hands on her hips, tilted her head back, and gazed toward the heavens. She sniffled from her tears and smiled at the same time. Though she still thought of Granny often, the image of Granny in her mind had begun to fade. Mehitable was grateful for just a little more time with her precious Granny. Knowing that she would be reunited with Granny in the spirit world was small consolation.

A couple of days later it was New Year's Eve, which of course meant that it was Mehitable's birthday again. Polly made a roast, drenched in gravy and flanked with carrots and potatoes. For dessert, Polly prepared Mehitable's mother's Shoo-Fly Pie recipe. Mehitable thought of Wilhelmina in her green dress all those years earlier, when Polly set the pie and a knife in front of Mehitable after dinner was finished. Then Mehitable, Polly, and Reuben played cards for a couple of hours before Mehitable returned to her space in the barn. Another birthday, Mehitable thought. She couldn't believe that she had turned 25-years-old.

Bosley weaved between her legs, indicating his affection for Mehitable by rubbing his sides up against her shins. The hours after dinner were usually their time. Mehitable understood that Bosley had missed her. Mehitable prepared for bed, picked up the book of fables and read one aloud. Though there were only farm animals there to hear her, Mehitable enjoyed the feeling of reading out loud. She thought it brought the words alive in a way that reading the same words within her head did not.

When she finished reading, Perry appeared to her again, the same way as before. Mehitable set her book down and waved happily. They chatted about their childhood for a few minutes, then Perry said, "Now that you are liberated, we can cross over now."

She said, "Aye, you really should cross over. I know you don't belong here." Tears cascaded down her cheeks as she added, "We'll all be together again, someday."

Perry waited quietly for Mehitable's sobbing to subside, then replied, "Aye, don't be sad. We like it when you are happy. Father would like you to play Adieu to the Village Delights."

"Oh my," Mehitable protested, "I haven't played that one in years!" She rifled around for the sheet music. Then she moved the virginal to her desk so that she could see Perry while she played. She smiled brightly, stretched her fingers and remembered how she used to play every night for her family. Then she placed her fingers on the keys. Sadly, Mehitable began with the hauntingly familiar words, "My Lucy alas is no more... is no... no more... my Lucy alas is no more." As she sang those words, her sisters and brothers appeared beside Perry, and then Wilhelmina and Horace manifested as well. Horace joined in, harmonizing instead of leading the vocal. Mehitable grinned and winked, winked and nodded at her family while she performed. As she neared the end of the song, one by one her family was absorbed in the warm embrace of the bright light. It reminded Mehitable of the pictures she had seen of European paintings where the subject of the paintings had a bright light surrounding their heads. Tear after tear ran down Mehitable's cheeks. Her lip quivered when Perry crossed over, the last of her siblings to do so. Wilhelmina and Horace smiled and waved as Mehitable reached the final lines, "Then soon, when life's sand is run out, we shall meet again, never to part... never to part... to part... we shall meet again never to part." She choked on the final phrase, but her family was gone by then anyhow.

After a few minutes, Mehitable returned the virginal to its table. She put away the sheet music to that sad song. *What a coincidence that her family had crossed on the exact same day of the year that they had perished in the fire, exactly nine years later,* she thought, and then she admonished herself, *You know better than that, Mehitable, that was not happenstance.*

She sat on her rocking chair, wrapped herself in a thick blanket and thought. She was aware of her breathing. It was unusual to just sit and not be busy doing something, and there was plenty of wool to process. Her family had been gone for years. Seeing them again was a miracle. This time they were gone and she knew they wouldn't be back. She felt honored that she had been able to help them find their way, yet now it felt like they were *truly* gone. Forever gone. Yet she felt the presence of her family and her distant ancestors within her. She felt as if the light of a million candles glowed within her bosom. She wanted nothing more than to just sit quietly and reflect on her memories.

Suddenly the air in the barn began to stir.

It no longer startled her when spirits appeared, yet she was surprised to see the ghost of a man she didn't recognize. She had enjoyed a few minutes of solitude and was sad that the moment had passed. She thought of the words that Perry had spoken. "You must embrace this gift and make it your life's work. It is how you can best serve God."

Mehitable spoke, tentatively at first. "Good evening, sir." She told the man her name and asked him how she might help. It was hard to look upon him. In one instant, he appeared to her as a strong farm boy, dressed for a day in the fields. Then in the next instant, he appeared as an older man, wrapped in a robe, dressed as she imagined an Indian would be dressed. The images blinked between the two at a dizzying speed. Yet his voice was constant and confident.

He introduced himself as Liam Mallory. As he spoke, she became aware of a presence behind him. Her eyes grew wide as it became clear to her. It was a buffalo. It stood, silent and still, and yet she could see its breath escape from its nostrils. It seemed to her that the animal was connected to the man in some way.

Speaking to ghosts was still new to her. It was easy to speak with the ghosts of people she had known and loved. She wondered what this man was doing in her barn and what she should do or say to help him. She took a deep breath, found her voice and said, "Pray, sir. How did you come to be here and how may I help?"

His wavering spirit crystallized and the countenance of the older man explained, "An ancient Indian woman led me here. She didn't speak a word, but I understood that I must follow her." He looked down and said, "It does not surprise me that the Great Spirit is a wise woman. It felt good to be in her presence, and something about you reminds me of her."

Mehitable offered, "Perhaps 'twas not the Great Spirit but some sort of guide you have encountered." She was quiet for a moment, and he did not fill the silence. Finally, she asked him why he looked like an Indian and spoke of the Great Spirit. He told her about his childhood on the frontier, the family of his raising, and the Mohawk people who had adopted him. She listened as he told her about the Mohawk man who had hated him at first and then had become as close to him as a brother.

Though he seemed comfortable confiding in her, she could tell that something was bothering him. She wondered whether he understood that he was dead. She asked, "What troubles you?"

The question seemed to be the key that unlocked his concerns. "I wander. Perhaps it was what I was meant to do. I like to discover new things, see new places, and explore new lands. I don't know what I seek. I don't know where I belong. I don't know whether I'm headed for heaven or hell. If it is heaven, will I live with Jesus or the Great Spirit? Which wife will I live with in heaven? Perhaps in between worlds is where I am meant to spend eternity."

She listened quietly and sympathetically. When he finished speaking, she said, "I don't think that's how it works. I don't believe the other side is full of jealous wives. I think you'll find your worlds come together there." She paused slightly then softly suggested, "Perhaps Jesus and the Great Spirit are the same, just as the farm boy and the man in the elk robe are one."

She watched as the man looked upward, his face full of joy. She spoke of the wonders his soul might experience, gently reminding him that he *enjoyed* making journeys into the unknown. She asked, "Do you see the way?" He nodded without looking at her and then he was gone. The buffalo that stood behind him remained for a moment longer. She noticed a patch of white on the buffalo's shoulder. The buffalo lowered its majestic head, its flowing beard seemed to melt into the floor of the barn. She couldn't help but think that the buffalo was bowing in thanks for having rescued the spirit of the man. The buffalo slowly evaporated.

Mehitable came back to her surroundings. She stood and yawned. It had been a busy day. Bosley jumped up on Mehitable's desk and pushed her hairbrush onto the floor. Mehitable shook her head, scooped up the cat, and rocked him into a roaring, snoring sleep on her lap while she tried to freeze the image of her family into her brain so that she would never be able to forget them.

Chapter 17
February 1809

Mehitable spent much of the next year helping soldiers cross over. Some were easy. Some were harder. There seemed to be an endless demand for her services.

One evening, Lieutenant Colonel Roger Townshend appeared in her barn. Mehitable had come to realize that many of the ghosts were confused and disoriented. Townshend was one of those. It was hard to talk with him because they would exchange a sentence or two, then Townshend would relive his death. And every time Townshend experienced the cannonball passing through his stomach, Mehitable felt like someone punched her in the gut. Finally, she gently inquired, "Sir, do you understand that you are dead, and that you are a *spirit* now? For some reason you appear to be stuck in some insufferable kind of *loop*, endlessly reliving the trauma of your death. It doesn't have to *be* like that. You can cross into the world of spirits. You really should," she encouraged.

It was just what he needed to hear. Mehitable had helped him break the cycle. She had stopped the cannons. Townshend looked at Mehitable, with a look of desperation on his face and said urgently, "I need to know if my family knows what happened to me."

Mehitable thought about Townshend's suggestion, "What year is it now?"

"1759," Townshend answered quickly. "The year is 1759."

"I don't know how to tell you this," Mehitable said, with a raised eyebrow. "You were killed fifty years ago. The year now is 1809. You have been stuck in Ticonderoga for a very long time."

Townshend said, "Nay, I was at Fort Carillon. We were trying to take it from the French. I know nothing of this *Tapioca*."

Mehitable answered patiently, "The British succeeded. They captured Fort Carillon and they renamed it. Ticonderoga, not tapioca." She placed one hand under her chin, stretched her opposite arm forward and said, "How can I help you, sir?"

Townshend asked, "Could you write a letter to my family?"

Mehitable raised an eyebrow and asked, "How old are you Mr. Townshend?"

"I am 28-years-old," he replied.

Mehitable asked, "So if you were 28-years-old, fifty years ago, how old would your parents be if they were still alive today? Perhaps one hundred years old?"

A worried look crossed Townshend's face. "Could you just try anyway? You could address it to Viscount Townshend, Raynham Hall, Norfolk, England. That way, whoever is viscount now could answer the letter, and then we'd know."

Mehitable sighed, took out a piece of paper, a quill, and a jar of ink. "Very well," she said. "You must tell me things that only you could know, and things that your family could verify, otherwise there is no chance that they will answer a letter from a strange woman in a distant land."

For the next two months, Townshend's ghost materialized frequently, checking to see if Mehitable had received an answer to her letter. One day, Mehitable was surprised when Reuben brought her a letter in a fancy envelope, all the way from England. It was from a distant cousin. His parents were long departed, but the cousin wrote that Townshend's mother, Audrey had commissioned a monument in his honor at Westminster. The inscription read:

This monument was erected by a disconsolate parent, the Lady Viscountess Townshend, In the memory of her fifth son, The Hon. Lieutenant-Colonel Roger Townshend, who was killed by a canonball on the 25th of July 1759, in the 28th year of his age, As he was reconnoitering the French lines at Ticonderoga, in North America. From the parent, the brother, and the friend, his social and amiable manners, his enterprising bravery, and the integrity of his heart, may claim the tribute of affection. Yet stranger weep not, for though premature his death, his life was glorious. Enrolling him with the names of those immortal statesmen and commanders whose wisdom and intrepidity, in the course of this comprehensive and successful war, have extended the commerce, enlarged the dominion, and upheld the majesty of these kingdoms, beyond the idea of any former age.

Mehitable thought to suggest that Townshend transport his ghostly self to Westminster or Raynham Hall directly, but he seemed pleased enough with the letter from his cousin. Mehitable warmly suggested, "You should cross over and be with your parents who cherish you."

Townshend looked at her innocently, as if he had never thought of it. "Can I do that?"

She nodded back, "Aye, I think you can."

Mehitable's next spirit was a soldier who appeared whenever she saw a tree that had been chopped down. His ghost sat on the stump with his hat in his hand. He always looked lost and confused, sad, and tired. One day, he spoke to Mehitable. "Can you see me?" he asked.

Mehitable nodded and answered, "Aye, sir. What is your name and how can I help you?"

The soldier answered, "I'm Nate, er—Nathaniel Wheat. I'm lost. I've been wandering these woods for days. One day I followed you here. Could you help me find my way home?"

"Oh dear," Mehitable answered sympathetically, "Pray, please permit me to inquire, where do you live, how old are you, and what year is this, Mr. Wheat?"

Nate looked surprised. "I'm just looking for some directions, ma'am, but if you must know, I live in Hollis, New Hampshire. I am 21-years-old, and the year, of course, is 1777. I promised my brother Tom that I would look after his wife Abigail and their daughter Lucy. Tom died at Bunker Hill two years ago. I haven't made it home yet."

Mehitable always hated having to ask, but she did anyway. "Do you know that you are dead, Mr. Wheat?"

Nate dropped his hat, surprised, "I am?" He looked at his hat on the ground. Disappointed, he continued, "Explains a lot, I guess."

Mehitable thought Nate would take comfort in knowing that the Battle for Independence had been successful. She informed him that it was 1809, not 1777. She thanked him for helping to assure freedom in America. Then she suggested that he cross into the world of spirits.

Nate had other plans which compelled Mehitable to send his niece, Lucy, a letter. Fortunately, Lucy was open-minded, and happy to hear her uncle's thoughts about her father's concern for her. He had died when she was just a baby. Mehitable had suggested that Nate try to materialize in New Hampshire so that she wouldn't have to send a letter and wait for a response, but Nate reminded Mehitable that he was lost and didn't have the slightest idea where to go. Mehitable discovered that she enjoyed writing letters for the dead, and so far, miraculously, both of her letters had received replies. Lucy's letter made Nate happy, and Mehitable was able to help him cross.

During late winter and early spring, a soldier named Daniel Cadwell visited in her barn each evening. He was the soldier that she had encountered at the edge of the woods in Skenesborough, on her way from Poultney to the mountains.

In the years since, she had sometimes seen him from a distance, his bright green eye peering out from under his hat, but mostly hiding his face from her view. Their visits were very brief. He didn't have a strong energy. He had been determined enough to quietly follow Mehitable, Polly, and Reuben on their trip from Poultney. He was a brave soldier but his spirit was not.

He had been stationed at Ticonderoga in 1777, but contracted smallpox. He was sent to Skenesborough, where he died in March of 1777. She learned that he was 44-years-old, had a wife named Eunice, and seven children. Again, Mehitable was asked to send a letter to a soldier's family. She was shocked to receive a touching letter from Cadwell's son, complete with updates on the entire family. As she read the letter to him, Cadwell's smallpox cleared from his face, and he quickly crossed over, a proud father and grandfather.

One early summer morning, Mehitable hurried through her morning chores. It had been too long since she had spent a day alone in the woods. She wasn't sure whether she wanted to hunt, fish, explore, or gather resources. She followed the road along the river toward the west for a mile, fished briefly, then spied a tiny clump of cedar trees across the river. She wondered if she could relocate the cedar trees and decided to try. She pulled her hook and line in and looked for a rock to dig with, wishing she had brought a shovel with her. Then she heard a voice calling, not far off in the distance. It sounded familiar. "Pendennis," he called, over and over.

She turned to the left, then she turned to the right. Nobody was there. She turned back toward the road and saw him. It was the man with the green coat. The ghost that she thought might be the famous war hero, Ethan Allen. She was swept with the same feeling as when she had seen him that New Year's Day, years before. He saw her, and he knew that she saw him. His ghost approached her slowly, as if it desired to make its arrival an event. The smell of oranges and cloves grew stronger as he got nearer, and she recalled the scent that accompanied her previous encounter with him. A scent that also included wood smoke and horse manure.

Mehitable turned to a nearby fallen tree and sat on the log, hiking herself up with a quick hop. A few inches of clearance allowed her to swing her feet beneath her without dragging them on the ground. From there, she waited for him to complete his slow approach.

Finally, he appeared before her. In his trumpeting voice, he said, "Good day, madam." He removed his tricorne beaver skin hat, held it at his chest, and bent slightly at the waist. He went on to inquire as to whether she was lost, and if she could use his assistance finding her way. His arms moved in a flamboyant fashion. He seemed to want to emphasize each sentence with some sort of flourish.

She replied, "Good day, sir. My name is Mehitable. I believe our paths have crossed before. I am not lost, but I must wonder, you seem to be searching for someone or something that *is* lost."

He answered, "But of course, my apologies, ma'am." He winked at her, and turned away, adding drama to the introduction he was preparing. He placed his hat back on his head and turned back toward her as if approaching her for the first time. He closed his eyes briefly and said, "I am Colonel Ethan Allen." He stepped his left foot forward, widening his stance, and placed his hand at the hilt of his cutlass on his right side, as if he were posing for a portrait. He tilted his head slightly upward and added, "You may know me as the liberator of Ticonderoga, and champion of hardworking patriots of the woods." He held his pose and left a brief pause before he stepped forward and looked into her face and said, "But alas, I seem to have lost my horse. He is a tall, flaxen chestnut with white socks, a narrow stripe on his head, a long blond mane, and a tail that flows almost to the ground." He described the horse as if he were describing the love of his life. "Pray, have you seen him?"

She said, "Oh dear, I haven't seen any horses that don't belong. How long has he been missing, and what is his name?"

He scratched his chin and looked bewildered. He wasn't accustomed to being confused. In life, he had been bold and impulsive. He acted according to reason and nature. He should be able to answer a simple question, but for some reason he couldn't say how long the horse had been missing. He made a motion with his hand, like he was flicking a fly from the neck of his horse and decided to focus his response on the other part of her question. "His name is Pendennis, after the castle where I was held prisoner in England. It was an impressive structure with a beautiful view of the ocean. I waited there, day after day for the proper hanging I was promised. People came from far and wide, from every corner of England to see me, and to smuggle gifts for me." He paused to marvel in the memory of the adulation, then continued. "When I finally regained precious freedom the name Pendennis stuck with me. A short time later, I found the best horse I have ever owned, and decided to name him after the castle. So his name is Pendennis. Voilà."

She could picture the shiny, alert horse that stood beside him. "Colonel Allen, sir, pray tell, what year is this?"

Again, Ethan looked confused. Finally, he concluded, " 'Tis 1789, I suppose."

She prodded, "And how old are you, sir, if you don't mind me asking."

He answered, "Fifty-two years old, I guess."

Mehitable frowned. She thought he looked 25-years-old, perhaps slightly older, but certainly not more than 30-years-old. "I don't know a polite way to ask this, Colonel Allen, but do you know that you are dead? You are an earth-bound spirit. 'Tis 1809. You have been a ghost for twenty years. You should depart the world of the living and join the spirit world." She noted his expression of surprise and softly concluded, "Don't you think it's time?"

She watched as he slowly transformed from crestfallen to his natural state, brash and intimidating. "I shall decide such matters, young lady." He twisted his head dramatically, and watched her from the side of his eyes, with a glare, like he was trying to evaluate whether she should be regarded as an enemy or as a kinswoman. "What is a young lass like you doing alone in the woods, might I ask?"

She answered, "Not at all, sir. I spend a lot of time in the woods and along the river, yet not as much as I should like to spend. I think today I am looking to find some small cedar trees to transport to my garden in town." It occurred to her to appeal to his ego and asked if he might share more of the historic story of his life. She was sure to emphasize it in the past tense, so that she might remind him that his life had ended. She was glad that most of the spirits that visited her were ordinary citizens, patriots, and colonists. Ethan was the most famous spirit she had encountered, and she had to admit that she was curious about him.

He couldn't resist the chance. He spoke of growing up in western

Connecticut, and working on the farm, chopping wood, plowing fields, harvesting grain, and taking the grain to the gristmill. "I was six feet tall by the time I was 16-years-old," he bragged. He became even more excited when he spoke of spending time in the woods with wild Mohawk Indians, learning how to survive on what nature provided. He told her about hunting rattlesnakes and wolves and collecting bounties for ridding the countryside of them. He frequently glanced at Mehitable to see if she was scared or impressed by the stories he was telling her. Then he talked about studying theology and philosophy before his father died suddenly, ending his hopes for a college education. He dreamily recalled courting the gristmill's daughter. Then he turned to Mehitable, and said, "She was plain and dour, a downright dowdy scold, possessing none of your mesmerizing beauty, charm, and mystique."

Mehitable's brow furrowed as she realized that the ghost of Ethan Allen was flirting with her. Who ever heard of such a thing? She had been drawn to his magnetism. The longer he spoke, the more fascinated she had become. He had amazing stories to tell, and was a gifted orator, but the more fondly he spoke of himself, the less she felt drawn to him. The more she realized that her ideal man would possess almost the exact opposite of Colonel Allen's personality. It also dawned on her that he might be extraordinarily difficult to dispatch to the spirit world.

Irreverently, Colonel Allen spoke of bundling with his fiancé, Mary Brown, which is to say sleeping with her before marriage, fully dressed, and with the blessing of her father, of course. Ethan winked at Mehitable as if he wished he were bundling with her at that very moment. "For some reason I can't explain, I couldn't get enough of Mary Brown, may God have mercy on her soul." He said the last part as if she had passed away, but he had gone on living. He explained that Mary had died, far too young, of tuberculosis.

Ethan told Mehitable about his writing, and the books he had published on philosophy and religion. The more he spoke of reason and nature and espoused his opposition to Christianity in favor of simple deism, the more shallow she found him to be. He quoted the famous poet, Alexander Pope, with great fervor. She smiled at the thought that Ethan was pompous and pretentious. He interpreted her smile as an invitation to continue.

An hour later, Ethan had told Mehitable about his role in helping to discover Poultney with his brother and cousin. They also discovered many other Vermont towns. She learned more about his role in the dispute between New York and New Hampshire over the land in between, which they had called the "Grants," prior to Vermont becoming the fourteenth state, subsequent to his death. He told the story of his role at Ticonderoga in a jocose way, as most of his stories went into elaborate detail about drinking in taverns on the way to or from his destinations. Then he spoke more seriously of his time in captivity. His story of starvation, dehydration, and torture mirrored the stories that Oliver Sanford had told at her sixteenth birthday celebration on New Year's Eve in Poultney.

When a quiet moment finally presented itself, Mehitable suggested that heaven must be full of beautiful horses and hot buttered rum. Most likely, he could find his beloved Pendennis there, and also his wife Mary.

Ethan turned toward her, his body bent at hips and knees like he was facing a clever opponent in a duel and he considered drawing his sword. "Ye are very clever. Not so fast, milady. I have unfinished business I must attend to." She inquired about what his business might be, and he went on. "I can't tell ye all of it, but I can tell ye I shall not leave this earth until I oversee the making of a statue portraying my physical likeness in a way that leaves a worthy legacy, and that inspires future generations to boldly fight for freedom. For liberty. Against oppression. Voilà." Mehitable noticed that he liked to use that word.

Mehitable kindly offered, "Very well then, Colonel Allen. I can assure you they teach schoolchildren all about those things, and I can remember learning about your role in the Revolutionary War and your captivity, as a girl. Thank you for helping establish our beloved America. Perhaps a statue is exactly what is needed. Perhaps one exists already, how would we know? I shall see if I can find out. Is there anything else I can do to help you, sir?"

Ethan thanked her for helping him understand that he should no longer search for his horse. He told her that she had been most kind, and made eyes at her as he slowly departed, as if he thought she might enjoy the sight of him leaving slowly. There was a reason the man that died in his fifties had manifested as a spirit in his twenties.

She sat on the log long after he had gone, shaking her head in wonderment. She had never encountered such a spirit before. She wondered, impossibly, *What shall I do about this one? Pray, God, I might need assistance with him. He seems so elusive. Perhaps his soul will remain for generations. It may be beyond my abilities to assist him. I'm sure this is not the last I shall see of Colonel Ethan Allen.*

The afternoon was disappearing quickly. She carefully hurried across the fast-moving river and dug up a dozen small cedar seedlings. On the way home, she prayed that the tiny trees would thrive in town. She intended to do her best to help them through the trauma of being transplanted.

Chapter 18
July 1810

Mehitable had spent the better part of two years living amongst the ghosts and helping them find their way. What had seemed like an endless demand for her attention had finally decreased to the point where Mehitable could go weeks without seeing a troubled spirit. Her daily wanderings led her farther and farther from home, and she filled most of her days widening the game trails in the forest and searching for all of the best fishing spots.

That summer, Polly's latest pregnancy had kept Mehitable closer to home. She couldn't take the chance of being beyond reach, should her friend need her. After chores and morning tea with Polly, Mehitable took her fishing to the familiar bank of the river near the house. Normally fish didn't feed at that time of the day in the heat of summer, but she found fishing to be a relaxing activity. If the big fish weren't interested in the worm on her hook, she was just as happy to watch the tiny minnows nibble at the skin on her toes at the edge of the river.

From that vantage point, she watched as most of the men in town labored to complete an enormous wooden dam across the river. The dam would serve as a bridge and power the tiny town's fledgling industries. Reuben organized the effort and paid neighbors generously to help construct it, and he promised to throw a town-wide celebration when it was completed. Mehitable frowned as she thought about it. She enjoyed watching the men work, and she was curious to see whether their plan would work as well as they hoped it would, but she was not looking forward to mingling with an entire town, small as it was.

She was counting the number of families, and she had gotten as high as twelve before a big fish hit her hook hard. She battled the trout for a while before she landed it amongst the sedges between the river and the meadow. Mehitable thought the fish was the biggest she had ever caught in the river, just a little shy of two feet long. She was so intent on that fish that she hadn't noticed Reuben standing nearby. She looked quickly to the dam. All of the men had left. She inquisitively looked back at Reuben.

Reuben complimented Mehitable on her catch and offered her a helping hand. As they walked back toward the house, Reuben explained that the work at the dam was finished and that he had invited everyone to celebrate its completion on August 4th, a Saturday. Mehitable raised her eyebrows, counting the days. Thirteen. As they approached the kitchen door, Mehitable asked, "What about Polly?"

Inside, they found Polly in an advanced stage of labor. Exasperated, Mehitable asked, "Why didn't you holler to me?" and hurried to assist. Polly had tended to all of the preparations herself.

Polly smiled. "How many times have we done this now? I thought I'd get as far as I could on my own, but I'm glad you're here now."

Mehitable handed 2-year-old Eliza to Reuben and sent them to the barn. Two hours later, Mehitable brought them back into the house to meet baby Ann. Eliza touched her baby sister's cheek with her index finger and said, "Baby." Then she toddled off looking for something more interesting to play with. Mehitable took Ann's tiny foot in her hand, closed her eyes, and smiled contentedly. No premonitions, just like when Polly had delivered Eliza. Mehitable shuddered ever so slightly, recalling the feeling of dread she had after the birth of baby Reuben, and her nightmares about Perlina.

Ann was a healthy, robust, summer baby, and Polly recovered her vigor after several days of moderate rest. Reuben had promised a party and planned out most of the details himself. He left the menu to Polly and Mehitable and offered to find them help if they needed it. Polly suggested that each family bring a dessert, and they could provide a picnic meal. Then she got an idea. "How about a blindfolded pie eating contest?"

Reuben liked the suggestion. "We'll have a picnic, then. I'll take care of the activities and I'll request that each of the neighboring families bring a pie. If you need help with the picnic lunch, I'll hire someone."

Polly suggested fried chicken, " 'Tis perfect for a picnic," she emphasized.

Mehitable agreed. All of the spring chicks had survived that year, and they could spare a dozen chickens. Mehitable offered to let Reuben wring their necks and pluck their feathers.

The day before the picnic, Polly baked one hundred biscuits. Mehitable made a dozen Shoo-Fly Pies. It was hard work, but Mehitable enjoyed thinking of her mother as she baked the heirloom recipe for the pie eating contest. The neighborhood pies would be shared amongst those who *weren't* competing in the contest. She also delighted at the thought of the contestants' faces covered in the sticky-sweet molasses pie filling. When the baking was done, they worked together to prepare the bacon, lima beans, and corn for succotash. With a 2-year-old and a newborn baby to tend to, it wasn't an easy day's work. They got lucky in the afternoon when Eliza and

Ann both took a nap at the same time. As they were scooping lima beans from their shells, Polly asked Mehitable if she would play the virginal and sing at the picnic.

Mehitable shook her head vigorously, a look of horror on her face. "Please don't ask me to do that, I just couldn't," she insisted. She explained that she would prefer not to be the center of attention. She understood the people in town judged her, and it didn't bother her, but most certainly, she did not want to perform for their entertainment. "I'm happy enough to make pies for their enjoyment. Pray, let us leave it at that." Polly frowned at Mehitable's mention of judgmental people and she abandoned her suggestion.

The next morning, Esther Partridge arrived with her 2-year-old baby, Marvin, just as Mehitable was headed out to the barn with Reuben to cull the chickens she had identified for butchering. Mehitable looked back over her shoulder. A thin gray ghost of a young woman hovered over Esther's shoulder. It looked like the ghost was trying to see the baby. Mehitable tripped over the tip of her shoe, a result of her distraction, and hit the ground on the path between the kitchen door and the barn door. She jumped to her feet and brushed the dust from her dress. Then she hurried to catch up to Reuben who had just passed through the barn door and was removing an axe from its hook on the wall.

After Mehitable helped separate the condemned dozen from the rest of her flock, she returned to the house. Esther was holding Ann. Marvin and Eliza were playing at her feet. Mehitable helped Polly lift the pot of fat onto a hook over the fire in the hearth so they could fry the chicken in it and then they prepared the batter. Mehitable frequently checked on Esther. The ghostly woman that looked just like Esther flitted from child to child, looking into their faces from just inches in front of their heads.

As they were grinding toasted bread into breadcrumbs, Mehitable asked Polly, "What do you know of this woman, Esther Partridge?"

Polly looked up at Mehitable, her brow furrowed. She spoke of Esther's father and her brothers who owned neighboring farms up the road.

As Polly told Mehitable about the members of the Partridge family, Mehitable rubbed her chin, furrowed her brow, and made listening noises. Finally, Mehitable asked, "Has someone close to them passed away recently?"

Polly thought a moment, and it came to her. "They had a sister named Eunice. I think she was just a little bit older than Esther. I believe she passed away three years ago from the winter influenza."

Mehitable was listening carefully and her expression conveyed to Polly that Polly had shared a very relevant piece of information.

Polly gasped, "Do you see her? Is she haunting her sister? Is she here? In my house?" Polly became flustered. "We have work to do today and a big picnic party this afternoon. We can't have a haunting. Not today." Polly began to hyperventilate.

Mehitable put her hand on Polly's shoulder, reassuring, "Nay, I'm sure it's nothing. Just a feeling or a vision. Nothing to trouble ourselves about."

Polly seemed relieved by Mehitable's reassurance, and Reuben disturbed their concern by knocking his boot into the kitchen door. His hands were full of dead, plucked chickens, upside-down, their heads swinging from their necks, inches from the floor. The kitchen table became a butcher's block, and the work of turning chicken carcasses into fried chicken began in earnest.

While they worked, Mehitable thought about the sister, Eunice Partridge. She wondered about her interest in the babies. She didn't want to worry Polly by asking any more questions. She wondered if Eunice had died before having any children of her own. Perhaps Eunice remained earthbound so she could share Esther's experience of motherhood. She nodded her head in confirmation of her thoughts. Then she filed the thought away.

Perhaps she would encounter Eunice later and help her to find her way.

Polly and Mehitable finished their work with less than a half an hour to spare, giving them a few minutes to freshen up before escorting picnic baskets to the meadow beside the river. Mehitable walked with Esther, Polly, and Reuben to the picnic, and they arrived just as the music began.

The senior Aaron Hayes, who went by the nickname Ron, was playing the fife, and he was accompanied by Andrew Hickok on the drums. Mehitable loved the jovial, whistling sound of the fife and the constancy of the pitter-pattering drumbeat, so different from the melodic sound of her virginal. Music always spoke to her. She perked her ears so she could hear the sound as she made several trips, fetching the rest of the chicken, then the biscuits, and finally the succotash.

Esther and her sister were busy watching the children, and Reuben and Polly were busy greeting neighbors. Finally, Mehitable was done carting the picnic lunch to the meadow when she realized, Mr. Hayes and Mr. Hickock had been playing that same song, over and over, verse after verse. She wondered if they knew any other songs, or if their repertoire was limited to "Yankee Doodle."

When they finished playing, Ron put his fife in his shirt pocket, and Andrew lifted the drum's strap over his head and set the drum on a stump. Andrew's wife handed their 2-year-old son to him, then she helped Polly uncover and serve the picnic luncheon.

Mehitable took over watching Eliza and Ann, allowing Esther to get in line for a plate of lunch. As they were parting, Mehitable didn't make eye contact with Esther. She was looking instead at her sister.

Eunice's ghost hadn't noticed Mehitable looking at her earlier. She was just about to float away with Esther, but instead she zoomed in front of Mehitable. Eunice whispered into Mehitable's ear, "You can see me." Even at a whisper, Eunice conveyed her amazement.

" 'Tis true," Mehitable said sympathetically while she gently rocked Ann. Eliza was rolling around in the grass and giggling. Mehitable followed her around the meadow, keeping her in sight. Mehitable glanced at the crowd. Everyone was intent on eating their picnic lunch and many were still in line to be served. Nobody was watching her. She turned her head and inquired, "Pray, are you Esther's sister Eunice?"

Eunice whispered sadly, "Aye, and Marvin is my nephew."

"But you wish he was your son," Mehitable said. She offered it as a question rather than a statement.

Eunice hung her head and added, "I wish I could hold him in my arms and smell the top of his head." She confirmed that she had always longed to mother a family of children. If only she had not wasted her life by starving herself to death for reasons she could not explain. She hadn't meant to kill herself, she just felt an overwhelming compulsion to be thin. Then Eunice looked out over the gathering of townspeople and noted how happy she was to see so many babies and children.

"You know, heaven is full of young 'uns," Mehitable whispered. "You should go with Jesus and be with them in heaven."

Eunice seemed surprised at the suggestion, "There is?"

Mehitable nodded. "How could it be heaven if there weren't babies and children there?"

Then Eunice expressed concern that she wouldn't get into heaven on account of having killed herself. Mehitable reassured her, reminding Eunice that she hadn't meant to kill herself, and even if she had, Mehitable was certain that she would be forgiven. Mehitable also suggested that Eunice could watch over her family from heaven just as easily. Delicately, Mehitable concluded, "Pray, go to God, Eunice."

Eunice's ghost appeared more brightly than she had previously, tilted her head and nodded, and clasped her hands over her heart.

Then she looked toward heaven. A rapturous, joyful look spread across her face and her apparition evaporated.

Mehitable stood for a moment, glad that she had been able to help Eunice. She could relate to her yearning for children. Polly's children filled her own heart with happiness, yet she often wished for children of her own. Eliza tugged at Mehitable's dress. She was hungry and she asked for her mother.

As everyone was finishing lunch, Ron and Andrew picked up the fife and drum and played "Turkey in the Straw." When they were done playing, Reuben stood on the stump where Andrew had rested his drum and gave a speech. Reuben didn't have a lot of experience speaking to crowds of people but found his voice among friends and neighbors. Before he thanked everyone for their help building the dam, Reuben expressed his family's gratitude over the arrival of tiny Ann. Then he talked for a few minutes about the possibilities for their small town. Truthfully, it wasn't a town of its own yet. The center of the town of Jay was miles up the road. "One day," Reuben predicted, "we'll have a town of our own right here." Then he shared his plans to build a potash factory, an iron foundry, and someday an inn. Reuben told a brief story about his friend and mentor, Tommy Todd, back in Poultney. Though he didn't mention it, Reuben had also been thinking about running for the State Assembly, a thought placed in his mind by his friend Farmer Weeks from the county seat in Elizabethtown. Reuben concluded by telling everyone about the activities that had been prepared for the afternoon, then he asked Reverend Hammond to say a few words. Eli blessed the gathered crowd, and he said a prayer for the brand-new dam across the river.

Mehitable stood in the shade of a maple tree, leaning against its trunk and watching as Leonard Owen presided over a whiskey barrel full of water and floating apples. Leonard was a balding, middle-aged man who owned and operated the grist mill.

It was late in the year for apples. The new season's apples wouldn't be ready for a month or more. Those that remained in root cellars from the previous year were punky, scabby, wormy, and bruised, but they floated.

Leonard's oldest son, Charles, kept track of the time, and his younger sons Chauncey and Thaddeus helped the younger contestants reach the top of the barrel. Eunice and Esther's brother, Stephen Partridge, won the contest with a blazing fast seven second time. Stephen opened his mouth extremely wide and forced his face into the water with such force that he was able to capture an apple in his mouth on his first attempt. To keep the afternoon moving, each contestant was allowed only a minute, and Charles kept everyone on task.

After the apple bobbing, Reuben released a plump pig into the meadow. The piglet had been rubbed in grease. Reuben had only used a little grease because a healthy pig was hard to catch. The crazed pig ran among the crowd as people chased it. Coriander Bump had a good grip on the piglet, but he slipped away from her before she could tuck him under her arm. The piglet darted between the legs of Thankful Bull, who screamed and jumped several feet into the air despite holding a baby and being pregnant. Fortunately, her husband Henry caught her, preventing her from falling to the ground. Finally, fast as lightning, 20-year-old Aaron Hayes, Jr. caught the fleeing pig before he could escape to freedom into the wilds of the forest. Aaron's little son Chester was delighted that his father had won the squealing piglet.

Mehitable had climbed up into a lower branch of the maple tree, which seemed like a prudent thing to do while everyone was racing around in pursuit of the *pink flash*. Although the piglet had safely been returned to captivity, Mehitable remained in the tree. She swung her legs contentedly and watched as a dozen contestants were blindfolded and placed in front of the tables that had held the picnic dinner an hour earlier. Mehitable wondered which Bump would win. There were so many townspeople interested in winning the contest that they had to draw names at random, yet Otis, Lester, and Dudley all won a chance, and so did Coriander. Mehitable leaned forward as the men dropped their faces into her Shoo-Fly Pies. It had been a big job making them on top of the rest of the work she had done the day before, but it made her happy and she laughed out loud watching the contest. Finally, Stephen Partridge lifted his face from the pie plate and hollered that he was finished. Stephen's brother, Reuben Partridge, had been placed in charge of judging the event, and despite his lack of independence, Reuben declared his brother the winner. Mehitable wished it were possible to freeze a moment in time so that an artist could draw a picture of the spectacle. Coriander and the eleven men were quite a sight, with faces full of molasses and crumbs. They looked even funnier when they removed their blindfolds. Reuben Partridge passed out the prize money put up by Reuben Sanford. One dollar for Stephen Partridge, 50 cents for Coriander Bump who had come very close to winning, and 25 cents for Aaron Hayes, who Mehitable thought had no chance of winning. He was as thin as a blade of grass.

The contestants cleaned up the best they could in a wash basin Polly had set out on a stump for them. The crowd dispersed. Most of the men played horseshoes. A couple of the older girls presided over hoop and stick races for the younger children in the meadow. Mehitable liked to watch the children push the large wooden hoops across the starting line and hit the top of the hoops with a wooden dowel as they wobbled their way across the field toward the finish line. Most of the women chatted and gossiped while they tended the children who were too young to play in the meadow.

Polly cleared away the pies from the contest, cleaned the tables, and set out the pies brought by the neighbors for dessert. Thankful Bull's mother-in-law, Mary, whipped a large batch of cream in Polly's kitchen during the contests to top off the pies.

While people ate dessert, Mehitable wandered off across the top of the dam like she was sleepwalking. She crossed the river without looking back, then wandered along the banks of the river on the other side.

Coriander's son, Bacon, followed Mehitable. He didn't feel like playing with the other children and he wasn't hungry for dessert. The men were busy talking about an Indian named Tecumseh and a French emperor named Napoleon.

Bacon was a strange boy who drew pictures that no 6-year-old boy should be capable of drawing. The people in his pictures looked like they were from India, perhaps hundreds or thousands of years before he was born. Neither Lester nor Coriander could write, and they had asked Mehitable if she could teach Bacon how to write his words. The boy quickly learned his alphabet and was writing complete sentences. He was fascinated by Mehitable and stared at her like nobody else existed whenever he was in her presence. Despite having asked Mehitable for her help, Coriander found her son's fascination with Mehitable disturbing.

Thankful Bull was nibbling on a slice of blueberry pie. Daintily, she ate tiny nibbles as slowly as possible, while her mother-in-law held her youngest baby, a little girl named Confidence, and her 2-year-old daughter named Perseverance. Thankful and Henry's 5-year-old son was named Tenacious, and their 7-year-old daughter was named Temperance. Henry and Thankful's family harkened back to Puritanical times, and the names of their children were reminiscent of names more typical of the 1600s. Thankful was about to nibble two blueberries and a breadcrumb from the tip of her fork when she saw Mehitable across the river. With her other hand, she tapped Coriander on the forearm and pointed at Mehitable. Across the river, Mehitable was having an animated conversation with herself. Thankful tsked. Coriander harrumphed.

Across the river, Mehitable stood talking to Daniel Sanford.

Daniel's presence was very weak and timid. She had seen him many times through the years, since she had first dreamed about his ghost, and since Reuben's father Oliver had told the story of Daniel and his son Jeremiah at the Livingston Sugar House in Manhattan during the Revolutionary War. When she saw Daniel that afternoon, she followed him across the dam and then along the river. He usually appeared during large gatherings, which made him difficult for Mehitable to talk with.

Across the river, Thankful had found one group of women and Coriander had found another. They whispered, pointed, and made scandalous accusations. Was she a witch? Was she possessed? Had the devil consumed her? Was she a danger to herself? To others?

Mehitable was sad to have to tell Daniel that his son Jerry did not survive captivity on the prison boat, but it warmed her heart to be able to tell him that America was free and proud, and that future generations of Sanfords were flourishing. She told him everything she knew of his family, especially Reuben and Polly.

Coriander found Reuben and interrupted his conversation with Leonard and Aaron. With a hand on her hip, she pointed across the river. "Just look at that woman who lives in your barn. Why do you tolerate that? What the *devil* do you suppose has gotten into her?" Coriander leaned forward aggressively and proclaimed, "She sleeps in a barn. She hunts for frogs. She talks to herself and she walks around alone in the woods all day. T'aint right," she concluded with her typical, "harrumph," and wandered off to share her observations with another little crowd of neighbors.

Mehitable felt elated after she helped Daniel Sanford find his way into the afterlife. After knowing how much he had suffered in the evil prison, it made her happy to think of him reunited with his loved ones in heaven. It surprised her to know that Daniel's ghost had no idea that he had been gone for over thirty years. She drew a deep, satisfying breath and felt the pride one feels when they know they have helped someone in need. When she turned around to walk back to the party, Mehitable was surprised to run into Bacon.

The boy asked, "Who were you talking to?"

Mehitable thought for a moment, and answered, "To God. Aye, Methinks I was talking with God."

Bacon was satisfied with Mehitable's answer. She bent down, picked up his hand in hers, and they walked across the dam.

When Coriander saw them, she shrieked. She blurted accusations, chief among them was the charge that Mehitable was trying to steal her son and give him to the devil, and she concluded by demanding, "To whom were you speaking, across the river, there," pointing to the spot where Mehitable helped Daniel Sanford find his way to heaven.

Mehitable opened her mouth, then closed it, not knowing what she was going to say exactly, when Bacon spoke for her. "She was talking with God, Mother. 'Tis it not okay to pray in the middle of the day?" he asked innocently.

Reverend Hammond took advantage of the opportunity to suggest that yes, saying prayers wasn't just for bedtime and before eating a meal. "God *is* always listening, especially to those who do God's work."

Thankful tipped her head toward the heavens and said, "Reverend, how do we know she speaks to God? 'Tis the devil that *she* speaks to."

Reverend Hammond suggested that it would be best to give a fellow human being the benefit of the doubt and challenged Thankful to name a time when Mehitable had done the devil's work. "Aside from the sinfully delicious pies she bakes, I can't find fault with Mehitable Munch."

Mehitable thanked Eli for the compliment and excused herself. It was late afternoon. She walked to the barn without looking back toward the celebration which was winding down anyhow. Inside the barn, Mehitable placed her milking stool beside Ophelia's daughter who had replaced her mother two summers earlier. Ophelia the second was just as good a listener as her mother had been. "Our neighbors would probably not understand me talking to you like this," Mehitable said to Ophelia as the first streams of milk pinged against the sides of the empty milk bucket.

The sun had set and Mehitable sat at the dinner table with Polly and Reuben. Eliza and Ann had gone to sleep quickly after the excitement of a busy day. They were relaxing with a cup of tea, and Polly put her hand on Mehitable's shoulder. "I think you should tell Reuben," Polly nudged, expecting that Mehitable would know what she meant. Polly had kept Mehitable's secret from her husband, as Mehitable had asked.

Mehitable understood. It had been two years since Polly had witnessed the confrontation in the barn with the demon spirit, the evil man, and the troubled boy. Polly had suggested several times that Mehitable talk about her gift with Reuben or with Reverend Hammond.

"Very well," Mehitable said. " 'Tis no better time than now, I presume." She turned to face Reuben, took a deep breath, and confided, "I can communicate with the dead. When they are unable to pass into the world of spirits, their souls remain stuck on earth. I am able to help them find the peace they need, and then they can follow Jesus into heaven." She went on to tell him about how she had helped his distant cousin, Daniel Sanford, find peace, by the side of the river that afternoon. Then she answered Reuben's questions about whether the work she did was dangerous or scary. She assured him that since the demon spirit, none of her work with the departed had been scary at all.

When Mehitable had retired to the barn for the evening, Reuben nervously paced back and forth, then stopped and grimaced. He looked Polly in the eye and said, "I'm not sure I can believe all that nonsense about talking to ghosts." He started pacing again and continued, "I believe in God and Jesus, but otherwise I have a hard time accepting things I cannot see or prove. But, I am happy to accept Reverend Hammond's conclusion that Mehitable was talking to God." He sat down next to Polly, draped his arm across her shoulder and finished, "I cannot agree with Coriander. Perhaps Mehitable is a *little* crazy, but there is no way she is a witch or talks to the devil."

Polly agreed. "Had I not seen it myself, I am sure I would feel the same way. Whether we fully understand her, she is our friend, and she has proven her devotion to us. I love her unconditionally, and yet, I can see why Coriander, Thankful, and others do not understand." Polly stood up, took Reuben by the hand, and they went to bed.

The next morning, Mehitable was having tea in Polly's kitchen when they heard a light, tentative tapping on the door. Polly flashed an *I wonder who that could be* glance at Mehitable as she hurried to the door to welcome a guest into her kitchen. "Pray, won't you come in Mrs. Bull," and invited Mary to join them for a cup of tea in the parlor.

Mary Bull told Polly she thought that would be lovely but assured her she would be just as happy to sit with them in the kitchen. Mary was a soft-spoken, timid woman, with gray hair and a friendly face. It was unusual for her to cross her daughter-in-law, Thankful Bull, or to willingly step into controversial territory. Mary's being in a room with Mehitable would have displeased Thankful. Mehitable had filled a teacup for Mary, and they finished with their small talk. Ann was sleeping in a basket nearby, and Eliza was playing quietly in the corner. Finally, Mary reached across the table and grasped

Mehitable's elbow gently, and admitted, "I have been watching you dear. I *do* believe you can talk to God. What do you know of heaven?"

To give herself time to contemplate how to respond to Mary's inquiry, Mehitable said, "Why do you ask, Mrs. Bull?"

Mary insisted that Polly and Mehitable call her by her first name, and then she shared her life story and most of her husband Leander's life story as well. Mary was born in 1750. He was five years older than she was. They had married in 1769. Mary lost her first two babies, and her third child was Henry. When Henry was a boy, Leander was killed at Ticonderoga. When Henry grew up and married Thankful, she moved in with them. Thankful had a deeply religious upbringing, and Mary was happy to live in a home that made religion such a high priority. Mary confided that sometimes she thought that Thankful jumped to harmful conclusions and didn't realize that she was judging people when she should leave the judging to God.

Mehitable had plenty of time to form her thoughts. "I do have an uncommon ability. I think that God has permitted me to be able to see into heaven." Mehitable astonished her neighbor as she accurately described Leander, just as if she were looking directly at him, decades earlier. She chose her words carefully. "God welcomes Leander into heaven."

A blissful look crossed Mary's face. She closed her eyes and she explained that she felt a tingling on her cheeks and a gentle touch on the tips of her lips. She recalled how Leander used to take her cheeks in his hands when he kissed her each morning before going about his day.

Mehitable encouraged Mary, "He will be with God and he will wait patiently for you until it is your time to join him."

With her eyes still closed, Mary whispered a prayer while Mehitable winked at Leander's ghost. They felt a breeze in the kitchen, although the door and windows were closed. Polly gasped almost imperceptibly, placed her hands over her chest, and exclaimed, "That was beautiful."

Mary was a frequent visitor from that day on, and Polly and Mehitable enjoyed the kindly presence of the sweet older woman. Sometimes Mary spoke on Mehitable's behalf around town, much to Thankful's chagrin.

Most of Mehitable's neighbors avoided her. Sometimes they nodded politely in passing without making eye contact. They rarely answered when Mehitable offered a *How do you do* in passing. It never bothered Mehitable when people didn't answer that question. She no longer expected them to, and merely offered the greeting out of habit. Perhaps if she were honest with herself, she would have to admit that she resented their lack of simple politeness.

As soon as the work at the dam was complete, Reuben took up the potash project. After watching Mehitable work the wood ash and water into lye to make soap, he had concluded that there had to be a better way, just as Tommy Todd had seen an opportunity with his carding factory. Reuben's distillery left a large amount of wood ash, and in addition to the ash generated in the hearth and ash from the neighbors' hearths, the potash operation grew nicely. Reuben hired Stephen Partridge and placed him in charge.

Mehitable cultivated rosemary, peppermint, and sage and produced enormous amounts of soap without the worst part of the work. Reuben had suggested dying soap red and using rose petals. Mehitable warned that red dye in the soap would make the water seem bloody, which might not be appealing and might dye light colored hair, but she encouraged the idea of using rose petals as a fragrance. It was nearly impossible to grow roses in the mountains, so far north. Mehitable focused her efforts on collecting cedar, which gave her even more of a reason to wander beyond the confines of the settlement.

Chapter 19

August 1812

And so, Mehitable's wandering in the woods continued. Each day she went farther into the wilderness than the day before, adding to her cumulative explorations.

One day her hiking brought her to a large rock at the edge of the woods. She followed the road that ran along the river as she often did. A red squirrel sat on top of the rock. Its big bushy tail followed the curve of its body to its ears which stood at attention. Its tiny brown eyes watched her intently and the squirrel remained prepared to scurry off into the forest at the first sign of danger.

Mehitable admired the beauty of the small animal. Her fear and hatred of mice didn't extend to squirrels. She admired their industrious nature, and yet, squirrels were also playful. Whenever she saw them, she felt as if she were being reminded to stop and take a moment to do something to feed her soul.

She made a chirping sound as if she hoped to converse with the denizen of the forest. It chattered back and she approached the rock. The squirrel jumped to a branch a short distance away and Mehitable climbed up onto the rock. Then the squirrel darted off to another tree, drawing Mehitable's eyes deeper into the woods.

She was intrigued. It looked as if a path led into the woods. The boulder seemed to signal that the trail was there and hide it at the same time. She followed the trail and the playful red squirrel down the path. Every once in a while, it would look back to see if she were following.

Eventually, that path led her to the shore of a large pond. She neglected to notice the small wickiup in a little meadow, two hundred yards away. She watched as the squirrel took a quick drink, twittered, and disappeared back into the woods.

Mehitable shed her clothes and walked into the lake. She splashed around like a happy, carefree child rather than a mature woman. She enjoyed the feeling of the cool, refreshing water on her naked body.

The commotion in his pond caught the attention of a young man across the lake. He leaned forward to see more clearly across the water. He rubbed his eyes, then squinted. It had been three years since he had seen another human being. As he watched, she finished her swim, turned her back, and walked away from him until she reached the edge of the lake. She turned, stretched her arms wide and tilted her head back.

The young man's heart pounded. It wasn't just a human, it was a woman. And she was naked. She had her arms stretched wide, welcoming him. Without giving thought to whether he should or should not, he began swimming.

She stood at the edge of the lake basking in the summer sun. Her long, wet hair cascaded down her back. She tilted her head back to magnify the surface area of her face that was exposed to the sun. Her eyes were closed and she thanked God for the glorious day. She thought she might store the sun's warmth and carry it into the winter, like a squirrel gathers nuts.

When she opened her eyes, she noticed something suddenly moving in the middle of the pond. At first, she thought it might be a bird. Maybe a loon, or a duck. It only took a moment to realize that it was something bigger. Her jaw dropped. She realized it was making its way toward her. She felt a rush of excitement. It was a man. She was so shocked, she lost her sense of modesty. She wondered how a man could appear from the depths of a pond.

She reasoned that she had come to accept that the dead appeared to her from out of thin air. Would it not be possible for God to deliver a real live man in such a manner as well? She remembered that she had said a prayer to God just before the swimming man had appeared. She gasped at the thought that this man was a gift from God, just as he found his footing and began to surface. Mehitable had never seen a fully naked man before.

In the three years that he had lived on the edge of the pond, he had never seen another person. He had long since dispensed with the notion of wearing a breechcloth in the summertime. He had been in such a hurry to make his way across the pond, he hadn't thought about what he would do when he got there. His chest heaved from the exertion of his swim. He simply stood there, dripping, staring intently into her eyes. His arousal was apparent.

Mehitable stood before him, frozen. He made no effort to cover himself. She couldn't help but look. His black hair was long, like her own. Beneath his serious eyes was a handsome, young face and a lithe, muscular body, like a yearling stag. Though she had never seen a naked man, it occurred to her as she quickly surveyed the totality of him that his appearance was as Polly had described. Mehitable breathed deeply as her heart pounded and she wondered if she were dreaming. This was not a spirit. It was one thing to have a naked man described, but it was quite another thing to be standing in front of one. Her lips moved. The words formed in her head: *God's plan.* She liked that this decision was made for her. *God will provide.* The notion filled her heart with wonder.

She felt herself reaching out to him even before she reached her arms forward and he stepped into her embrace. For the longest time she had resisted, waiting for the right time to accept suitors. If it were left up to her, she might never find a match. She liked the looks of the man in her arms. She felt surrounded by the smell of the forest as he wrapped his arms around her, his hands slowly stroking the soft skin on her back, making her skin tingle. Ever so briefly, she thought of the lasting, lingering impression that Reuben's hand had made on her shoulder, so many years before. She had thought of that touch so many times throughout the years. The strong, yet gentle caress of the stranger's hands on her back wiped away the distant memory.

She dismissed thoughts, reason, worry, and doubt, instead deciding to do what came naturally. *I shall place my trust in God. I will let him take control*, she thought, as the man pressed his chest against hers. She felt like her heart was strangling her lungs and her breathing became shallow. Her cheeks felt red and hot. She felt his strong hands gently lift her from the ground. She could feel his powerful heartbeat as if his blood were coursing through her veins as well as his own. He guided their bodies together, ever so slowly. His dark eyes gazed intently into hers. She felt as if his soul had found its way through her pupils and she melted into him.

He was eager, and she was ready. They fit together as if they had been made to stand there, united in motion, clinging to one another desperately, urgently. Mehitable felt a rush of freedom. Her troubled past evaporated. The future was exciting. When the present exploded within her, she collapsed, weightless. His arms held her tightly and prevented her from falling to the ground. His intimate stare never diverted from her eyes. Even then, his look of longing remained.

When they separated, Mehitable moaned, wishing the moment could have lasted forever. He looked at her face as if he were trying to memorize every feature. It occurred to her that she had never known such rapture. She thought she had been happy before but had never truly felt the explosive joy she felt at that moment. As Mehitable's feet returned to the sandy dirt on the shore of the pond, her eyes met his and they became startled by a commotion in a large tree behind them. They turned to look and watched as one red squirrel chased another up an enormous tree, then down another tree, recklessly flinging their bodies from branch to branch.

They looked back at each other and laughed at the squirrels' amorous antics. It crossed Mehitable's mind that she liked the sound of his laughter, and she felt him take her hand in his. He pointed at the water with a flick of his head and he led her into the pond. For a moment she wondered if he was taking her back to wherever it was that he had come from in the first place. Instead of being dragged beneath the surface and forced to live in an underwater kingdom, they enjoyed a playful swim. They splashed around like a couple of children, taking their cue from the fun-loving squirrels until they found themselves in each other's arms, caressing each other under water.

It took a long time for them to realize that they had spent a little too long in the chilly water. Eventually, they made their way to the shore. With his open palm indicating the path, he showed her the ancient loop trail that had been left by generations of his people around the perimeter of the pond. Then he showed her his home, the small wickiup in the clearing that overlooked the water. He pointed at things he wanted her to see and grunted for emphasis. For each thing he showed her, Mehitable nodded her head and said, "How lovely."

Just outside the wickiup, there was a fire circle and a stump, partially hollowed out. He gestured for her to sit. It fit her shape perfectly, and she thought that it felt as comfortable as a fancy parlor chair. She watched as he blew on the embers and ashes and brought the fire back to life. He tossed a couple of round pinecones into the fire, and she noticed that there were many pinecones in the little meadow. They were gathered into conical piles.

A few feet away, she saw a perfect looking pinecone next to a handmade knife. She sat forward, picked it up, and was surprised at the weight of it. It was strong and delicate at the same time. She realized that it was carved from a block of wood rather than collected from the branches of a tree or the forest floor beneath. She looked at him and she thought that he seemed proud that she had noticed its beauty. As she held the sculpture, she heard the distant murmur of a familiar spirit. She wished she could understand what the voice was saying. She wrapped her fingers around the carving and held it in her cupped hands. She felt a bright light within her core as she closed her eyes. She felt a sense of enlightenment and two words very clearly appeared in her mind.

She stood up and joined him at the other side of the fire circle. She pointed her fingers toward herself and said her name. Then she repeated it, tilting her head down slightly, looking into his eyes expectantly.

He muttered a few garbled syllables. "Me-hit-a-bull."

She shook her head vigorously from side to side, slowly annunciating, "Muh-hett-a-BELLE." With a little practice, she thought that he said her name better than anyone else she knew. Then she pointed at him and said those two words, "Magnificent Destiny."

He repeated crisply, as instructed, "Des-tuh-knee."

Destiny smiled at Mehitable, inquisitively raised an eyebrow then bent over to pick a wildflower. She watched as he picked them, one after another. Then he gathered some tall grasses. He rushed around the small meadow, never taking his eyes from hers for more than a second or two. She watched as he twisted the grasses together, expanding their length by overlapping them. Then he bent the switch of grasses into a circle, weaving the beginning onto the end. He wove all of the flowers of August onto the grass circle—purple coneflowers, black-eyed Susans, white daisies, bee balm, and penstemon. She was aware of her nakedness as she marveled at his unclothed body. She felt like the first woman, the center of the universe, Eve at creation, in the Garden of Eden. Destiny brought the ring of flowers back to where she stood and lifted them onto her head. She felt honored and loved, even if she couldn't see the splendor that he had made for her. She took his hand in hers and brought it to her face, breathing deeply. That scent impressed itself on her spirit. To her, that was the smell of him. Wildflowers in August, with a woodsy compliment.

Mehitable watched him make a series of gestures. His movements became more pronounced and she watched him with mystification. As she continued to study his actions, it dawned on her that he was performing some kind of ceremony. When he finished and stood proudly in front of her, she realized that it was his version of a marriage ceremony. She offered her hand to him. Destiny laughed heartily, joyfully. She thought that he seemed pleased.

Then he hurried into the wickiup and returned with the furs from his bunk. He laid them over the grass in the meadow, sat and patted the fur with his hand. She sat beside him, removed her crown of flowers and they enjoyed the quiet closeness of lovers who know only the language of love.

Finally, late in the afternoon, Mehitable sat up, faced him, and ran her fingers through his long hair. She touched his face with the tips of her fingers, then she cupped his cheeks in her hands. She felt the muscles in his jaws as he clenched his teeth. She placed her open palms on his chest and said the name she had given him. *How strange*, she thought. *I just married this man, and now I must leave, and I must hurry. I am late already.* She hoped he understood that she must go, but that she would be back. Soon. Very soon.

Then Mehitable stood up from the furs and looked at his body, stretched out across the blanket. She wished she could stay. She thought the movement of her hands and arms signaled to him that she had to leave, but that she would return. She spoke the words in

English, not knowing whether he understood any of them. Perhaps with her pantomime and the tone of her voice, he might understand. She picked up the floral crown and then she hurried from the blanket. Her dress and pack basket sat where she had left them at the side of the pond. She thought she could feel the intensity of his gaze on her body as she walked away. She turned to wave at him before she set out down the path toward home. He held up his hand without waving. She thought she saw tears in his eyes.

As she hurried along the path, she wondered about the expression on his face as she left. Did he expect her to stay with him? Maybe she should have. She remembered the time that she had gotten lost in the rain and spent the night in a forgotten cave. Her friends had gathered half of the town to search for her. If she were to decide to leave her home in the barn, she couldn't just disappear. She must tell her friends first. Good manners and duty forced her down the path, though she longed to turn around and immediately head back to the magical pond.

She felt a sense of urgency about her responsibilities. She knew she was supposed to be home milking the cow. She was way behind her normal routine. Nevertheless, she couldn't help herself. A big tree had dropped a large quantity of perfectly symmetrical cones, and she felt compelled to fill her pack basket with them. As she lingered under the pine tree, she thought about the nature of love. It hadn't occurred to her before that she could love a man from the moment she met him. She had always thought of love as more of an evolution, from acquaintance to friendship, then to love. *Can love occur in an instant, like a flash of lightning? Does it require the tests of time? Must it be proven, and re-proven?* She had long believed in unconditional love, though that was for family and friends she had known since she was a child, or for precious newborn babies and children. She felt the tug of a wish unfulfilled, a wistful pang at the thought of children, and then she realized that dusk was fast approaching.

She stood up and shook her head at the basket full of pinecones and she wondered what she was going to do with them. It was as if she were gathering them as a gift for him, though she was headed in the wrong direction, besides, he already had what looked like a million pinecones. Even so, she hefted the full basket onto her shoulders.

As she hurried along the road toward home, she thought about the look of surprise on Destiny's face as she prepared to leave. *He looks at me like I am a miracle. He makes me feel like I am the queen of the forest. But he is the miracle.* She replayed the afternoon in her mind with the motions slowed, savoring the memories as her feet hurried along beneath her, following the familiar road. She had his face burned into her memory. She pictured his smoldering eyes, his strong jaw, and his fierce cheekbones. She breathed deeply and imagined that she could smell him. She recalled his flirtatious smiles as they splashed each other in the pond. She remembered the feel of his body as she caressed him under the slippery water. She longed to hear his comforting laughter again. Mostly she thought about the intimacies they had shared.

She thanked God for sending her such a precious gift. The gift of love. She thought about having a man of her own. A man she wouldn't have to share. A man that didn't belong to someone else. She told God that she was married to the man and would be true to him always. "What God has brought together, let no man cast asunder." *I hope he feels the same,* she thought. The closer she got to home, the more she began to worry. *What next? What about tomorrow. What if I return tomorrow and he's gone? How will I ever find him again? What will my friends think?* Then it dawned on her that her husband was an Indian. A wild man from the forest, no less. What would the townspeople think? After a couple of minutes contemplating their neighbors, she thought, *Dash it, who cares. I shall become a wild woman of the forest if that is God's plan for me.*

After she had left the pond, Destiny grabbed his pack basket and filled it with a few essential items. He didn't know how long he would be gone. He lifted the woven basket to his back. The cordage straps hung over his shoulders. He was just about to put his feet on the trail he'd seen her take, when he realized he was still naked. He shook his head, admonishing himself for his recklessness and returned to the wickiup to retrieve his breechcloth. He dropped the pack from his shoulders and put on a shirt before lifting the pack again to his back.

His head filled with wonder. For years he had built a life alone by the beautiful pond in the forest, beneath the majestic mountain. And now, the Great Spirit had given him the gift of love, but just for the afternoon. He wondered why she didn't stay with him. Didn't she understand that they were married now? He couldn't understand why she left, but moments after she had gone, he knew he couldn't let her go without finding her. They had to be together, together forever. He had never been more certain of anything in his life.

He knew how to move quickly and quietly through the forest. Mehitable never knew she was being followed. She was preoccupied with her thoughts and with her pace. It was a long hike to make before the sun set, given the late start she had gotten. He had a little harder time concealing himself when they went through meadows or the cleared land from the new farms that had begun to spring up. In August, the crops grew high and he was not tall, so he managed to remain concealed.

From a short distance away, he saw her enter the barn. He watched for a while and eventually he saw her leave the barn with a bucket in one hand and a basket in the other. She brought them into a house and reappeared a couple of minutes later. Then she went back into the barn. He waited for some time to see if she would come back out, then tiptoed through the open door.

Mehitable gasped when she saw him creeping down the dark, shadowy hallway. She had just changed into her nightgown and was passing the brush through her hair, dreamily recalling their afternoon together.

When he knew that she had seen him, he held out his right hand, palm forward, in greeting. She stood, stretched out her arms to welcome him, and said, "Magnificent Destiny."

He said her name, then he said, "How lovely." He held the carved pinecone in the palm of his left hand and spoke in his native tongue. She bowed her head in appreciation. She thought about the many hours he must have spent carving the keepsake. She was honored that he wanted her to have it. She thanked him in English and kissed him briefly before setting the sculpture on her table.

She gestured to her chair. He looked at the chair, then looked back at her. Mehitable sat on the chair, looked at him, then stood back up and gestured again. He got the idea. Next, she pointed at her hairbrush, then pointed to her hair, then to his hair. He might not have gotten the idea of what she meant to do until she started passing the brush through his hair.

Then Mehitable spread her blankets in the stall next to her sheep and gestured for him to join her. They both fell asleep quickly, happily nestled together between the sheep. Mehitable awoke before Destiny and lay there thinking about how she was going to explain everything to her friends. She breathed deeply, then the rooster crowed and Destiny woke up and jumped to his feet, eyes wide open. Mehitable took him by the hand and led him down the ladder to the lower level of the barn. She showed him the chickens through the slats in their coop, then she tiptoed in and retrieved an egg. She placed a large brown egg in his hand. Then she introduced him to Ophelia.

He watched her as she put the milking stool next to the cow, and the bucket beneath the udders. With years of practice, she quickly went from teat to teat, squeezing from the top to the bottom and directing the steady stream of milk into the bottom of the bucket. After a minute, she stood up and gestured toward the milking stool.

Reluctantly he sat on the stool, grabbed onto a teat, and smiled when the stream of milk came forth. He tried each one, then stood up, gesturing back to the seat. Mehitable finished milking the cow, then she picked up the pail and walked to the doorway. She turned back toward him and said, "Destiny, stay." She pointed at the stool by the cow. He sat down and Mehitable nodded, repeated the word stay, and then she rushed out of the doorway with the milk pail.

Mehitable found Reuben and Polly at the breakfast table as usual. She set the pail on the table and breathlessly gasped, "I have to tell you something. I don't know how to say it, so I guess I'll just say it. I met a man. We got married in the woods. I have him in the barn. He is an Indian."

Reuben laughed and asked, "Does he read Shakespeare and play the violin?" It was very unusual for Mehitable to joke around, so he should have taken her seriously, but he couldn't help himself.

Mehitable looked at Reuben, shrugged and left the door open as she quickly left the kitchen. Back in the barn she found Destiny where she had left him, thought, *There's no time like the present*, took him by the hand and led him to the house. Reuben met them just outside the kitchen door. Mehitable introduced them, saying Reuben's name slowly, "Roo-ben."

Instinctively, Reuben said, "How do you do," and extended his hand. He couldn't help but look back and forth between Destiny and Mehitable, as if to say, "Is all of this really happening?"

Destiny repeated what Reuben had said and stared at his hand. Mehitable filled Reuben's hand with hers, then gestured to Destiny. He held out his hand to Reuben and repeated, "How do you do?"

Then Mehitable introduced Polly and the children. Polly covered her mouth with her hand and slowly looked at Destiny from his feet to the top of his head, then back to his feet again. Then she looked at Mehitable and her eyes grew wide in surprise. She stammered, "Indian. He *is* an Indian. Oh, Mehitable. Is he wild?"

Just then Destiny said to Polly, "How do you do?"

Polly raised an eyebrow and answered, "Very well, I'm sure." She tilted her face toward Reuben to see how he was reacting to the presence of the refined, wild stranger. His civility had disarmed her concerns, yet she couldn't resist protectively wrapping her mother- ly arms around her children who stood at her side. She glanced at Mehitable who was looking at Destiny like he had hung the moon and sprinkled the stars in the sky. Then Polly smiled at Destiny.

When the introductions were finished, Mehitable took Destiny by the hand back to the barn and showed him how to do the rest of the chores, from feeding the animals to shoveling manure.

Reuben and Polly looked at each other in amazement. After years of trying to convince Mehitable to entertain suitors, the last thing they expected *that* morning was to meet Mehitable's new *hus- band*. Reuben joked, "I guess she finally found a man who won't mind sleeping in a barn. After she teaches him English, she can teach him to sing!" Despite his jokes, Reuben wasn't in favor of al- lowing Destiny to stay in his barn. The tendons in Reuben's neck expanded widely, and his mouth spread across his face as it did when he wasn't sure he liked the sound of something. "Maybe this town can accept an Indian in our barn, but only under the condition that they have a Christian wedding."

Polly asked, "What shall we do if he isn't tame? We can't have him in our barn, or in our town. We also can't let Mehitable go away with him. What shall we do?" Polly burst into tears. Reuben com- forted Polly, assuring her that everything would work out.

When Polly stopped crying, Reuben hurried over to the barn. He had many questions for Mehitable. Mehitable watched Reuben's eyebrows jump around on his forehead when she told him that she had just met Destiny the day before. She watched his face pinch inwardly as if it might collapse within itself when she answered his question about her plans by telling him that she had no plan.

Mehitable told Reuben about Destiny's wickiup on a small pond a couple of miles away. Reuben asked her if she planned to move into the wickiup or if she planned to move him into the barn. Mehitable answered, "My home is here, but I will follow my husband if he wants to move there."

Reuben shook his head from side to side. "We've known each other a long time. We are like family and we will support whatever decisions you make. You're a grown woman. We'll honor your wishes. We'd like to have you make your wild woodland wedding official by having a Christian wedding with a preacher officiating. Would you do that for us?"

Mehitable nodded, tears in her eyes. Though she had rejected him as a suitor, she had always loved him. Almost as much as she loved Polly. She was glad that Polly let her *share* her husband and her family with her all those years. She was glad that he was her friend, and she finally understood why she had waited so many years.

Reuben put his hand on Mehitable's shoulder and said, "Then Destiny is welcome here. If Destiny doesn't want to sleep in a barn, maybe we could build him a wickiup by the sawmill." Mehitable thanked Reuben, and Reuben added, "Now see if you can get Destiny into some suitable wedding clothes, and I'll ride out and see if I can find a man of the cloth."

Chapter 20

September 1812

Two days later, Reuben returned with the Reverend Eli Hammond. Reuben put Lucy in her stall and turned Reverend Hammond's swayback old nag into an empty stall next to Lucy's.

Eli joined Polly and Mehitable for a cup of tea and some wedding planning. Reuben gestured to Destiny to join him, and they went for a slow walk across the dam, into the cemetery and back. After a couple of days with Mehitable, Destiny's vocabulary had reached about thirty words. Reuben laughed and said, "I might say these same words even if you could understand them." He reached out and patted Destiny on his shoulder a couple times. He could see Destiny looking at him from the corner of his eyes as they walked side by side. Reuben said, "Let's see. I don't think I've ever told anyone this before, but Mehitable was my first love. I thought about her every day for a year before I asked her to walk the village green with me." Reuben turned and looked at Destiny briefly. There wasn't the slightest indication that the young man understood a word of it, but he could see that Destiny was listening. "She suggested I ask her friend to stroll with me instead. She joked that I might marry them both. Believe me, nothing would have made me happier. But that isn't how a God-fearing man such as me conducts himself. Even so, we have loved her like family, and I would do anything to see to her safety and happiness. I can see that you make her happy, Destiny. I'm not sure it is a good idea to have you sleeping in our barn in the middle of our town, but let's give this a try." Reuben exhaled sharply. " 'Tis a lot to process, but somehow, I feel like we'll be friends too. So, I guess I don't have a choice but to trust you and offer you my approval." The slightest indication of a tear formed in the corner of Reuben's eye. "I have to admit it, I don't have any right to be so, but I am a little jealous. I have always found Mehitable to be spellbindingly mysterious, a little scary even." Reuben took another deep breath, offered his hand to Destiny, and said, "Wherefore they are no more twain, but one flesh. What therefore God hath joined together, let no man put asunder."

Destiny stood with Reuben, awaiting some signal as to what he should do or where he should go next. The only expression Reuben could detect was a sad, sympathetic dropping at the corners of Destiny's mouth when Reuben had gotten emotional. Reuben decided that Destiny was a good listener, even if he had no idea what was being said.

When they returned to Polly's kitchen, Reuben showed Reverend Hammond to the guest room. Polly and Mehitable had worked on altering the suit that Reuben had worn at Mehitable's party twelve years earlier. There wasn't much chance it would fit him again in the future. It was the smallest of his three suits, but still it required tailoring in order to fit Destiny's slender frame.

Reuben smiled when he returned to the kitchen and saw Destiny standing there in his old suit, with Polly and Mehitable poking, pinching, and prodding, trying to decide what needed altering, and how to make the adjustments. Destiny smiled awkwardly, like he didn't know what else to do. Reuben said out loud, "Looks like Destiny doesn't mind the attention." Then Reuben walked out the door toward the mill, shaking his head and recalling what it was like to be a newly married man.

Half an hour later, they had finished with Destiny's fitting. Polly turned her head, and Destiny quickly donned his regular attire. He stood by the door, held up his hand without waving it, and then he was gone.

Polly noted, "Destiny uses the same sign for hello, goodbye, and stop."

Mehitable replied, "I know. 'Tis quite perplexing, yet he looks just as good coming as going, and even when he's standing still." She sighed, dreamily.

Polly jokingly suggested, "Maybe he'll be a better husband if you *don't* teach him how to talk."

After dinner they practiced the ceremony in the barn, with an audience of sheep. Polly stood by Mehitable's right elbow, and Reuben stood by Destiny's side. They all faced Reverend Hammond who stood on a small stool to make up for the fact that both Destiny and Mehitable were taller than he was.

After some work, Destiny understood that he was to repeat what Reverend Hammond said whenever Hammond looked in his eyes and pointed at him. Reverend Hammond fed the lines slowly, two or three words at a time. "I Destiny take thee Mehitable to be my wedded wife, to have and to hold from this day forward, for better or worse, for richer, for poorer, in sickness and in health, to love and to cherish, till death us do part, according to God's holy ordinance, and thereto I plight thee my troth."

It got better after Destiny watched Mehitable repeat her lines. "I, Mehitable, take thee Destiny to be my wedded husband, to have and to hold from this day forward, for better for worse, for richer, for poorer, in sickness and in health, to love, cherish, and to obey, till death us do part, according to God's holy ordinance, and thereto I give thee my troth."

The happy couple ended their day with a long walk by the river after dark. She wasn't nervous about getting married. In her mind she already was. Having to stand before the town to perform a ceremony had her stomach unsettled, but holding Destiny in her arms made her feel better. She marveled at the reflection of the stars in his eyes.

Reuben got up early in the morning to bathe in the river before the sun rose. Then he dressed in his best suit and sat for a while in the parlor while he waited for others to wake up. He saw an envelope on a shelf that hadn't caught his eye before. He spent most of his time in the study, and rarely sat alone in the parlor. The envelope had his name on it. He opened the envelope and found the letter his wife had written to him eight years earlier, when she had labored for days with baby Perlina. He thought about the sweet baby they had lost so long ago. More tears streamed down his face as he read the words that his wife hoped he would never have to see, her instructions that she would like him to marry Mehitable if anything happened to her during childbirth.

In the morning, Mehitable brushed her hair twice as long as she usually did. Then she slipped into the burgundy dress, the one she had worn so many years before. It brought her happy memories, and sad memories too. She took a deep breath and resolved that today would be about making good memories. She motioned to Destiny by pointing at him, then holding up her hand, then pointing at the ground. He understood that he was to stay where he was.

In Polly's kitchen, Mehitable took a seat at the table and Polly fixed her hair into a bundle on top of her head. Mehitable never wore her hair up like other women her age did, but that day, she allowed it. Reuben took his suit out to the barn and handed it to Destiny, then turned his back while Destiny put the suit on. While he waited, Reuben said, "I wonder if you have any idea what is going on, young man." When Destiny had finished changing he stood like a soldier at attention, awaiting orders, but there was a hint of a smile at the corner of his lips, and his eyes always followed Reuben when they were together, as if looking for clues from the man that would add meaning to the words he couldn't comprehend. Reuben gestured toward the barn door, then Reuben led him to the kitchen so that Polly and Mehitable could inspect his appearance. Mehitable took her brush to Destiny's long hair and gathered it into a ponytail which spilled down from the nape of his neck to the small of his back.

Reuben went to check on the arrangements. He had hired Otis and Dudley to tend the fire at his kiln. All night long they had slow cooked a whiskey pig at the perfect temperature, with a vigorous basting regimen. Three times each hour, they slid the pig out and brushed on a paste made of Reuben's rye whiskey, scallions, cayenne pepper, horseradish, maple syrup, tomatoes, garlic, and applesauce. It was enough to feed the town, and all night long the smell was carried on a light breeze across the valley, assuring that everyone in town would want to attend. Reuben gave final instructions to Otis and Dudley. He had learned to be very specific with them, and to repeat instructions several times. Then he went to the meadow which overlooked the dam, the same meadow where they had held the dam bridge picnic two years earlier. He nodded as he went along. Everything had been set up according to his instructions. It would be a short, simple ceremony, and guests had been asked to bring their own picnic blankets. There was a table at the top of the hill for Reverend Hammond's use, and there was a row of plank tables on which the pig would be served.

At noon, Andrew Hickok began drumming and the wedding guests headed up onto the hillside, leaving a wide path for the wedding procession up the hill. Thankful stopped Andrew's drumming with her hand on his shoulder. She whispered a suggestion in his ear that the drumbeat would rile up Destiny and remind him that he was a wild Indian. Andrew told Thankful that he had his orders and returned to tapping on his drum, despite her objection.

Five minutes later, the ceremony was underway. Instead of waiting by Reverend Hammond's side, Mehitable and Destiny walked up the path together. On the way past, Mehitable heard Thankful say to her husband, "If Reuben wasn't your boss there is no way we would attend this *heathen* wedding ceremony." Further up the path, Mehitable was sure she heard a harrumph. She would have been happier to get married with just Reuben, Polly, and Reverend Hammond as witnesses, but Reuben had convinced Mehitable that the town would have an easier time accepting Destiny if they were a part of the ceremony. Mehitable wondered how many decades it would take. Confound them all anyhow.

Mehitable was proud of the job Destiny did repeating his lines. She was appreciative that he did whatever was asked or needed, and she wondered at least a hundred times that day what he was thinking. Around other people, his expression was usually stoic, but when they were alone together, she could often guess at his thoughts. She had learned to read his face and many of his gestures.

After the ceremony, Otis and Dudley grunted and strained under the enormous weight of the pig. They carried it on what looked like a stretcher. As a final touch, they filled the empty eye sockets with Concord grapes, and they shoved a bright red apple in the pig's mouth. Again, Mehitable heard Thankful's voice in the crowd. "Savage, devil pig!" Sometimes others in town agreed with Thankful, but never when Reuben was present.

Reuben put on a thick apron over his best suit and handed another apron to Eliada, Polly's brother from Vermont who had just moved to town with his new wife. Eliada helped Reuben carve the pig, placing a generous amount of pork on everyone's plates, starting with the bride and groom who were seated at a private table. Everyone else dined on picnic blankets spread across the meadow.

Then dinner was cleared away and Otis and Dudley brought out lemon cake. Reuben and Polly hand-delivered cake to everyone in the crowd. Most folks were talking about the war that had just been declared. Polly heard Thankful talking about Tecumseh who had evidently teamed up with the British, and she heard Thankful suggest a concern that Destiny might suddenly follow Tecumseh's lead and slay them all in the dead of night. Polly only bothered to intervene long enough to inform Thankful that Destiny's people weren't from the same tribe as Tecumseh, and that Tecumseh was all the way out in Ohio or Indiana. As Polly withdrew to deliver another slice of cake, she heard someone talking about the Battle of Tippecanoe.

War was on everyone's minds.

When everyone had their lemon cake, Otis and Dudley followed Reuben to Destiny and Polly's table. Destiny had learned a new word: cake. He had decided that he liked the cake, and it was clear he would like another piece of it. Reuben went to get him another slice.

At that moment, Otis asked Mehitable if he could touch Destiny. He said, "I've never touched an Indian." Lester and Coriander wandered over to join Otis and Dudley.

Mehitable suggested, "How about if you shook his hand? Would that count as touching an Indian?" Otis vigorously nodded, giggled, and held out his hand for a handshake. Destiny smiled and offered his hand. Dudley decided he would like a handshake as well, and not to be left out. Lester extended his hand too. Coriander harrumphed and muttered the word *pagan* loud enough to be heard ten feet away. As she walked away, the baby she had clutched to her hip flopped around, as if it were trying to sit on a bucking horse. Despite what Coriander thought, the Bump boys decided *they* liked Destiny, and each one giggled through a second handshake before Reuben returned.

People began wandering away toward home. In front of her family, Mary Bull told Mehitable that it was a lovely ceremony, she told Reuben that dinner was delicious, and she kissed Mehitable *and* Destiny on the cheek. Mehitable was glad she couldn't hear Thankful at that moment or experience her thoughts.

The morning after Mehitable and Destiny were married, attention turned to the harvest. After breakfast, Reuben invited them to tour the fields where Otis and Dudley were hard at work, tying bundles of rye into cylinders of stalks. Lester was on a slightly tilted wooden platform, using his bare feet to separate the kernels of wheat from the stalk-bundles, a process called thrashing. The light brown, nut-colored seeds rolled down the platform into a collection bucket. The straw bundles were set aside for use as bedding in the barn.

Mehitable and Destiny held hands and stood a short distance from where the Bumps were working. Reuben ran his hands through the collected kernels in the catch basin. He nodded and verbalized his satisfaction with the quality of the grain. With his inspection complete, he looked at Mehitable and Destiny. Destiny's upper lip was raised in a sneer, and he shook his head judgmentally.

Reuben misunderstood. "Would you like to try?" he asked.

Destiny had learned enough words to say, "Women farm. I hunt."

Reuben looked down at his feet and said, "Oh, I see." He was glad that Destiny had spoken quietly and that the Bumps hadn't heard. Even so, there was no mistaking the forcefulness of Destiny's conviction regarding men in the field. He understood that must be part of Destiny's heritage and knew Destiny would find his own way to contribute.

They walked from the farm to the still, housed in a twenty-five by thirty-five-foot building along the river, a short distance from Reuben's barn. Coriander worked in the yard, winnowing the harvest, separating the wheat from the chaff. It was a perfectly breezy morning. She poured the harvest from one bucket to another. The heavier seeds fell directly into the bucket, and the breeze carried away the lighter bits of debris. Coriander's children played in the mud a short distance away, under her watchful eye.

Reuben complimented Coriander on her work. The seeds in her bucket were exceptionally clean. She stood up, put her hands on her hips and grumbled in complaint, "Three of them and they can't keep up with one of me. Dunderheads!"

Reuben patted Coriander on her shoulder. "You work hard, and nobody can match your quality."

Coriander seemed pleased with Reuben's attention, handed him a bucket full of clean kernels, then set out to corral one of her children who was on his way toward the river.

Next Reuben took Destiny and Mehitable to Mr. Owen's gristmill. He said to Destiny, "I shall show you how these seeds are ground into a powder." Destiny raised an eyebrow, not comprehending Reuben's words. "You'll see," Reuben encouraged.

Inside the mill, Reuben pointed to the inner workings, the water wheel connected to a series of wooden gears. Reuben made a large circular motion with his hand and arm. Then he pointed to the intake and the outflow. Reuben ran his hands through the bucket of wheat kernels, for emphasis, then he poured them into the intake. A fine powder began to flow from the outflow, and Reuben used both hands to direct Destiny's attention to the flour. Reuben picked up a pinch of the white powder and let it fall, smiling proudly.

They walked back to the still. Coriander was back at work.

Lester had brought her a new batch of rye to winnow. Coriander grumbled about the useless babies and said she looked forward to when they would be big enough to be put to work.

Reuben led Destiny and Mehitable into the large shack. Excitedly, Reuben explained the distilling process, pointing at a series of barrels, fireplaces, and copper piping. He seemed particularly excited about a snowman-shaped apparatus on the top of the biggest barrel, which he referred to as the "onion." Most of the lesson on distilling was lost on Destiny, but he did comprehend that Reuben needed wood for whatever it was that he did. Destiny held out his right arm, made a muscle, grasped it with his own left hand, and proudly said, "I chop."

Reuben nodded vigorously, "T'would help a lot. I'd be most grateful." Then Reuben excused himself, telling them he planned to return to the field to help Otis, Lester, and Dudley. "Maybe if I help those boys, we'll be able to keep up with Coriander."

Mehitable kissed Destiny sweetly on the lips, then headed toward the house. Destiny removed his shirt, took up the axe, and began chopping wood for the still. A couple of hours later, Mehitable returned carrying a picnic basket. Coriander stood beside her winnowing buckets, hands on her hips, gawking at Destiny a short distance away. She hadn't heard Mehitable approaching, and she jumped when Mehitable suggested, "Handsome man, 'aint he." It wasn't like Mehitable, but she said it anyway.

"He works hard, I'll give him that," Coriander replied.

Mehitable handed Coriander a sandwich from her basket. She was halfway to the woodpile when she heard Coriander snort, "Heathen." Mehitable turned to look at Coriander and watched as she stretched her lips around the sandwich in her hand, taking half of it into her mouth in one bite.

Mehitable sat for a moment in the shade and she watched Destiny work for a while before interrupting him. He was making fast work of it, and the bins were about three quarters full. After lunch, she took him by the hand and they headed toward the river. Coriander hollered after them, "Hey. There's work yet to be done. 'Twont do itself, you know."

Mehitable pretended not to hear her, and Destiny pretended not to understand.

Chapter 21
September 1812

Polly's baby arrived at the end of September. Eliada's wife helped Mehitable tend to the delivery. Instead of waiting anxiously nearby, Reuben worked at the still. The harvest, threshing, winnowing, and grinding processes were finished. The fermentation process was underway and would wait for no one.

Destiny spent the morning replenishing the wood in the bins and then, without a word to anyone, he walked off into the woods.

Reuben monitored the mash personally, cooking it overnight, and stirring the contents of the big barrel with a huge paddle that looked like an oar. At the top of the barrel, a thick, bubbly, crusty mass formed. Just before dawn, Reuben mixed in malted barley, making the mixture smoother and easier to stir.

After laboring through the night, baby Jane was born just after sunrise. Mehitable cleaned up in the house then walked to the shed. " 'Tis a girl! Congratulations, Reuben. Come see." On their way back to the house, Mehitable asked, "Where is Destiny?"

Reuben shrugged. "I haven't seen him since yesterday." He had just finished mixing malted barley into the barrel. Reuben apologized for asking Mehitable to stir the mixture. It required constant stirring to become perfectly smooth. Fifteen minutes later, Reuben returned and thanked Mehitable for helping Polly overnight. Polly and baby Jane were sleeping comfortably, and Eliada's wife was re-laxing in a chair nearby. Reuben suggested Mehitable get some rest also.

Mehitable looked around for Destiny. Failing to find him, she lay down and took a nap. It had been a long night, and Mehitable fell asleep easily and stayed asleep until after noon. When she awoke, she devoted more effort into looking for Destiny. They had been married less than a month, and it was the first time since they were married that she didn't know where he was. At the end of the day she lay awake, wondering. Had he returned to the woods? Did he decide he would rather not be married? She shuddered at the thought. She hadn't minded being alone. Having found love, she felt a pang of grief just at the thought of experiencing loss.

The next morning Destiny returned, carrying a small deer and a string of trout. He smiled, set his catch down, and wrapped Mehitable up in a tight embrace. Mehitable clung to him, thinking she never wanted to let go. When they separated, Destiny said, "I hunt." Instantly, she understood that she must accept that he would come and go. It was his way of providing for his family, of contrib-uting. She could identify with him. She had no desire to be tamed, to fit within civilization's expectations, and she should not expect that of him either. She praised the bounty he brought and she could tell that pleased him. She decided that if he must leave to hunt and provide, she would make his returns joyous occasions.

When all the rye had been converted to whiskey, Mehitable ar-ranged for Reuben to tend the animals in their absence. She packed a couple of baskets with blankets, food, and clothes, and took Destiny by the hand. They walked down the road, crossed the river, then followed the road to the left. A couple of miles later, they arrived at Copperas Pond. It was early October, and the fall colors reflected brilliantly on the perfectly still water.

Mehitable was glad that Reuben and Polly had accepted Destiny. Nevertheless, she was glad to be alone together with her husband, and away from the judgmental eyes of Coriander Bump and Thankful Bull.

She stood at the edge of the water next to Destiny, pointed to the middle of the lake, and suggested, "Let's do it again." Somehow, he understood. The air was cold, and the water was brisk. Destiny dropped his clothes at the water's edge, swam a short distance into the lake, then turned around. Mehitable's pulse quickened as he swam back toward her. She would never forget the feeling that he was a special gift, and that he had been meant just for her. She would never forget their first encounter and she enjoyed the reenactment almost as much. Mehitable resolved to never take that gift for granted.

That night, two hours past midnight, Mehitable woke from a dream. Her eyes blinked open. She was fully awake and could vividly remember a vision which had come to her in her sleep. Even in the dark, windowless wickiup, she could faintly see Destiny's sleeping face, so close. She loved to watch him sleep. She looked at his long lashes and thought he looked almost like a young boy rather than a grown man. Her heart raced. *If the dream is real, I know Destiny's story.*

Mehitable turned to lay on her back. With the tip of her finger, she traced the spiral on the face of the medallion that hung heavily at the center of her chest. She saw Destiny with his family in a longhouse. He looked several years younger, but she could tell that it was him. Their family had a compartment in the middle of a longhouse that housed many family units. She saw several scenes of Destiny fighting with his older brother and arguing with his parents as his three younger sisters looked on. She watched a vision of Destiny's life that played out like reading the pages of a book. Mehitable watched as Destiny fell in love with a young woman, and then she watched as Destiny's mother secretly arranged a marriage between that woman and Destiny's older brother. The whole family was in on it, everyone knew in advance except Destiny, including grandparents, cousins, aunts, and uncles. Then Mehitable watched as Destiny packed a basket full of the things he would need to survive on his own. Though they spoke a language that was strange to Mehitable, somehow, she understood the meaning of their words. Angrily, he told his family never to utter his name again. If they must speak of him, they could refer to him as He Who Walks Alone. Mehitable could feel the bitter bite of betrayal as she experienced Destiny's departure from his people and the village of his birth.

Her finger continued tracing the endless interconnected spiral triplets on her chest. She saw Destiny heading north. He didn't look sad and he didn't look back. She heard him shouting into the wind, "I am He Who Walks Alone. I live like my brother, a wolf alone, my spirit animal." She understood that Destiny's name for himself was Wolf Alone. That was before she renamed him. She smiled at the thought, *Sometimes the wolf walks alone, sometimes the wolf needs his pack.*

A final vision came to Mehitable that night. Destiny had an ancestor that watched over him. She sensed that ancestor was a powerful spirit. He appeared to her as a strong young man, and yet, at the same time he seemed as if he were ageless. An old soul. The man told her that the symbol on the necklace was a symbol of fertility, and that he would watch over *her* just as he watched over Destiny. The words of advice that she retained from the vision were *Treasure one another,* but she couldn't remember whether she had heard him say those words in the vision, or whether those words had just appeared in her mind.

Before she fell back to sleep, Mehitable thought, *I don't know anything about you. I don't know how old you are. I don't know all the things you like, or all the things you don't. All I know is you make me happier than I ever imagined being. We shall start with that.* She wished that he understood enough English so that she could tell him about her visions, and perhaps he could confirm them. He had added to his vocabulary, but he was a long way from fluency. After years of speaking with no one, he had become unaccustomed to phrasing thoughts for others to hear in his own language, not to mention in a strange tongue.

The next evening, they were sitting by the fire outside the wickiup. The flickering flames were casting tall shadows from the pine trees along the banks of the pond. Suddenly, an ear-piercing scream came from the darkness. It sounded like it was just an arm's length beyond the circle of light from the fire. It reminded her of the screams she heard in the woods just before Perlina died.

Mehitable turned to face the darkness. She felt an overwhelming sense of sadness and dread. Years of remembered torture tumbled back into her mind. Mehitable grabbed the medallion in her hand and stepped forward into the darkness.

Like ants crawling across a log, Mehitable saw tiny devilish spirits spilling from a knothole in a giant, ancient, gnarled white pine tree. She stood erect and confident. Recalling the prayers that had worked when she faced the demon, Mehitable ordered the evil spirits back into the knothole, and she ordered them never to return. The last spirit though the knothole tried to resist, tried to scream again in the night, but ended up swallowing its scream in a gulp, almost as if it were drowning. Then it was gone. Mehitable prayed for the tree, asking Jesus to bless it for eternity. She laid her hands over the knothole and said a final prayer.

Just as suddenly as evil had appeared from the dark of night, tranquility seemed to fill the air, and the clouds drifted off leaving a bright, full moon, and stars that sparkled brightly. Mehitable turned back toward the fire, and Destiny stood there, mouth hanging open in astonishment. "Shaman," he uttered with amazement.

Mehitable nodded, confirming Destiny's conclusion. They returned to the warmth and comfort of their fire. Mehitable pulled a long, thin stick from the fire and scratched with the black, coal end of the stick on a rock. She drew a picture of a wolf with its snout pointed toward the sky. Then she drew a full moon around it. She pointed at the wolf, then she pointed at Destiny. Destiny nodded excitedly, placed his hand on his chest, and affirmed that the spirit of the wolf lived in his heart. Then she pointed at the moon, and then at herself. Mehitable whispered in her husband's ear, "Does the wolf howl for want of the moon?" Destiny raised his eyebrow, and smiled, lips closed, like he had discovered a secret.

The next morning as Mehitable was making breakfast, her stomach started to churn. At first, she didn't know what to think. She briefly wondered what she had eaten to cause the pain in her stomach. Then it hit her. After years of tending Polly's pregnancies, she suddenly understood that she had morning sickness. Then she recalled the all-knowing smile on the face of the spirit that had told her about the fertility symbol on her necklace, the spirit she knew as Wanders Far. She softly rubbed her stomach and thought about the new life beginning within her. So many questions flooded her mind. Would it be a baby girl or boy? Would the child look like his father or his mother, or maybe a more distant relative? She thought of Granny. Then worry crept into her thoughts. Would her child have to deal with the horrors of hauntings and the burden of helping ghosts? She thought of how Granny had tried to prepare her. Would she have to do the same for her child, or children? She hung her head, understanding that it wasn't up to her. Then she thought of Coriander, Thankful, and the rest of the town. Would her child be welcome in their town? Through the years, whenever she had thought about being a mother, she never realized how much doubt and worry would come along with motherhood. She knew that all she could do was love her baby and raise her child as best as she could.

Mehitable hoped that in the years to come, when Destiny learned more English, he could confirm his story. She wondered what he would think about the fact that she had seen his story in a dream. Would he be surprised to hear that his ancestor watched over them? She would be happy to use his old name if he preferred, but she hoped that he would prefer to keep the name she had chosen for him. She thought about what it would mean to their child to know Destiny's story.

While she waited for her baby to be born, Mehitable found herself spending most of her time helping Destiny's ancestors find their way to Jesus. One day, she helped a hundred of Destiny's earthbound ancestors pass into the world of spirits, all at once. They had been earthbound since an epidemic of smallpox had swept through their village. One prayer, a sympathetic thought, and three short empathetic sentences was all it took. One by one, she watched the ghosts sail into the loving arms of their creator.

Mehitable thought about what Granny had told her about the importance of her gift, and she never felt so grateful for that blessing as she did the day she helped the smallpox victims. That thought was interrupted by Mehitable's first labor pain.

Chapter 22

May 1813

Stubbornly, Mehitable argued for delivering the baby in the barn. It was the first time she and Polly had fought since they were schoolchildren. "You can't have your baby among the farm animals," Polly exclaimed, shuddering. Mehitable argued that it was good enough for Jesus, and it should be good enough for her too. Polly made the point that it would be a whole lot easier for her to help Mehitable if she was in the house, in bed where she belonged, and that Mehitable should think of Eliada's wife as well. Destiny looked back and forth between Polly and Mehitable as if he had never seen people argue before. He aimed his left shoulder slightly forward and tucked his chin toward his chest, like a bull preparing to charge. It was as if he were preparing himself to assist Mehitable in their squabble, only he had no idea what they were talking about. After the delivery, Polly promised to help Mehitable back to her place in the barn. Mehitable consented, and Destiny looked relieved despite the fact that Polly had prevailed. Then Polly promptly led Destiny to the barn, pointed her finger and firmly said, "Destiny, stay."

After twelve hours in labor, Mehitable gave birth to a baby boy, an hour after sunset on a warm day in the middle of May. Eliada's wife held Mehitable's hand, and Mehitable held her baby on her chest as she rested. Polly went to the barn to get Destiny and shared the news that he was a father and that the baby was a boy. As she approached, he quickly covered up whatever he was working on. Polly had tried to get a look at what she thought looked like a hunk of a deer antler on a worktable, only with a picture carved into its surface. She was curious to see it more closely, but there were more urgent matters to tend to.

Polly shooed Destiny out of the barn, and they hurried along the path between the barn and the house. He reached out a finger and touched the baby, as if he thought perhaps the baby might be a spirit instead of flesh and blood. Then he placed his hand on the back of the little boy and smiled proudly. He gently kissed Mehitable and then she requested assistance getting to the barn. She thanked Polly for talking some sense into her. Polly took the opportunity to suggest that Mehitable spend the night right where she was. Mehitable told her not to push her luck and reminded her of her promise. Polly disapprovingly shook her head from side to side as Destiny took one arm and Reuben took the other. As they passed through the barn door, Mehitable declared officially what she had intended all along: "I shall call him Moses."

The next morning, Destiny tended to the chores in the barn. Mehitable begrudgingly accepted his assistance with what she saw as her responsibility, but she refused assistance up the path to the house. Polly had prepared a large breakfast. Eliada and his wife joined them, and just as they were sitting down to eat, there was a knock on the door. Polly asked Mary Bull to join them for breakfast too.

Mehitable sat happily at the table, holding Moses in her arms. She was already used to his presence and felt like he had been with her for an eternity. She half-listened to her friends as they discussed the news that American troops had captured and burned the city of York on the shores of Lake Ontario. The war seemed to be getting closer. Mehitable wished that the Europeans would fight their war in Europe and leave them alone.

After a plentiful meal of bacon, eggs, and buttered biscuits dipped in maple syrup, Mehitable strolled slowly down the road toward the river. Destiny walked with her, protectively at her elbow. At the side of the rushing river, despite the onslaught of blackflies, Mehitable held Moses in the palms of her hands and lifted him forward slightly toward the water, as if she was sharing him with the mountain spirits. She resolved to expose him to the forest, field, and stream, as frequently as possible. On the way back, they passed Henry and Thankful. Henry tipped his hat politely, perhaps by habit. Thankful turned away as they passed, intentionally ignoring their presence. Mehitable heard the word, "Half-breed." She wasn't sure whether the word had come from Thankful's lips or whether she had thought it so powerfully that Mehitable heard her thoughts. She tipped her head up slightly, proudly, and reminded herself that she didn't care what Thankful thought anyway. A little later, another neighbor passed, muttering something unintelligible when Mehitable said politely, "How do you do?" The disrespect didn't bother Mehitable; she neither craved nor needed their respect. Ever since she had resigned her position at the mercantile in the aftermath of the fire that had killed her family so many years earlier, she had avoided people, except for Polly's family. She enjoyed living in a frontier town at the edge of civilization. Nevertheless, she resolved that the people that she did encounter, she would greet politely whether they deserved it or not.

Six months later, Mehitable was alone with Moses in the barn after dinner. It was the middle of November, and Destiny had been gone for two nights. Usually, he just seemed to vanish, but on that occasion, Mehitable had seen him gather his bow, knife, pack basket, blanket, and warm clothing. With the leaves gone and the fresh snowfall, Destiny had hunting on his mind.

She set Moses on his belly on a blanket and turned her back to him. She picked up her hairbrush and enjoyed the familiar feel of the bristles separating the strands of her hair. When she was done, she set the brush down on the table, and turned back to look at Moses. He was gone. Her eyes grew huge in panic, and then she saw Moses in the stall where they slept with the sheep. Emmeline was licking his face, and he was giggling contentedly. *How is it possible? Moses can't crawl. Nobody could have moved him, and the sheep couldn't have come to get him.*

Mehitable prepared for bed. She pondered the situation. She couldn't think of any way to explain it. It defied explanation. *Could it be my sanity? Did I place him on the blanket or in the stall?* Eventually, Mehitable fell asleep without finding answers to the questions she asked herself.

Mehitable spent much of the next day with Polly. It was windy, cold, and snowy outside. Mehitable enjoyed spending a quiet day indoors. While the older girls played upstairs, Mehitable and Polly set the babies down for a nap in the middle of the afternoon and sat together sewing. Moses napped in a wooden rocking cradle in the parlor where they worked. Mehitable was in the middle of telling a long story, and her fingers were flying as her needle poked in and out of the shirt she was mending. Then she realized that Polly hadn't made a sound in some time. As she continued her story, she looked up at Polly to make sure she was listening. Clearly, Polly was not. The color had flushed from her face, and she sat there gawking, amazed, staring at the cradle where Moses napped. The cradle was rocking, gently, on its own, as if an invisible someone was sitting in the chair next to it, pushing the cradle with their foot from time to time, just as Polly had done so many times with her feet while her babies slept in that cradle while she sewed.

Mehitable reached her hand across the space between their chairs and placed her hand on Polly's shoulder. "There, there," Mehitable comforted, "no need to worry. Spirits are drawn to children, and sometimes they can't help themselves."

Polly looked from the crib to Mehitable, "And you approve?"

Mehitable nodded.

Polly's eyes got even wider. "Why can't they just stay in the barn?"

Mehitable understood that her friend was uncomfortable in the presence of ghosts. She reassured her, "There is no cause for fear, Polly."

Polly asked about the ghost that pushed the cradle. "Is it your mother? Is it your Granny?"

Mehitable shook her head. "Nay, 'tis one of Destiny's ancestors." She noticed that her answer made Polly uncomfortable. Mehitable reassured Polly, "Don't be scared. This is one of the gentlest, most highly evolved souls I have ever encountered. The only thing I can't understand is why this spirit remains earthbound. This soul must know that heaven is waiting." As Mehitable spoke to Polly, the spirit of the man in the chair rocking the cradle smiled up at her. Mehitable felt a surging within her chest that reminded her of the feeling that she got when she said her prayers. She was struck by the handsomeness of the spirit, and how similar his features were to those of her husband. It was the spirit she had interacted with before, the one that told her that he watched over Destiny. The spirit of the elderly man who told her she would find the spiral medallion now appeared in the form of a young father. It didn't matter that he manifested as a younger man. She immediately knew him by his ageless eyes. She heard his name in her heart once more: *Wanders Far*. It made her happy to know that his spirit watched over Moses also. Mehitable's gaze was locked onto the face of the spirit as she concluded, "I think it is my job to help this ghost pass into the spirit world." She saw a smile on the spirit's countenance, and the spirit shook his head in disagreement and vanished. A light breeze blew through the parlor, and the rocking cradle slowed to a stop.

Polly whispered, "Is the spirit gone?"

Mehitable nodded.

Polly told Mehitable that the years hadn't made it easier to understand. How Mehitable could see the spirits. How the spirits could manifest. She admitted that the thought of stranger's ghosts popping in and out of her house scared her when she thought of it, which was far too often for her taste. "I'm sure the old Indian woman who rocked Moses in the cradle was a lovely, sweet soul. 'Tis hard to stomach the notion of someone you can't see, sitting there staring at you."

Mehitable didn't bother to correct her friend. She sensed that it wouldn't make Polly more comfortable if she knew the spirit was masculine, and that he manifested as young rather than old. "Pray, try to put it from your mind, dear. Most of these spirits are gentle, kind, and calm, much more so than the living. It's just that some are a little confused." Just then, Mehitable's thoughts wandered off. *Why is Destiny's ancestor's spirit confused, and how can I help him find his way?*

For the next six months, whenever Mehitable put Moses down to nap, the spirit would appear and rock the cradle with his foot. She grew to accept it as normal, and she enjoyed the company of the quiet soul who seldom spoke, but always had a sympathetic expression on his face. When she tried to speak to the spirit, he held his finger to his lips, as if he were saying, "Hush now, mustn't wake the baby."

Chapter 23
April 1814

In late April of the following year, Moses was 11-months-old. He had found his feet and had begun to toddle awkwardly.

It was election day and Reuben had been on the road for several months, giving speeches and attending meetings in all of the neighboring towns. With Farmer Weeks of Elizabethtown's encouragement, Reuben had put together a compelling case and a winning strategy and was elected to the State Assembly. The news of his election reached Polly and Mehitable before Reuben had returned home from the county seat, where he had spent the final days of his campaign, making his best case.

They were busy in the kitchen preparing a celebratory meal. The children ran wild throughout the house. Moses was standing on his wobbly legs, holding on to the leg of the kitchen table, when they heard the buggy pull up to the barn outside. Mehitable turned to look toward the kitchen door, and she saw Moses speed through the distance between the table and the door, like a blur. She gasped. *What just happened? How is it possible? Is this what happens when I set him down in one place only to find him in a different place?* She felt a prickle of alarm.

Moments later, Reuben came through the door. Moses grabbed onto his leg, and the girls came running from every corner of the house. Polly kissed him on the cheek and congratulated him before returning to the cookpot on the hearth.

At dinner Reuben thanked his family and spoke of the honor. He was looking forward to serving in the 38th New York State Legislature. "We shall be in session from the 26th of September to the 24th of October, then again from January 31st through April 18th."

Polly took the opportunity to share the news that Reuben was going to be a father again in the fall. She pouted at the thought that he might not be there when the baby was born. Reuben reassured her, "This is wonderful news. We are truly blessed. Perchance this time, we shall welcome a little boy to the family."

Mehitable knew that if they did have another boy, it would also be named Reuben. He may have only lived four days, but there already was a Reuben, Jr. She didn't approve, but she kept her opinion to herself.

Late that summer, as Reuben was making plans for harvesting the rye crops, a rider galloped down the road, and came to an abrupt stop in front of the house. A man jumped from his saddle and told Reuben that the British had retaliated for the burning of York by attacking Washington, ransacking the city and setting buildings on fire. Breathlessly the man spoke of Dolly Madison's running from the White House carrying George Washington's portrait. The man handed Reuben a uniform, appointed him Major, assigned him to lead a battalion, and declared that said battalion was officially part of New York State's 9th Regiment of Infantry. Then the man ordered him to muster a militia of men from all of the area towns for the defense of Plattsburgh and Lake Champlain. The war had come to them. He had ten days to gather men and arrive on the lake shores.

Reuben tried on the uniform. How had they known his size? Somehow it fit perfectly. He looked down at his shoulder, wiggled it, and watched the movement of the tassels. Reuben frowned. Regardless of what Reuben thought of the uniform, he tipped his shoulders back, pushed his chest forward, and wore it proudly.

With less than an hour's notice, Reuben was prepared to ride out. Polly stood in front of him, curled her lip, and asked, "Don't you do enough? Do you have to do this too?" Tears of worry streamed down her face.

"I must go, I am a public servant now," Reuben whispered, having just taken a solemn oath, not an hour earlier. "I shall exercise caution," he assured her. Moments later, Lucy carried Reuben off to war, leaving a yard full of crying women behind. Women who feared the worst. It was a similar scene throughout the North Country, as Reuben went from house to house gathering men to join him. Men like Dudley Bump, Stephen Partridge, Reuben Partridge, and Andrew Hickok. Men from Jay, Keene, and the outskirts of Elizabethtown.

Mehitable thought that Reuben looked distinguished in his dark blue coat with the yellow trim at the sleeves, white breeches, and tall black hat adorned with silver braided rope. She held Destiny's hand tightly, protectively, and clutched Moses to her chest. She said a prayer for Reuben's safety, then she handed Moses to Destiny. Mehitable stretched her arms wide and wrapped them around Polly. Polly sobbed as if she had just gotten the news that Reuben had been killed in battle.

They didn't hear anything over the weeks that followed. Then one September afternoon, several weeks later, the men returned.

Reuben stood in the yard, in a somber mood. As soon as Reuben's boots hit the ground, 6-year-old Eliza practically jumped into his arms and buried her face in his neck and hugged him like she never planned to let him go. Ann, 4-years-old, hugged Reuben's leg, and 2-year-old Jane stood beside Polly, waiting her turn. When Reuben picked up Jane, she giggled and flicked the fringe that dangled from the shoulders of his coat.

After the children went to bed, Reuben told Polly, Mehitable, and Destiny about the weeks he had been away. The group of men that Reuben recruited had come to be known as *Reuben's Battalion*. They had heroically removed the stringers from an important bridge. All the while, they were under heavy rifle fire. Reuben showed them where a bullet had chipped the wood on his axe handle, and another place where a bullet struck a gouge in the stock of his rifle. Their mission succeeded in delaying the British from crossing into Plattsburgh and played an important role in America's victory at the Battle of Plattsburgh.

When Reuben finished telling the rest of the story, he hung his head and told everyone that the reason he relayed the happy news of victory with such modest enthusiasm was because of the sadness over the tragic loss of their friend and neighbor, Stephen Partridge. Mehitable thought of the young man who had won the apple bobbing contest at the dam bridge party four years earlier, and she thought of the time that she had helped his sister Eunice find her way into the world of spirits. Reuben relayed the pain that he felt at having to inform Stephen's wife, Lois. She would have to raise her boys on her own, with the modest help of generous neighbors. Mehitable prayed for Reuben Partridge, who lived next door to them. He would probably have to work harder and feed both his and his brother's family. Then Mehitable prayed for Stephen's soul, and hoped that his spirit would swiftly find his way to Jesus.

Somehow that fall they managed to harvest the rye, without

Reuben and minus a Bump brother. The grain would have to wait to be converted to whiskey. Reuben had little more than a week in between serving in the war and his obligations in the State Assembly. As Reuben was leaving for Albany, Polly was in the last trimester of her pregnancy. She pouted the entire week, complaining that Reuben would be gone when the baby came, and as Reuben was leaving, she said mournfully, "I feel like I have been pregnant for half of my life."

As it happened, the baby came late, and Reuben was home when Polly gave birth to their fourth daughter. Mehitable had begged her not to re-use Perlina's name for another daughter. Polly had begrudgingly taken her friend's advice three times. She rationalized the new baby's name, saying, "Perley is not the same as Perlina," though that was what she had always called Perlina. She couldn't explain why she was so compelled to name a baby Perley. Mehitable knew her friend never completely got over losing that sweet child. Coincidentally, Perley very closely resembled Perlina. She had the same haunting, bright blue eyes and tiny, button nose.

A couple of days after Perley was born, Polly got a letter from her brothers in Vermont. After building a house in Jay, Eliada and his wife had moved back to Vermont with their baby, Elizabeth. Eliada's wife had grown homesick and couldn't bear the separation from her family in Poultney. As Polly read on, she learned that her younger brother Albert was planning to marry a girl named Jane in the middle of January. Albert's letter reminded Polly that when they left Vermont ten years earlier, he had told them to save some wilderness for him. The plan was for Albert to take over the house and farm that Eliada had built. Polly was glad to hear that her baby brother was finally making his dreams come true.

A couple of weeks later, they received news about the signing of The Treaty of Ghent which effectively ended the war between the Europeans. Everyone assumed that would also mean the end of the war between Great Britain and the United States. Reuben wanted to share the news of the treaty, and Polly wanted Reuben to check on the house Eliada had built, to make sure it was ready for Albert's arrival. Polly and Mehitable spent a day baking, then Mehitable accompanied Reuben on a day trip in the sleigh. Everything was just as Eliada and his wife had left it, so they could reassure Polly that the house was ready for Albert and Jane. On the way back, Reuben stopped to visit Reuben Partridge. Mehitable visited across the road with Lois, Stephen's widow.

It had been a very difficult year. In addition to losing her husband in the Battle of Plattsburgh, she had lost her 5-year-old daughter to influenza. Her husband's father had moved in with Lois. He was a great help and comfort. Friends and neighbors truly had helped Lois provide for her children. Her two older boys were active youngsters that required constant supervision. The babe in her arms, a boy named Martin, had been born a few months before her husband's death. Work, worry, and grief robbed the pallor from her face and left her skin gray. Mehitable couldn't detect any joy within her soul. Lois politely accepted the biscuits, bread, cakes, and pies and she dutifully offered Mehitable a cup of tea. Her older boys played with their grandfather while Lois visited with Mehitable in the sitting room. Martin slept comfortably in Lois's arms and the two women talked softly.

Finally, Lois looked over her shoulder to make sure that her father-in-law wouldn't hear her. Then she said, "Mary Bull told me you can see into heaven and communicate with the dead. Is it true?" The faint light of optimism spread across her face as she twisted to look more directly at Mehitable. Lois told Mehitable about the unspeakable despair that comes with losing a spouse, not just for her but for the whole family. "If I could only visit with Stephen one more time, I declare, I'd feel like the luckiest woman alive."

A tear sprang to Mehitable's eye, rolled down her nose, and jumped from her upper lip. She answered, "Sometimes I can, only Stephen's spirit remains earthbound. Maybe you can feel his presence at times, in subtle ways. He doesn't think he can bear to leave you here alone, and he worries for you, but he needs to go to God, in heaven, and wait for you to join him there someday."

Lois's lip quivered. "Oh my goodness. I don't know if I believe all that."

Mehitable asked Lois, "What would you say to Stephen if he were here right now? What would you want him to know? Talk to him out loud, I think it will make you feel better."

"I don't know if I could," Lois hesitated.

Mehitable cocked her head, as if listening for a distant sound, then she whispered the words, "My precious, tiny turnip."

Lois's eyes grew wide in astonishment, "Nobody knows he called me that." It convinced Lois of Stephen's presence. Through sniffles and tears that almost woke Martin from his nap, Lois looked at Mehitable as if she were her husband, and spoke of all the sadness, disappointment, and grief that she had felt over the last couple of months. Then she sat up straight, and bragged, "But we are strong, and we shall overcome."

Mehitable suggested a short prayer, after which she spoke to Stephen's ghost. She told him that he could watch over his family from the world of spirits, and that was where he belonged. Then she passed Stephen's final thoughts to his wife.

Lois thanked Mehitable for helping her speak with her husband. " 'Tis just what I needed," she said.

Mehitable told Lois that she was glad she could help. Lois's cheeks were rosy instead of ashen. The two women sat silently in the parlor as the energy of the room shifted.

Chapter 24
February 1815

Polly's brother Albert and his new wife, Jane, arrived on the 12th day of February. It was slow going, as winter travel always was. They made many stops along what they called their wedding trip. They spent at least one night in every town they passed through. Sometimes they spent two nights. They carried little with them in a small wagon.

Albert brought gifts from old friends and neighbors back in Vermont. Mehitable and Polly's girlhood friend Aurilla still made beautiful hatpins and had made a special pin for each of them. Albert told them about Aurilla's husband and their 10-year-old twins. Mehitable was happy for her friend but couldn't help but feel jealous on behalf of her brother, Perry. Mehitable thought of the fox skin that Perry had wanted Aurilla to have and hoped that she still wore it.

Four months later, on a foggy spring morning, Destiny raced around the barn preparing for a trip into the woods and mountains. Mehitable watched him get ready to go. She wished he would stay.

She had something she wanted to tell him. He seemed to be in a hurry. She had been waiting for a quiet, tender moment. She had imagined a lazy, romantic stroll in her garden, the smell of herbs at her feet, and the intoxicating fragrance of the bright pink piney blooming just inside her garden gate. She pictured them embracing and looking into each other's eyes. She wished he wouldn't go. She was eager to tell him her news. It would have to wait.

Usually Destiny would disappear without a word. It rankled when he didn't let her know he was leaving before he was gone. Usually he was gone only one night, but sometimes it was two, and occasionally it had been as many as five nights. She looked at him sadly, her lower lip distended. How long would she have to keep her happy news to herself? *Should I just tell him anyway?*

When Destiny finished gathering his things, he embraced her. They kissed as if they were reuniting rather than parting. Then he backed his head away, looked her in the eyes and said, "I am not me without you." Her mouth fell open briefly in astonishment. It was the most complex thought he had given voice to since she had started teaching him English. Most of his words were nouns or verbs. He had learned to say, "I love you," but that was the full extent of his vocabulary when it came to expressing tender emotions. She quickly nodded and repeated his words back to him. Moments later he was gone, but his words stayed behind with her. *I am not me without you.* She stomped her foot impetuously, angry with herself. *I should have told him.*

All day, Destiny was never far from Mehitable's thoughts. He had been gone for five days. She kept waiting for him to wander into town with his basket full of the forest's bounty. She couldn't remember him being gone longer. She thought, *Today must be the day he comes home. I think I can feel his presence nearby.*

She kept herself busy with a shovel in the chicken coop. The stench had become overwhelming, and the task was long overdue. She stood up straight for a brief break and massaged her lower back with her hands. Then she peeked through a crack in the walls of the coop. Moses was happily playing with some wood blocks on the floor of the barn just outside of the coop. She sniffled and frowned, desperate to share the news of her new pregnancy with her husband. She figured the baby would come in late February. Polly was also expecting again in February, and Albert's wife Jane was a couple of months ahead of them. The small town was growing fast.

Later that evening, Mehitable worked on her spinning wheel while Moses slept. She thought about how Destiny had spent years alone in the woods. It must have been hard to go from being a wolf alone to living in a town, having a wife, and being a father. She smiled to think of his light-hearted nature and shook her head. It amazed her that a man who was so pleasant to be around could be just as happy to be entirely alone as to be surrounded by friends. Frequently Mehitable fantasized about moving to the pond to raise their family there instead of living in Polly and Reuben's barn. She had told herself that Polly and Reuben needed her, but Reuben could hire people to do the work she did. Polly had frequent visitors. Albert's wife Jane spent a lot of time with Polly, and Mary Bull's visits had increased from weekly to every other day. She knew Polly didn't *need* her, though she knew Polly cherished their friendship as much as she did.

Mehitable felt a chill and shivered. It was unusually chilly for June. She lifted her shawl from the back of her chair, covered her shoulders, and tied the ends in front of her. Mehitable chided herself for worrying. She always worried when Destiny was away, though he had survived just fine on his own for years by himself in the wilderness.

The chill in the air became a swift breeze. Mehitable tried to smooth the gooseflesh from her arms. She stood up from her spinning wheel and stepped to the edge of the light that her lantern provided. In the distance she heard the rhythmic knocking of wood. It sounded like the noise Moses made with his toy blocks while she was mucking out the chicken coop.

Then, deep within the darkness, she saw the faint white ghost of her husband. Her heart felt like it had sunk from her chest. She felt like someone had kicked the legs from a chair as she sat in it. She took off her shawl. She let her nightgown fall to the ground. She stood naked, arms stretched wide, like she did the day Destiny appeared from the depths of Copperas Pond. Tears streamed down her cheeks. She wanted to be strong but felt the urge to curl up on the ground and sob. Only, Destiny was there with her. She could feel his presence. She welcomed the ghost of her husband, eyes wide open. Destiny's ghost passed through her body as she stood there. She turned around, arms still stretched wide. His ghost passed through her a second time. She felt his presence at the same time as she felt his loss. She watched as Destiny kneeled over their son and she watched as he kissed the sleeping boy on his forehead. Then Destiny's ghost moved about the barn as if he didn't know where he was going or what he was doing. She understood that he was confused. She wondered, *Does his spirit know that his body has passed?* Her heart ached. She longed for the man. She welcomed his ghost. She must wait for his baby.

With another swift breeze, Destiny was gone.

Mehitable sobbed for hours. She didn't want to wake Moses, so she retreated into the darkness and sat at the open door of the barn with her face buried in the fabric of her magic shawl. Eventually, she talked herself into the notion that her encounter with Destiny's ghost was in her imagination. She returned to the side of her sleeping child and curled up beside him. She let herself believe the lie she told herself, and finally fell into a fitful sleep. When she awoke the next morning, she prayed that she had been mistaken, but she couldn't escape the truth that gnawed within her. *How could I mistake a ghost after all the ghosts I've seen?* She wondered why the spirit world didn't warn her so she could prevent his death. *Why would God bring him to me only to take him away?*

Moses began to stir. She didn't have a choice but to believe everything was alright. She couldn't get through the day if she didn't. As she got dressed and prepared for her morning chores, Mehitable experienced the familiar vision of a terrible memory. Many times since she almost fell over the edge of the cliff, seven years earlier, she had envisioned arms and legs flailing and her body crashing into the running water below. The vision always vanished before the moment of impact.

She hurriedly milked Ophelia and brought food and water to the animals in the barn. Then Mehitable left Moses with Polly. Polly raised her eyebrows when it was clear that Mehitable had no intention of answering the question that Polly didn't ask. Reuben was out of town on official business. Albert and Jane were having breakfast in Polly's kitchen, and Mehitable asked Albert to follow her.

Mehitable was led along the river in an unblinking trance. She let unseen spirits guide her. A monarch butterfly also seemed to be leading the way. She looked up and recognized the cliffs way above as the trail she had been on years earlier when she almost slipped and fell to her death. Even though she had not gone over the edge, she was left with the memory of having fallen. The feeling of speeding through the air. An almost imperceptible sense of having shattered upon impact after the fall. A sense of having been released from her body and seeing her smashed body on the rocks below her as she floated above her remains.

The path along the ferocious river was rough, and they had to crawl through dead limbs of trees to trace the riverside. They had to crawl over enormous boulders and scale up and down the other side of steep hillsides to get to where they needed to go. Polly's brother was about to sound the alarming voice of reason and suggest that they should give up searching along the river, when suddenly, Mehitable gasped and pointed at an enormous hawk that had just landed on a crag of rock twenty feet from them. Then Mehitable saw what remained of her husband's body. She screamed in horror and crashed to her knees. Her vision had been real, only it was Destiny's misfortune, not her own. Her hands flew up to cover her eyes, her body folded at her waist, her arms rested along her thighs in a snail's position. Mehitable wailed in grief on the cold, hard rock beneath her.

Albert put his arm across her shoulder. He tried to offer her some comfort, but she was inconsolable. He aimed his words into her seemingly deaf ears, telling her that he would attend to Destiny's remains. He stood for a moment before moving, as if trying to decide how to face what he needed to do. Fortunately, he had brought a large blanket in a basket he carried strapped to his back.

Mehitable turned her back on Albert and picked up a weathered gray stick and smashed it into a boulder in the river, sending punky slivers of half rotted wood flying in all directions. Her jaw clenched, and she reached for a large piece of driftwood. She swung it savagely over her head into another large boulder along the river, as if she were exacting her revenge against the rocks that claimed Destiny's life and shattered his beautiful body.

Albert worked as quickly as he could. His face twisted in revulsion and his stomach tumbled, promising to spill its contents, though breakfast had been hours before. Destiny's body had been ravaged by the impact. An arm had separated from his body, yet the hand on that arm was gripped into a tight fist. Albert opened the hand on the arm and a four-inch cylindrical piece of the antler of a deer rolled onto the top of a rock. He looked at the intricate carving on the antler and quickly put it in his pocket. Then he placed the arm and gathered the rest of Destiny's remains into the blanket and tied it up as best as he could, ducking splinters and chunks of wood that flew from the impact of Mehitable's rage against the boulders.

Mehitable dropped to her knees at the edge of the river, not feeling the discomfort of the rocks that pressed into her kneecaps. She tilted her head back and looked up into the sky, and begged God for a miracle. Couldn't God return him to her from thin air, just as he had sent him to her from the depths of Copperas Pond. She promised God anything, anything except Moses, and the new life she was carrying. Instead of God answering her prayers, Albert cleared his throat to catch her attention, telling her it was time to go. Destiny's legs remained visible at the bottom of the blanket that Albert had wrapped him in. It couldn't be helped. Albert hefted the dead body up and over his shoulder.

The trip back was excruciating. The terrain was difficult enough without a heavy load. Mehitable couldn't go very far before she stopped to bury her face in her hands again. She kept thinking, *I never got to tell him we are going to have another baby.* She never imagined that something terrible could happen to him, and that she might never get the chance to tell him about the new baby. She had been waiting for that perfect moment which never came. Grief and regret kept bringing her back to her knees throughout the afternoon.

Albert took advantage of those grieving moments to rest. Then when Mehitable was able to proceed again, Albert grunted and strained to lift the corpse up to his shoulders again.

Finally, they made it home late in the afternoon. Albert placed the body in the back of the wagon just outside of the barn and covered it with canvas. Then he guided Mehitable into Polly's house, and into Polly's arms. Mehitable wailed, "He's gone." She didn't care that the children were watching, or that she was upsetting them. Albert and Jane did their best to calm the children, and Polly rocked gently from side to side, with Mehitable in her arms, and made comforting shushing noises as Mehitable's grief waxed and waned.

Polly told Mehitable that Moses could stay with her that night. Before Mehitable retreated to the familiar comfort of the barn, Albert stopped her, and pulled the section of antler from his pocket. "I found this in," Albert almost couldn't finish his sentence, but regained his voice, "in Destiny's hand at the river," and placed it in Mehitable's hand.

Polly gasped. "I saw that once before. The night Moses was born, Destiny was working on that carving while he was waiting for the news that he had become a father."

Mehitable clutched the carving to her chest. Tears sprang to her eyes again, and she ran from Polly's house to the barn. When her eyes cleared enough to see, she lit her tiny lamp and held the antler as close to it as she could. She stared at it for hours. There was a carving of a woman and it looked exactly like herself, holding a baby. There was a wolf, head tipped back, and an enormous full moon behind the three of them. It was just as she had drawn it with the stick at Copperas Pond after she had seen the vision of his past.

She wondered where his ghost was. If he was still earthbound, she knew she would have to help him find his way to the world of spirits. She wished she could keep his spirit with her, and never let him go. She knew it was selfish, and that it was wrong to keep his spirit with her. *He must go to Jesus, like all the others.* This time, Jesus would have to wait until she was ready to let his spirit go. *Maybe someday I'll be strong enough, but I can't let his spirit go now. Where are you, Destiny?* She had never pleaded with a spirit to appear before.

She held the carving to her cheek and cried herself to sleep. The last words she said to herself before she fell asleep were the last words he said to her, "I am not me without you."

Chapter 25

June 1815

Reuben returned the next morning. Albert dug a grave in the cemetery, and Reuben quickly fashioned a coffin. A large gray stone was placed at the head of the grave to mark the spot until a stone could be placed. At sunset, the small family gathered in the cemetery. Albert and his wife Jane stood with Reuben, Polly, and their girls a few feet behind Mehitable. Reuben began saying the Lord's prayer, and everyone joined in. Then Polly started singing "Amazing Grace." When the song was over, Mehitable walked forward, put her hands atop of the marker rock, and began to speak in a language nobody understood. Mehitable knew she was speaking in Destiny's native tongue, but she had no idea what she was saying. Even so, she felt better having been able to give him that. Sadly, she stood tall, took Moses from Jane's arms, and solemnly led the mourners from the cemetery back toward home.

Polly invited everyone in for a cup of tea. The children played in the living room, and the adults sat at the dinner table. Polly draped a shawl across Mehitable's shoulders and placed a hot cup of her favorite tea in her hand. Reuben passed a little bowl of sugar and a spoon across the table. As Mehitable stirred the tea, Reuben asked if he could get a stone for Destiny's grave. "What would you like the marker to say?" he asked.

Mehitable looked up from her tea, her eyebrows arched, and she asked, "Can you have them carve a picture of a wolf on the stone? The words should say Magnificent Destiny, beloved husband of Mehitable Munch, died 1815. Is that too much? Can they do that?"

Reuben nodded slowly, his spoken words seeming to betray the nodding of his head. "I'll see what I can do," he said slowly. Then he repeated it again. "I'll see what I can do." His voice trailed off at the end.

Months later Reuben returned from a long trip, delivering whiskey and attending meetings. Reuben's returns always became noisy celebrations. As the wagon approached, the children appeared and began to cheer. They had been conditioned to expect gifts. Polly and Mehitable also looked forward to Reuben's arrivals. Every child got a sweet stick of cinnamon flavored stick candy. Reuben took Polly in his arms, hugged her tightly, and pressed his lips to hers. Then he gave her three fat bolts of fabric, two yellow and white checked, and one solid yellow, the color of lemons. Then he hugged Mehitable. Afterward, he tipped his hat, and said, "The headstone is finished. I picked it up in Elizabethtown. Let me show you."

Reuben climbed up into the back of the wagon and held out a helping hand. Mehitable took his hand and jumped up into the wagon. She looked down upon the stone and tilted her head. She bit her lower lip, and placed her hand over her heart, her fingers loosely closed into a fist. Then she looked up at Reuben as tears streamed down her face. She had never seen such an elaborate picture carved onto a headstone before, and Reuben had purchased an extra-large slab. He fit all of the words she had asked for. In addition, he asked the mason to carve, "Devoted father and cherished friend."

Mehitable looked into Reuben's eyes and almost choked on her words. " 'Tis beautiful." She squatted down and traced the wolf design with her fingertips, and then she traced the words, as if she were writing them on paper with her fingertip. She knew the stone must have cost Reuben a tremendous amount of money. Finally, she stood back up in the back of the wagon, and said, "I am eternally grateful."

Otis, Lester, and Dudley Bump had helped Reuben place the stone at the head of Destiny's grave. The boulder that had marked the head had been moved to the foot of the grave, at Mehitable's request. She planned to sit on the rock whenever she visited the cemetery. When their work was done, Reuben draped a sheet over the headstone.

The following Sunday, Eli Hammond came to town, as he did once every four or five weeks. It was a warm, early September day. The sun shone brightly. The light blue sky contained almost no clouds. Friends, family, and neighbors walked at a comfortable pace up the hillside toward the cemetery. The tiny town wasn't very old and it wasn't very large, but there were already fifteen stones marking the final resting places of the dearly departed in the fledgling cemetery. When they got to the gate, Mehitable set Moses on the ground in front of her. He ran straight toward the newly placed stone, which had a sheet thrown over it. Mehitable clasped her hands at her waist in front of her and walked slowly up to the graveside.

Reverend Hammond said a few comforting prayers, and cited several poignant Bible verses, then he recited Mehitable's favorite, the one her Granny had always loved. "God indeed is my savior; I am confident and unafraid. My strength and courage is the Lord, and he has been my savior." He looked around at the gathering of people with a serene look on his face, and concluded by citing the reference, confidently, "Isaiah 12:2." Then he gestured toward the covered gravestone with his right arm and said, "Shall we?"

Reuben stepped forward, faced the crowd, and repeated Reverend Hammond's gesture with his left hand, then snapped the sheet from the gravestone.

Someone gasped at the sight.

Thankful Bull whispered loudly to Coriander Bump, "Is that some kind of pagan symbol?"

Another woman could be heard making a *tsk* sound from the corner of her mouth.

Mehitable basked contentedly in the disapproval. She walked forward toward the stone and placed her hand on top of it. Then she patted it a couple of times, like an older woman might tap a small boy on the top of his head. She turned and shook Reverend Hammond's hand. She quickly hugged Reuben, then she embraced Polly. She whispered in Polly's ear, "I thank God every day for you and your family, and all your kindness, through the years."

Polly's lips trembled. She held Mehitable's arm as if she expected her to swoon and stood ready to help her keep her feet beneath her. Polly told Mehitable that they were sisters, and that they stood together.

As the gathered crowd dispersed, Polly asked if she could take Moses back with her. She understood that Mehitable would want to remain in the cemetery by herself for a while. Mehitable nodded and stood alone, hands clasped in front of her again, watching everyone walk down the hillside. The late summer smell of goldenrod, echinacea, and sundried meadow grass swept across her senses on the heels of a warm breeze. The scent of leather also surrounded her. She stood still but she felt like she was twirling, spinning in circles, and the sense of movement made her feel better than she had felt since discovering Destiny's body at the river.

Mehitable sat on the boulder, her feet inches from the ground. It made her happy to sit there alone on the rock, talking to her husband. It was as if he were sitting across from her, on the marker, his feet dangling over the edge of the gravestone, his buried body lying under the ground between them. She talked with Destiny as she would have if she had seen him just a couple of days earlier. He had learned many English words, and he could communicate basic thoughts about actions and objects. Destiny had never achieved the fluency necessary for lengthy conversations about thoughts, feelings, emotions, hopes, and dreams. Even as a spirit, he communicated about such things sparsely, conveying his thoughts more with his eyes and his expressions than with words. It didn't matter to her. Now that he had passed, she could read his thoughts and didn't need to hear his words anyhow.

Finally, Mehitable knew it was time to go. She stood up and turned to leave. At the cemetery gate, she turned around and looked back into the cemetery. She saw three spirits moving toward Destiny's gravestone from the right, and two moving in from the left. Mehitable smiled. She was glad that Destiny would have some company. *A wolf pack, perhaps,* she thought. In the future she would help them all cross over. Mehitable thought it was nice that the spirits would gather at Destiny's grave. It also pleased her that Destiny's marker was unlike any other. *How fitting,* she surmised. Then she walked away. She felt a sudden need to spend some time among the living.

When she got home, Polly had Sunday dinner ready. The house smelled warm and inviting. Polly had doused a ham in maple syrup and baked it slowly all day. She mashed potatoes with plenty of butter, and her mother's recipe for Apple Brown Betty was cooling on a table by the window. There was a pot of minty tea at the hearth. Albert and his wife Jane were there, as well as Reverend Hammond, who was telling stories and making everyone laugh. Mehitable closed the door behind her, patted her chest above her heart, her signal to herself that her husband was with her, and she joined her family at the table.

It was an exceptionally warm, early November day, three months later. Most of the trees had lost their foliage. Mehitable carried a heavy picnic basket filled with lunch. Polly was way ahead of her, Jane on one hip, and Perley on the other. The older girls walked along slowly, lost in a conversation. Moses toddled in front of Mehitable, stopping to investigate frequently. He was fascinated by anything that moved, and tried to catch every insect, toad, or tiny snake that crossed his path.

Mehitable wasn't in any hurry. It had been months since she had lost her husband, and she was only just getting to the point where she could think happy thoughts on a regular basis. She enjoyed hearing her feet crunching the crispy leaves under her feet as she walked. She felt a strange sensation in her belly and wondered if it was a tiny foot giving her a kick, suggesting she hurry along and have lunch soon. She thought about how her baby would never know his father. Moses, also, would never remember Destiny. She wiped a tear from the corner of her eye with a finger. Just ahead of her, Moses tripped over a fallen branch, giggled, rolled head over heels, and sprang back to his feet, then continued along as if he had never fallen. Mehitable chuckled.

For weeks, Mehitable and Polly had been joking about whose baby would be born first. Mehitable thought to wonder who would deliver the babies if they both ended up having them on the same day. She shuddered at the thought that they would be at the mercy of Coriander Bump to midwife their deliveries, or worse yet, Thankful Bull. Mehitable was still thinking about that when she caught up with Polly. Mehitable watched as Polly set the babies down on the grass and then she helped Polly spread a large picnic blanket on the grass, right next to the gravestone which marked the final resting place for Polly's first two babies. Mehitable asked what Polly thought would happen if they both went into labor at the same time.

Polly stood up and absentmindedly caressed her belly, one hand on each side rubbing in circles. She frowned at Mehitable. "Fie! What *would* we do?" Before they could resolve the issue of the day, hungry children interrupted the women's concerns.

Mehitable arranged the children in a circle on the blanket. Polly dug fried chicken out of the basket, passing out drumsticks to each of the children before sitting down on the blanket herself. Baby Perley set to nursing while Mehitable passed out freshly baked biscuits to the rest of the children.

After half a biscuit and a few bites of chicken, Moses toddled off after a grasshopper. One by one, the other children followed, until Mehitable and Polly were alone. The baby had fallen asleep on the blanket after having nursed.

Polly looked at her belly, patted it proudly, and said, "Thankful Bull says 'tis a boy. She said she feels it in her bones."

Mehitable gasped in horror, and mocked, "Blasphemy. Witchcraft! How could she claim to *know* it's a boy?" They shared a brief grin at Thankful Bull's expense. Mehitable placed her hand on the spiral medallion that hung on a string around her neck, then she reached forward, put a hand on Polly's belly, closed her eyes and was silent for a minute. When she opened her eyes and looked up into her friend's face, Mehitable corrected knowingly, "You will have *another* baby girl."

Polly said, "Oh, really?" Then she leaned forward, put her hands on either side of Mehitable's belly, closed her eyes, then opened them. Polly proclaimed randomly, "You will also have a baby girl," and she smiled proudly, having committed to her prediction. She waited half a second and then added, "How did I do?"

Mehitable laughed and instructed Polly to put her hands back. When Polly's hands were placed on Mehitable's belly again,

Mehitable placed her hands on Polly's cheeks. Mehitable closed her eyes. When she opened them, she shook her head and said, "Nay, 'tis another boy and he will look just like his father. I will name him Noah."

Polly nodded approvingly, and said, "I shall name my baby Phebe, after Reuben's mother." She shook her head, bemused, and muttered, "Five girls. Be still my beating heart."

Just then, Moses took off running, as fast as his chubby legs would carry him, like he had a purpose. He ran directly to Destiny's grave, stopped, tilted his head back and looked up as if he were listening to a parent lecture him. Then he began running around the cemetery with no sense of purpose or direction, like a butterfly flitting from one flowerhead to another. Mehitable watched as Moses ran, stopped, and pointed. Then a couple of seconds later, he ran in another direction, stopped, and pointed again. Finally, he ran right up to the edge of the blanket, pointed, giggled, and looked at his mother. She watched her son gesturing to the air as if to someone else. She asked, "What are you doing, baby?"

A radiant smile filled Moses's cherubic cheeks and he said, "I'm playing hide and seek with Father. Don't you see him, Mommy?"

Mehitable shook her head slowly in amazement and looked at Polly. Then she looked back at her son. She clasped her hands beneath her chin, looked to the sky and said, "Pray, Jesus, please let his *gift* be a blessing."

A Special Offer

As a special gift for joining my email list, I'll send you a FREE digital copy of my book: *The Curse of Conchobar—A Prequel to the Adirondack Spirit Series*. It's the best way to meet this ancient ancestor of Wanders Far and his progeny. The Adirondack Spirit Series is an epic, multi-generational family saga and it all starts with Conchobar. Are supernatural tendencies hereditary? If you guessed yes, maybe you're descended from old souls too.

Your FREE digital book is waiting. Click here:

https://dl.bookfunnel.com/iwczowhp8q

My Humble Request

As a new indie author, I'm striving to help my books find an audience. Nothing is more valuable in helping people find my books than reviews from readers like you. Even a very short review is enormously helpful, and I will be eternally grateful. Thank you so much for your interest in my book.

Also by David Fitz-Gerald

From The Adirondack Spirit Series

Wanders Far—An Unlikely Hero's Journey

Wanders Far lived in dangerous times. From a very young age, his wanderlust compelled him down one path after another. No village could contain him. He was happy living a simple life in the physical world. The spirit world had other plans. One lifetime was not enough for Wanders Far's old soul.

https://books2read.com/wandersfar

Information about future installments in the series can be found at https://www.itsoag.com/

Not part of the Adirondack Spirit Series

In the Shadow of a Giant—Remembering Paleface Ski Center and Dude Ranch

The story of a dreamer who fought Mother Nature, Father Time, and a dwindling checkbook balance to build a family-owned resort in the heart of the Adirondack Mountains. Take a trip back in time and enjoy a one-of-a kind, vintage, Adirondack vacation experience. https://books2read.com/itsoag

Acknowledgements

I don't know if every writer can say this, but I sure can: I LOVE MY EDITOR. Sure, she's my cousin, but she is also a fantastic collaborator. Lindsay, I have become so dependent on your loving, patient, gentle guidance. From the bottom of my heart, thank you, Lindsay.

I'm grateful to the community of readers, reviewers, and authors for their encouragement and support. Special thanks to my Adirondack Spirit Guides group for their early feedback. If you'd like to join the club, you can find us on Facebook at https://www.facebook.com/groups/adirondackspiritguides. I'd especially like to thank author Elizabeth Bell (Lazare Family Saga: *Necessary Sins*, *Lost Saints*, and *Native Stranger*) for her input and feedback at a time when I was trying to make important decisions. I'd also like to thank author Paul Bennett (The Mallory Saga: *Clash of Empires* and *Paths to Freedom*) for lending me his character, Liam Mallory. It was fun having a special guest star from his series drop in for a couple of pages in my book.

I've found my pastime has turned into an enormously pleasurable hobby. I couldn't do it without the support of readers like you. I look forward to welcoming you back for the next installment in the Adirondack Spirit Series.

Finally, I'd like to emphasize that this is a work of fiction. Actual historical characters have been fictionalized. Also, the real towns of Wilmington, New York and Poultney, Vermont have been fictionalized. Even so, many details are factual and verified. As a reader and writer of historical fiction, I enjoy the coexistence of fact and fiction. Thank you for spending time in Mehitable's world.

CPSIA information can be obtained
at www.ICGtesting.com
Printed in the USA
FSHW011300091220
76749FS

9 781977 233578